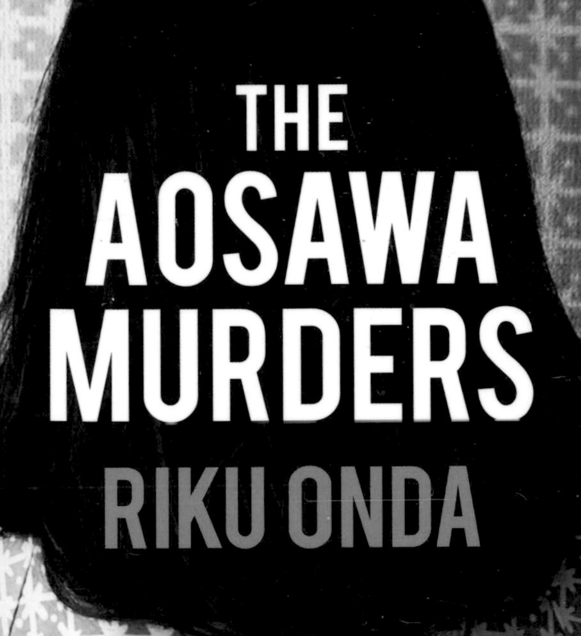
THE
AOSAWA
MURDERS
RIKU ONDA

Riku Onda, born in 1964, is the professional name of Nanae Kumagai. She has been writing fiction since 1991 and has published prolifically since. She has won the Yoshikawa Eiji Prize for New Writers, the Japan Booksellers' Award, the Yamamoto Shugoro Prize and the Naoki Prize. Her work has been adapted for film and television.

The Aosawa Murders won the prestigious Mystery Writers of Japan Award for Best Novel. It is Riku Onda's first crime novel and her first work translated into English.

THE AOSAWA MURDERS

Riku Onda

Translated from the Japanese
by Alison Watts

BITTER LEMON PRESS
LONDON

BITTER LEMON PRESS

First published in the United Kingdom in 2020 by
Bitter Lemon Press, 47 Wilmington Square, London WC1X 0ET

www.bitterlemonpress.com

First published in Japanese in 2005 as *EUGENIA* by
KADOKAWA CORPORATION, Tokyo.

English translation rights arranged with KADOKAWA CORPORATION,
Tokyo through Japan Uni Agency, Inc., Tokyo

English translation by Alison Watts 2020

A CIP record for this book is available from the British Library

ISBN 978-1-912242-245
eBook ISBN 978-1-912242-252

Text design and typesetting by Tetragon, London
Printed and bound by CPI Group (UK) Ltd, Croydon, CR0 4YY

For Michel Petrucciani,
who never lived to see the twenty-first century.

CONTENTS

Eugenia, my Eugenia.I journeyed alone all this time
That I might meet you again.
And I tell you this:
That days of shivering in a long-ago dawn
Also end today.
From here on we will be together, forever.
The song that rises to my lips,
The insects of the woods crushed beneath my shoes in the morning,
And this tiny heart of mine ceaselessly pumping blood,
All this, I offer to you.

PROLOGUE

Transcript of a police interview with Hisako Aosawa. Interviewer: Detective T—. File: Aosawa Murders, City of K—, I— Prefecture

What do you remember?
Being outside an old, dark, blue room.

Where was this room? Whose house was it?
I don't know.

Why were you in the room?
I don't know. But someone – an adult – was holding my hand. That person must have taken me to the room.

Who was it?
I don't know.

Tell us about the room. Which part was blue?
The walls were blue. A deep, cold blue. The room was Japanese-style, with tatami mats. Very small and compact. It was an unusual design, I think – two walls faced the corridor. Parts of it were a reddish-purple colour too. I remember thinking I would hate it to be my room and have to eat meals surrounded by those walls.

Did you enter the room?
No. At least, I don't remember going in. We just looked in from outside.

What happened next?
I don't remember.

Can you remember anything else? Anything at all, no matter how trivial.
The crepe myrtle.

A crepe myrtle tree? With a smooth bark trunk?
No, the flower. A white crepe myrtle flower.

White? Are you sure? Not red?
Yes. I remember a pure white crepe myrtle flower. In full bloom.

Take your time and try to remember. What did you think as you looked at this white crepe myrtle flower? What did you feel?
It was so beautiful. In full bloom, with not a blemish. It was so beautiful, I was frightened.

You were frightened? Why?
I don't know. But for some reason I was very frightened by that white flower.

1
FROM THE SEA

A conversation with Makiko Saiga, the author, thirty years after the murders

I

As always, the new season brings rain.

No, I take that back; new is not the word I'm looking for, it's *next*. The next season always brings rain. That's what it feels like in this city.

The change of season in this part of the world is never dramatic. It's more like the gradual erosion of a boundary line every time a rain shower arrives to paint the old season over bit by bit, as the new one takes its time to turn gradually, in a vague, almost apologetic fashion.

On this side of the country rain rolls in from the sea.

I was always very aware of that as a child.

These buildings block the view from here now, but almost anywhere in the city that was even slightly elevated used to have a view of the ocean. You'd see undulating waves of ominous rain clouds, weighed down with stifling heat, creep in from the sea and rise up over the land, threatening to dump their load over the city.

When I moved to the Kanto region, I was astonished to discover that wind blew *off* the land there, and out into the Pacific Ocean. On the Kanto coastline you don't get the same sense as you do here of the overbearing presence of the sea. You can be right up close to the water's edge and still not feel it. Heat and smells that rise off the land escape out to sea. Towns throw themselves open to the ocean. And the horizon is always far in the distance, like a picture in a frame.

But the ocean here isn't refreshing at all. Gazing at it doesn't give you any sense of freedom or relief. And the horizon is always close, as if waiting for an opportunity to force its way onto land. It feels like you're being watched, and if you dare look away for just a moment the sea might descend upon you. Do you see what I mean?

It's so *hot*, isn't it?

This heat is so heavy. It's like the city is sealed up inside a steamer. Heat like this is cruel, it robs you of energy, far more than you expect.

As a child I found summer unbearable. I'd lose my appetite and barely eat. By the end of the summer holidays my diet would consist of *somen* noodles and barley tea, that's about all. In photos I look thin and goggle-eyed. Have you noticed how walking over this hot asphalt makes your legs feel shaky? Now everyone has air conditioning, it's not the summer heat that takes its toll so much as the shock of the difference between the temperature indoors and outdoors. It's getting hotter and hotter every year, don't you think? Climate change, I expect.

It's been a long time.

You do realize we only lived here for four years, when I was in primary school? We came here in the spring of grade two, when I was seven, and moved to Nagano in the spring of grade six.

Yes, I spent a year going back and forth between here and Tokyo in that period.

Did you bring an umbrella? The guidebook recommends you do. The sky's clear now, but you can't be sure how long that will last.

As I was saying, this humidity is lethal. It saps you of all energy. Notice how the sky is a murky blue colour and the clouds have a dull glowing outline? They seem so close you feel you could reach out and touch them. *That's* when you get heavy showers. Before you know it low clouds fill the sky and dump rain mercilessly on the city. An umbrella is hardly enough protection to stop ankles and shoulders getting wet – it's enough to make you miserable and fed up.

Nobody seems to wear wellies any more, do they? I loved wearing them as a child to play in puddles, skipping through them or deliberately jumping in with both feet to make a big splash.

It doesn't snow so much in this area. We lived in Toyama for a while before moving here, which isn't far geographically, but the snow there was something else. It was a heavy, *wet* snow. The kind that would hurt if someone threw a snowball at you. The sliding paper screens in the house used to swell up with moisture and stick shut. You don't get that kind of snow in this city.

Human beings are strange creatures, though. We soon forget. When the weather gets this humid it's hard to believe that just a few months earlier it was wintry and cold, and we miss it.

Oh, it's so *hot*.

II

Doesn't the layout of this city strike you as odd?

It hadn't occurred to you? Well, most cities have some kind of commercial district near the train station. That is, if a station wasn't added later for a new bullet train line or to provide airport access. Typically, old regional cities like this one develop outwards from the station. But that's not the case here. All you find around the station in this city is a few hotels, while the centre and main shopping area are further off.

In my experience prefectural capitals all tend to look alike. At the front of the station you'll find a traffic circle surrounded by department stores and hotels. Then, leading from the station, a main road lined with shops, and an entertainment district in an area parallel – not quite connected, but not exactly separate – to the zone for offices and local or regional government buildings. There's also usually some kind of redevelopment on the other side of the station, with rows of sterile new buildings. Do you see what I mean?

As a child I had trouble grasping the layout of this city. I knew where the bus stops were, and the area around each one, but I didn't know where they were in relation to each other.

Do you mind if we just wander about?

As I was saying, other cities have visible boundaries where the centre ends. It's clear that beyond a certain point the land is either for residential or agricultural use. The divisions are obvious.

Here, though, there's nothing to show where the city centre ends. You can walk one way and find yourself in a teahouse district. Or if you go in another direction it's all temples and shrines. Walk a bit further and you find old samurai houses, then the prefectural offices, then the entertainment quarter. Wherever you go, there are loosely grouped small communities that seem to go on forever. Walking around the city, as we are now, is like a synaptic experience – it's all connected but separate. There's no centre anywhere, only a series of loosely linked neighbourhoods. You could walk and walk and never feel like there's any end to it. It's like moving pieces on a Chinese chequers board.

I enjoy rambling about old towns. Going to an unknown place and glimpsing the lives of strangers. Walking around an old city is like a journey through time. I get a lot of pleasure from discovering remnants of times past, like a milk box outside an old house or a retro enamel sign tacked to the wall of a tiny shop.

I like this city in particular because you can take a winding route through it. In a big city like Kyoto, for example, the streets are laid out systematically like squares in a computer game, and having to follow them makes you feel overwhelmed and powerless. Or maybe it's the flatness of the downtown district that does it. It can be surprisingly tiring to walk only on flat ground, with no change in your pace or breathing.

Oh yes, I'm sure that military and historical circumstances greatly influenced the development of this city's layout.

See on the map how this hill is at the centre of the city and flanked on two sides by rivers. The city is a natural fortress, you see, surrounded by hills on three sides and sea on the other. It would be difficult to invade with a hilltop castle and the town on the slopes below, built around a network of narrow roads and slopes. Another thing about this city is that it has never been destroyed by fire, so the old layout remains to this day.

It's a long time since I've heard the phrase *destroyed by fire.* As a child I often heard adults use it. Was that place ever destroyed by fire, they'd ask, or say in reference to such-and-such a place that it *never burned.* Of course I didn't understand at the time, but what they were really asking was whether or not somewhere had been firebombed in the Second World War. Isn't it horrifying to think it happened so many times that *destroyed by fire* and *never burned* became part of everyday speech?

III

I haven't been here in a very long time. Not since I came on a school excursion. When you live near a famous sightseeing spot, you hardly ever actually go there. Look how few people are here today. It's too hot and humid even for tour groups. That's good for us, though, we can take our time looking around. A lot of tourists come in winter, of course, to see the trees and shrubs all wrapped up to protect them against the snow. You must have seen it on the news.

But it's obvious why this garden is known as one of the three great gardens of Japan. Just look at the size and scale of it, the variety of landscapes, and how meticulously it's kept. The greenery here is also very striking, almost defiantly so, I always think.

Authority is an interesting phenomenon, isn't it? Who would be able to create such an awe-inspiring place as this garden nowadays? Of course this is a wonderful achievement. It's beautiful, a piece of cultural heritage to be proud of and necessary as a bastion of the Japanese spirit. But at the end of the day, it's a garden, not something essential in the way that farms, or schools, or irrigation systems are. The powers that be who created this garden and maintained it for hundreds of years are beyond the understanding of ordinary people like us.

That's right. Sometimes people get caught up in events beyond their understanding. They get ambushed under the guise of chance. Things happen and it seems as if they're in another world or dimension. When something like that occurs, nobody can explain what's really going on... Well, of course they can't.

What do you think a person should do when they come across something they don't understand? Should they reject it, pretend they never saw it? Be angry or resentful? Grieve or simply be confused? Those would be natural reactions, I suppose.

In my case, I moved to Nagano not long afterwards and apparently that was enough for me to get over it, being a child. I did in fact forget about the whole affair rather quickly.

Or so I thought, but in fact it was still with me, like a sediment that had settled deep down inside.

Recalling the events didn't make me feel uncomfortable. I hadn't been directly involved. But as I grew older, every time I saw an injustice or something I couldn't understand, I felt something surreptitiously stirring deep down inside, slowly working its way up from the depths. Over time this sense of unease built up and felt more solid.

I don't remember what the trigger was, but one day I realized I had to do something about it. I knew I couldn't go on with life as usual until I'd removed that accumulation of uneasiness. If I didn't, I knew I'd suffocate.

I thought a great deal about it, about what I could do to bring everything to the surface.

Given how much I didn't understand, I knew that realistically it could only be within the limits of my ability to comprehend.

Then I set about researching the subject, which I also did to the best of my ability and within the limits of my understanding.

That was how I chose to deal with it. I felt I had no other choice.

The result was *The Forgotten Festival*, which I wrote eleven years after the murders.

IV

This far in you can't hear the traffic any more.

Cars, cars, cars, everywhere you go there are cars. Why are there so many cars on the road? Where's everyone going? Sometimes I stop and think about it. Why is there so much traffic? See, as I said before, the roads in an old city like this are narrow. The traffic jam around the prefectural office here is *always* horrendous.

These cedars are magnificent, aren't they? And the pines. Such a deep, dark green. More black than green, really. Green that verges on darkness.

Even the pond water looks heavy and stagnant in this heat.

Note how high above sea level it is. Piping water up here used to be a terrible struggle. Everybody knows the story of the local lord who had water diverted uphill from the river by an inverted siphoning technique, but every time I see this pond I remember the legend of artisans who were killed to protect the secret of that technology. I don't know if it's true or not, but that's the beauty of it – the fact that it seems likely.

Fear is a spice that lends credibility. Just the right amount sprinkled in any story makes it plausible.

That's the kind of thing I remember.

An odd craze swept through my class afterwards. All the girls were doing it. Can you guess what it was?

Well, I'll tell you. It was making pressed flowers. Yes, everybody was pressing Asiatic day flowers.

Apparently the glass used to weigh down the letter found at the crime scene had a day flower in it. I don't know why, but for some reason everybody started to believe that day flowers were a charm against evil. Rumour had it that carrying a bookmark made from a pressed day flower would protect the carrier from being targeted by a homicidal maniac. So everybody went looking for day flowers to press. There was absolutely no basis to it, but a lot of strange rumours floated around at the time. The flowers had to be pressed in a telephone book, or a science textbook, or inserted into folded newspaper and placed under somebody's futon, and if that person didn't notice it was good luck – things like that. One girl I was friendly with gave me a bookmark and told me in all seriousness that I'd be safe if I kept it on me at all times.

Oh yes, they enjoyed themselves all right. Adults too, as well as the children.

Of course people were traumatized. I mean, it was unthinkable that something like that should have happened in the very city where we lived! The disruption to our lives was enormous. Fear spread like wildfire, and we were all on edge, jumping at shadows. It was as if we were in the grip of a feverish hysteria, brought on by living day after day in a state of high tension – something that normally you'd never experience in daily life. In my memories of that time, I have a distinct sense of being part of a major event.

That's why I used the word *festival*. That was honestly how it looked to me.

Of course, I'm aware people disapproved of me choosing *The Forgotten Festival* as the book's title. But ultimately it's fiction, although it is based on facts and research. It was all a kind of festival, that's what I honestly think.

Non-fiction? I'm not keen on the word. No matter how much a writer tries to adhere to the truth, the notion of non-fiction is an illusion. All that can exist is fiction visible to the eye. And what is visible can also lie. The same applies to that which we hear and touch. Fictions that exist and fictions that don't exist – that's the level of difference, in my opinion. Do you see what I mean?

Oh, this *heat.*

The sweat's running into my eyes. And my shirt's soaked as well – it's most unattractive.

This section of the garden is for cherry trees, but you'd never know at this time of year.

That's the odd thing about cherry trees. Other trees keep their identity all year round. It's easy to tell whether they're a ginkgo, or camellia, or maple, or willow. Only cherry trees seem to become inconspicuous. When not in bloom, they're just nameless trees. Everybody remembers where they are only when the blossom season arrives. Otherwise, they're forgotten. At least that's my impression.

Every section of this garden has a different theme. Long ago it would have been the equivalent of an amusement park.

In one section apparently someone decided to put together a collection of unusual things, since there was so much space available.

Bring together lots of unusual trees and stones in the one place – that was the idea. When you see it, the word *singular* comes to mind.

Yes, singular, and conjuring up mysterious vistas.

This is just my opinion, of course, but the concept of *singular* is a subtle but important factor in much of Japanese culture. It implies taking a step back to admire something that might be slightly deviant, or unsettling in some way. To coolly observe something repellent and unpleasant and appreciate it as a form of beauty for entertainment. I find that psychology fascinating. Take the ideogram for "singular" for instance, which also contains the meaning of "suspect and unusual". I see in that a kind of warped humour. With echoes of a sadistic joke, a brutal awakening, or a detached gaze.

I wanted to write that book from the perspective of a singular gaze. I'm still not sure if I succeeded or not.

That's right, I have no desire to write another. People said I was a one-hit wonder, but from the outset I only ever intended to write the one book. The storm it caused when it was released took me completely by surprise. But I knew if I kept my head low and stayed quiet, it would soon be forgotten. Those were the days before the internet, and it was harder to get hold of personal information than it is now. The media were more laid-back too. I had several strategies that helped me get through that period.

I feel satisfied at having written it. Nobody knows what the truth is. It never even occurred to me to wonder if what I wrote was the truth.

V

What do I do now? Nothing in particular. I'm a housewife, I have a daughter who started primary school this year. I'd like to go out to work again soon but don't have any special skill, which makes it hard to find a job in this day and age. My husband never reads books, only newspapers. We first met sometime after all the excitement over the book had died down and he doesn't even know that I wrote it. That's fine by me. I don't think he's ever noticed it on my bookshelf.

It's easy to tell this is the top of a hill. This garden was originally once part of a castle. Over there is Mount Utatsu, with the teahouse district at its base.

My goal in life? For my daughter to grow up safely into adulthood, I suppose.

I don't have any great ambitions for myself. It's enough for me if the three of us can lead safe, healthy lives. A peaceful life is best. But such a modest ambition is becoming more and more difficult to achieve. People may try to live quiet, retiring lives, but things can happen. They might get caught up in a crime, or ill from food additives. The way society works or businesses operate can change in a flash, and even as you wish things would stay the same, a giant wave engulfs everything. It's tragic when people think the wave won't reach them but get swept away by it anyway. The wave takes everything with it, you hurt all over, and you're left holding on to nothing.

I wasn't swept away by the wave. It simply lapped at my feet. That was the extent of it. Even so, up until I wrote *The Forgotten Festival* I could see its white foam in the depths of night and could not escape its persistent roar.

After the book came out I received a lot of correspondence.

Many letters were critical, of course, and some were even threatening. But most were insightful and sympathetic. As I read them, I could hear the bewilderment and doubts of the writers. I sensed their struggle to process the experience of being caught up in the wave resonating from between the lines. Those letters confirmed my feeling that my work was done with this one book.

No, I don't mean that. It was anything but over, but the weight of those letters was more than enough to be burdened with in one lifetime.

VI

That's the famous two-legged Kotoji stone lantern. It's shaped like the bridge of a koto.

This particular scene often appears in travel brochures and on postcards.

The pines are wrapped up in winter to protect them against the snow. *Yukitsuri*, it's called. It's very beautiful, I'm sure you've heard of it. Bundled cones of radiant lines point skywards with a geometric beauty.

There's a concentration of spectacular pines and unusual trees in this area. Isn't the view magnificent?

This garden is more like a backgammon board than a theme park. Square one is the spindle tree slope. Then there's the cherry tree garden, and a curving river, and a bridge. I wonder where upstream is?

You're a curious person too, aren't you? What do you want to know?

I wrote down in the book everything I learned from my research. Frankly speaking, anyone who's interested in that book – which literally has been *forgotten* – must have time on their hands. Even if I do say so myself as the author.

It's all very much over and done with now. The suspect, although dead, was charged. A lot was never made clear, but it's all in the past. The investigation finished a long time ago.

Although I use the word *research*, all I did was listen to people connected with the case talk about their memories. That's the only approach I could think of, and realistically speaking, all I was able to do.

That said, I can see in retrospect how rash, insensitive and heedless I was.

The only reason I *could* do it was because I was a foolish university student who had the time. People still remembered my older brothers and me, and I guess my earnestness and general ineptness must have worked to my advantage.

Ten years had passed by then, which I think had given people enough time to put some distance between themselves and events. Enough, even, for some of them to recall that period with nostalgia.

Many of the people I interviewed told me that at the time they had felt extremely pressured by the media and curiosity seekers when all they wanted was to be left alone. But over time they had become more able to look back and reflect on everything that had happened. Some people told me that the more time passed the more they felt the need to talk things over again and express their opinions. But by then the affair was old news, forgotten by the world. Others, however, wished they *could* forget about it, but were too afraid to.

So, you see, my timing was good – I think that's what it came down to in the end – and was a big reason why I was able to write the book.

I was lucky. If there's such a thing as fate, then it was in my favour that summer during my fourth year of university.

Yes, that's right. At first it was supposed to be a substitute for my graduation thesis. I was studying marketing and hit on the idea of researching different interview and survey techniques to see what difference they made to the volume of information that could be obtained and the quality of that information.

Why did I think about researching an event from my childhood? I don't even remember what set me off now. But it was entirely unrelated to marketing.

Once I'd decided to do it, though, I never wavered. I persuaded friends to help me, I wrote letters to people with connections, I made phone calls, and from May until September that year I came here four times to interview people. Some people I saw every visit and others only once.

It was surprisingly effective to visit regularly with intervals in between. Sometimes my interviewees were too nervous to find the right words, even if they were willing. But often after I left they recalled things. And with repeated visits their memories started to come back. Some people said almost nothing to my face but would always send me a letter afterwards.

That summer was special.

The summer that it happened, and the summer I spent coming to this city to interview people connected with it, are joined in my mind.

I associate both summers with the colour white. White summers, white days. I'm sure I was in an abnormally feverish state during both.

By the time I'd finished listening to everybody, I was filled with their words. I couldn't even begin to think about a graduation thesis any more. When I started to write I felt possessed. I didn't know if I was writing a novel, or what it was.

If anything, it was after I finished writing that things got complicated. Unfortunately I'd written something that wasn't even remotely close to what a graduation thesis should be. It had taken me all summer, and I'd poured all my energy into it. So I was horrified when the reality of my position hit me. But I didn't have the time or energy to write another thesis.

At some point, however, my tutorial group found out about this strange document I'd been obsessed with writing, and then my professor got wind of it, and after reading he recommended I turn it into a thesis. Then, to my surprise, someone at a publishing company read it too – my professor's former student. And from there it quickly progressed into becoming a book.

Thinking back, it seems like a dream now. If that hadn't happened, you and I wouldn't be here together now. It was fate.

VII

The thing that stuck in my mind most at the time was all the grown-ups saying it reminded them of the Teigin Incident. I didn't know about that as a child. It wasn't until I studied Japanese history in high school that I finally understood what they were referring to. Teachers are hard-pressed to squeeze in everything up to the Second World War into the curriculum for Japanese history, so post-war history tends to get short shrift, and is something of a blind spot, don't you think? Personally, I prefer post-war history myself, I read a lot about it.

There are a few similarities to the Teigin Incident, but not much of significance, in my opinion. One day a man came along and gave a large group of people poison to drink – that's the sum of it.

The Teigin Incident occurred more than twenty years earlier, soon after the war ended, during the Allied Occupation. A man calling himself a doctor arrived at a branch of the Imperial Bank and said that he had been ordered by the Occupation forces to carry out inoculations because of an outbreak of dysentery. He then distributed what he said was an oral vaccine and asked everyone present to drink it.

Dysentery is a dated word now, but it was a common occurrence then. The so-called vaccine was in fact deadly poison and while the victims writhed in agony, the man made off with money from the bank. Twelve out of the sixteen people who drank the poison died.

A large group of people all poisoned at once. I suppose that similarity was striking. The post-war era was still fresh in the memory of the adults around me during my childhood.

This incident was carried out in a similar fashion. That day, celebrations were being held for two auspicious birthdays:

the sixtieth of the head of the family – the doctor – and the grandmother's eighty-eighth. Plus one of the grandsons had a birthday too. Everybody in the neighbourhood knew three generations in that family shared the same birthday. That's why nobody was suspicious of sake being delivered as a gift. The sender's name was given as a friend of the doctor, who lived in another region, and the delivery included soft drinks for the children. Such thoughtfulness made an impression, and of course nobody dreamed that it was all poisoned. The sake and soft drink were shared between everybody in the house for a toast.

The result was tragic. Neighbours, and a tradesman who happened to be there at the time, were also victims. Seventeen people died altogether, six of them children. There were three children in the family, so children from around the neighbourhood had come to play at the house that day.

Junji had a narrow escape. As you may know, he was always restless, someone who can never keep still, which was lucky for him that day. He was given some of the soft drink but came home without having any because he was so excited by the celebrations that he wanted to fetch me and my other older brother to go back with him and have some too.

The three of us arrived at the house to discover a scene from hell. People were scattered everywhere, writhing in agony. At first, we didn't realize they were in pain, because we couldn't comprehend what we were seeing. It looked like they might have been dancing about in celebration. But there was also vomit everywhere, and a sickly, sour smell drifting through the front entrance.

It was a long time before we could get that stench out of our nostrils. Just the sight of a soft drink was enough to bring back the smell for my brother, and he couldn't drink any for a long time afterwards.

My eldest brother was the first to realize something was wrong and ran straight for the police. Junji and I were terrified, and we ran back home to tell our mother.

In no time a huge commotion began.

The road outside the house, which was quite narrow, was blocked with ambulances and police cars, and a huge crowd of curious spectators gathered. That alone was almost like a festival crowd. We stayed inside, close to our mother, while outside the whole neighbourhood was in uproar. It sounded like the roar of the ocean, and I remember feeling that our house was like a boat. I had this vision of us floating through the crowd, drifting off into the distance.

Have you ever heard it said that in extraordinary circumstances the air changes colour?

Well, that day the air seemed to separate into two layers. A murky layer that hung over the floor, and another layer closer to the ceiling that sparkled, hard and clear. The air around our feet felt heavy and stagnant, but higher up it was as though the air was being sucked upwards by someone way up high. I really can't explain it.

It was a day like today, towards the end of summer. Humid, with no wind.

But summer lingered long after that day. The summer dragged on for us, and for everybody in the city that year.

VIII

Oh, careful. Look, see the fishing line strung out in a grid, like a go board.

It's to protect the moss. That's moss, not grass. Isn't it superb? That fishing line must keep the birds away, too. I expect it prevents large birds from landing there.

That large wooden building over there is the Seisonkaku Villa. It was built by a feudal lord as a retirement house for his mother and is listed as an Important Cultural Property. Shall we go inside? It's rather interesting.

Traditional houses are so dark inside, aren't they? The houses I lived in as a child always were. I remember the gloomy, mysterious interior of my grandmother's house in the daytime. There was always a sickly sweet-sour smell, a mixture of incense and medicinal poultices and food simmering on the stove, which used to make me feel depressed for no particular reason.

Chilly in here, isn't it? The sweat soon dries once you're out of the sun. What a relief. But it would have been cold in winter. The cold creeps in upwards from the feet. People in the olden days must have been chilled to the bone.

As I was saying, over a hundred police were assigned to the murder investigation. Naturally, since the whole city was in a panic. People in the neighbourhood were questioned so often it quite wore them out. My mother was a bundle of nerves. She wouldn't let us buy any snacks or cold drinks outside the house. All we were allowed to drink was green tea made at home. I suppose it was much the same in all households with children.

I was in grade five at primary school at the time, so I must have been ten or eleven. My brothers, who were very close in age, were thirteen and fourteen and in their second and third years of middle school.

The police interviewed us repeatedly. A detective and policewoman came to the house and had us talk about the same thing over and over. They questioned Junji many times, because he was at the house on the day. He was a sociable boy by nature, but even he became tired of it. I understand why the police did that, though. Almost everybody who was in the house had died, and the doctors didn't allow survivors to be questioned for quite some time afterwards.

As nothing was taken from the house, the police's first line of inquiry was a revenge crime. But the family was highly respected in the community, a family of doctors going back generations. They were all upstanding people, so it was hard to think of anyone who might have a grudge against them. The investigation soon reached an impasse.

When the investigation stalled, the atmosphere became tense. Despite a huge investment of manpower, and persistent questioning by police to the point that everyone was fed up with it, no picture of the suspect had emerged. Police and residents alike were stressed by the situation.

We were all on edge. A mass murderer was among us and we didn't know who. All anyone knew was it had to be someone nearby.

And of course the murderer *was* close.

The man in the black baseball cap and yellow raincoat.

Although he'd become notorious, no one had actually seen his face. Police created a composite photograph based on neighbours' testimonies, but it wasn't very useful.

The man who had ridden a delivery motorbike loaded with a case of drinks.

He wasn't the usual man from the liquor shop, but he gave a convincing impression of having been asked to bring the drinks round. As I told you before, the name he gave as the sender was a friend of Dr Aosawa's, the head of a hospital in Yamagata Prefecture who was a friend from the doctor's medical school days. So the doctor didn't question it.

Yes, it was raining at the time. A low-pressure system was approaching, and it was working up to a storm, blowing wind and rain. That's why nobody thought it odd that the man's face was hidden by rain gear.

Next day, the yellow raincoat was found in the river downstream. The man must have discarded it immediately after delivering the drinks. Apart from that strange letter, that's all the physical evidence the culprit left behind.

IX

We were in limbo, that white summer, while the police investigation dragged on through the late summer heat.

The longer it went on, the more worn out and depressed people became.

Practically the whole Aosawa family had been wiped out in one fell swoop, and the house looked like it was slowly crumbling away.

I crept past that house many times, but it was always deadly silent. You'd never have guessed there was anybody in there, although relatives from Fukui and Osaka had come to deal with the aftermath.

After the murders everybody treated the place like a haunted house – nobody went near it.

But of course it wasn't unoccupied.

She was still living there. And the people who took care of her.

I caught sight of her in the window a few times, but always sneaked away quietly, though she couldn't have seen me.

There was a large crepe myrtle tree out the front of that house. Crepe myrtle is most often associated with red flowers, like the decorative paper flowers used on sports days, but the flowers on that tree were pure white. And it always used to be in spectacular bloom over summer.

I remember walking past the house and staring at the crepe myrtle.

Maybe that's why I associate that summer so strongly with the colour white.

x

I think it was around the end of October that the investigation finally picked up.

The trigger was a suicide. A man living in a rented apartment hung himself. When the landlord who found him read the suicide note he called the police.

In his note the man confessed to being guilty of the mass poisoning at the Aosawa house. He wrote that he had delivered the poison after receiving notice that he had to kill the Aosawa family. This man had been plagued by headaches from an unknown cause for many years, and suffered from insomnia and delusions. He also had a history of psychiatric treatment.

Understandably, the police didn't take it seriously at first, because several other people had made similar claims by then. But they saw things differently when a black baseball cap, the keys to a motorbike and the dregs of an agricultural poison exactly the same as that used in the crime were found inside a cupboard in the apartment.

The clincher was the discovery that his fingerprints matched those found on a glass and the letter left at the scene. All at once the police and mass media were fired up again, and all people could talk about was the discovery of the culprit. But the excitement didn't last long, since he was already dead.

It was something of an anticlimax after the investigation had stalled for so long.

People had mixed emotions. Relief for one thing, but also a feeling of being let down. And, equally, an overwhelming emptiness.

They were glad the culprit wasn't a neighbour or acquaintance, and relieved that there was no reason to hold a grudge against the Aosawa family, but they still couldn't make sense of why all those people had died. Of the absurdity of so many innocent people losing their lives because of one man's delusion. Quite a few people became depressed once the crime was solved. It seemed so pointless. If the culprit had at least had a strong motive, it might have been easier to understand.

Once it was all over, people felt as if they had been left in limbo.

Yes, they did. Many people expressed doubt as to whether the man who committed suicide really was the culprit.

The biggest sticking point was his connection with the Aosawa family – what was his link with them, where and how had he met them? He didn't live near the Aosawas, and ultimately it wasn't clear how he knew them. In the end it was put down to an indirect connection through the Aosawa Clinic. It was a large facility, and there was also the possibility he'd seen an advert for it somewhere.

Another point of contention was how he knew the name of Dr Aosawa's friend in Yamagata. That doctor was cleared of suspicion, but *he* had no connection with the culprit either. That was another unsolved mystery.

General opinion was the man had delivered the sake, but some raised the possibility of someone else having actually put the poison into the drinks.

His acquaintances testified to his long medical history, his lack of confidence, and personality traits such as a tendency to dwell on things and be easily suggestible. There was speculation that he could have been persuaded by someone into believing he was responsible, and that *that* someone had planted the poison and baseball cap in his room.

It was only speculation, though – there was never any evidence to support this theory. In the end, the man who committed suicide was deemed the culprit.

XI

Impressive, isn't it? For a house of this kind the ceiling is quite high, and the stairs are rather wide.

The garden is magnificent too.

See how the wide eaves along this walkway are entirely unsupported? It's held up by a kind of cantilever structure. Wouldn't it be nice to take a nap here? It looks so cool and pleasant with the breeze blowing through.

What do I think? I don't know what the truth is really. I don't even know if I believe that the man who committed suicide is the culprit. Though I do think he is connected somehow.

The Forgotten Festival doesn't have a conclusive ending. I was criticized for leaving it open-ended, but I couldn't reach a conclusion. I never even thought I would reach one.

If I may speak frankly – and please don't misunderstand me – I wonder if a crime like this, something beyond our comprehension, is more of an accident than anything else. At some point it begins to roll down a slope, like a snowball, rapidly picking up speed. Moment by moment it gets bigger until, before anyone knows it, anyone at the base of that slope gets mowed down by it. Of course, human agency and contrivance are at the centre of this particular snowball, and probably repressed emotions have something to do with it as well, but I believe that terrible things – terrible beyond anything that humans could devise – *can* happen due to a series of circumstances coinciding with some kind of trigger. Such events are then presented to us in the form of a great calamity, as if to mock our puny human desires. Do you see what I mean?

My feeling is that this crime was something like that.

XII

Look at this room. It's so elaborate for such a small space.

It's called the ultramarine room. See how the walls are bright blue. That's lapis lazuli, a colour used a lot in ancient Egypt, apparently. It's made by grinding up highly prized minerals.

The author and scholar Kenichi Yoshida mentioned this room in his writings about the city. He said it was probably contrived so that when you go upstairs and walk along the veranda past the tatami-mat rooms to reach this corner room, your eyes will fall on the bright-blue walls, whose colour is enhanced by the slanting light from outside.

I don't know if it's a calculated effect or not, but in this city the walls of old houses are usually painted a deep red, so these blue walls are unexpected.

The light in winter reaches as far as that wall. It's an unusual, unsettling kind of room.

When she – Hisako, that is – was questioned, she was confused at first, and apparently started talking about this room all of a sudden. No matter what the policewoman said to her, she'd only speak of things she had seen as a child.

I can well believe it. She'd been alone and listening to her family dying all around her with no one to tell her what was going on. It must have been terrifying. Of all the people who lived in that house, only she had survived.

Hisako Aosawa... She was in her first year of middle school at the time, so she would have been around twelve.

Hisako was very beautiful. When she started middle school she had her long, straight hair cut short into a bob. It suited her – made her look like one of those traditional dolls. It also highlighted the contrast between her pitch-black hair and pale, delicately textured skin.

She was smart, and very composed. All the children in the neighbourhood admired her. My brothers, too. They idolized her.

But she had health problems, a condition called auto-intoxication. She turned pale sometimes and had to lie down. She was often absent from school, but the teachers weren't strict about that as she was a good student.

Autointoxication... Apparently children with unstable autonomic nerve systems often have it. The body manufactures toxins, just like with pre-eclampsia in pregnancy. Hisako said that on the day she had been sitting in her special chair with the armrests because she was feeling exhausted and drained of energy. Isn't it strange the things that can decide your fate one way or another? That day she didn't put anything in her mouth because of the auto-intoxication, which had always been an affliction but turned out to be her saviour.

I have to say, that was very like her. I realize she must have suffered, but that weak, delicate air did suit her perfectly. It added to her mystique. She was quite the young lady from a grand house.

I know how insensitive this sounds, but it was my impression that even the aftermath of such an awful tragedy was in keeping with her image. It was dramatic. She was the survivor of a tragedy – a role she was made for. Nobody actually said it, but I think the other children thought so too. She was a tragic heroine in our eyes, and the crime only ensured that she was imprinted that way in our memories forever.

XIII

When I did my research for *The Forgotten Festival* I spoke with Hisako only once.

She ended up living in that house for a long time afterwards, but when I met her she was packing up to leave.

She was about to be married. Her fiancé was a German guy who she had met at graduate school, and they were going to live in America, where he'd found a post. Apparently he was planning to have her eyes examined again by doctors in America.

She was happy to meet me again, and we spent a whole day together.

My conversation with her then was central to *The Forgotten Festival.*

Hisako's powers of memory were outstanding. She hadn't forgotten anything of what she'd touched and heard that day. Ten years after the event her memory was still astonishingly sharp. So much so that I felt able to recreate her experience in my own mind as she had lived it.

If she had been sighted, things would have been different, I think. I'm sure the case would have been solved much more quickly if she had been able to see the culprit. She heard somebody walking in the kitchen. She heard the letter being put on the table, and a glass being placed on top of it. If she had been so inclined, she could have seen the person's face.

If she had been able to see, of course.

Her thoughts ran along the same lines as mine.

She told me she couldn't have endured seeing everybody's suffering as they died. To have seen that would have destroyed her and made it impossible to keep on living afterwards.

She also said that she had always felt the weight of two conflicting emotions in equal measure. One was frustration that the perpetrator might have been caught earlier if she had been able to see, and the other was the certainty that she would never have survived if she had.

I think so too. If she had been sighted, she also would have died, either from having drunk the poison or being killed by the culprit.

Nobody knows what would have happened.

It was fate – *that* much is for sure.

XIV

Hisako lost her sight before she started school.

I don't know the details, but apparently she was injured falling off a swing and hitting the back of her head, then she developed a high fever and gradually her sight went.

Her parents were desperate and had her examined by numerous doctors in Tokyo, but no one could give them any hope of recovery.

She didn't lose heart, though. Being still young, and a bright, sensitive girl, she got used to being blind very quickly and didn't appear to be at all incapacitated in daily life. If you spent time with her, you'd see what I mean. When you're with her it almost feels as if you're the one at a disadvantage, despite being sighted.

She didn't go to a special school for the blind, either. Her parents must have done everything they could to get her into an ordinary school. She memorized the school layout and the exact details of the route our group had to walk to school every morning, so she was always confident. After she learned how to use an abacus she could calculate with such extraordinary speed it made everyone wonder what she might have been capable of if she were sighted.

She was very mysterious.

I did wonder more than once if maybe she actually *could* see. I always had the feeling that she picked up on everything, despite being blind. If you were in a room with her, she immediately perceived changes in people's facial expressions or what was happening around her. Adults often remarked on it too.

Sometimes she made mysterious comments. Things like *I became able to see after I lost my sight.* She often said that.

She said once it was as though she could see with her hands, or ears, or forehead. I remember feeling very spooked when I heard her say that.

That's why I tried to visit her in that house several times after it all happened, because I wanted to ask her privately about it. I thought she must have seen everything.

She *had* to know who the culprit was.

XV

I really don't know where Hisako is now. Still overseas, I expect.

We corresponded several times when I was writing *The Forgotten Festival*, but I've lost touch since then. With her intelligence, I'm sure she's managing perfectly well wherever she is. She might even have regained her sight. I enjoy imagining her being able to see again and prefer to leave it that way. I'm not inclined to look her up and find out for certain.

Oh, I knew it would still be humid outside. It's almost closing time but the heat hasn't let up at all, has it? My handkerchief's soaking wet.

Letter? Ah, *that* letter, you mean.

Ultimately it remained a mystery. Everything about it – who wrote it and left it there, why, and for whom? What did it mean, and who was this Eugenia?

It was never established anyway that it was he who wrote it. The handwriting was analysed, but experts couldn't say whether it was his or not as his writing hand was injured at the time. There's no doubt he touched the letter, but we don't know whether he took it there or simply touched it by accident when delivering the sake.

In the end, however, that letter was treated as evidence of his crazed delusions.

Eugenia…

It's not a name that strikes a bell, is it, so the assumption was that it must be a quote from somewhere. But despite extensive research the police never did find any clue as to who or what it might be.

I wonder if that letter ever reached its intended recipient.

That will remain a mystery forever.

XVI

Oh dear, a sudden shower. The rain here creeps up on you before you even notice it getting dark and overcast. Let's take shelter somewhere.

The raindrops are very large, so I don't think it'll last long.

Fate… The world spins on fate.

An amazing coincidence happened to me today.

When I arrived at the station, I saw a familiar face. We both recognized each other, but – as often happens – couldn't remember each other's name.

We stood there talking for a while, sizing each other up, and then we both remembered at the same time.

It was the policewoman who assisted in the investigation, interviewing women and children.

Meeting her again really took me back. She's retired now, apparently.

We chatted a bit, then she suddenly brought up the topic of Hisako Aosawa's interviews, and I learned something that I hadn't known before writing *The Forgotten Festival.*

It was about the blue room that I mentioned to you earlier.

Well, it might have been because of the shock, but apparently the first things Hisako spoke of in interviews were memories of when she could see, and she mentioned the ultramarine room in Seisonkaku Villa.

Another thing she mentioned was the white crepe myrtle.

That was a shock – I mean for me. It was a big shock that Hisako had spoken of the ultramarine room and the white crepe myrtle immediately afterwards.

If I'd known this before writing *The Forgotten Festival,* it would have been completely different.

XVII

What exactly do you want to know?

Do you intend to use my *Forgotten Festival* to write your own *Forgotten Festival*?

Me? Write a new *Forgotten Festival*?

Yes, I could possibly write another *Festival*, but that would belong to me – not you. There will most definitely *not* be another *Forgotten Festival*.

The real culprit? No, that's not what I was saying. Well, I'm not sure… I really don't know.

You see, it's a very simple story.

If there are ten people in a house and nine die, who is the culprit?

It's not a whodunnit. The answer's easy – it's the survivor, of course.

That's what I'm saying.

Hisako did it?

Well, I don't know what to think. I can't confirm or deny anything. There's no evidence or grounds to think that. But after coming here today, I know this – the last remaining person was the culprit. That's all.

Oh, it's so *hot*. Look how big the raindrops are still. This rain doesn't look like stopping any time soon. It simply stirs the heat up even more.

Such dreadful heat…

How long will this last, I wonder?

2
TWO RIVERS AND A HILL

The assistant

I

It's a long time since I took a stroll along this river.

The humidity's as oppressive as ever.

Indeed it is, and today's another sultry day. It's like being in a sauna. This clammy sensation on the skin brings back vivid memories.

Well, from my observations of the city so far, it's hardly changed in some respects, yet in others it's considerably different. In all honesty, I don't recall much. I was an utterly average student back then, not given too much to deep reflection. And it's been more than twenty years since I helped Makiko Saiga with the interviews for *The Forgotten Festival.* Well now, let me think, how old was I when the purpose of my travels began to change…

As a young man, I'd travelled with the intention of seeing things I'd never seen before. If memory serves me rightly, I used to say I'd go and see anything once so long as it was new, or had curiosity value, or was out of the ordinary in some way.

However, after I graduated and got a job, I became so consumed by my work that I lost interest in seeing new things. In fact, the aim of my travels became to not see anything I didn't have to. They were an escape from the daily grind, basically.

Yes, as time went by, I began to travel again in order to see things I had a fancy to see. Mind you, they didn't necessarily exist in reality any more. My travels became a quest for the sources of memories, things that I had ostensibly seen before. Scenes from childhood, for example, or locations with nostalgic associations and the like.

I do believe that's why I'm here now. It never would have occurred to me otherwise to visit this city, other than for work-related reasons. I'm here in search of nostalgic memories.

I say, the sky is rather low and gloomy, don't you think? One almost feels as if tears might fall from it at any moment.

And indeed, here comes the rain.

II

Makiko Saiga? I haven't heard her name in a long while.

She was a year above me at university. We belonged to the same club. Our official name was the Travel Club, but we weren't a particularly gung-ho group. In reality, it was simply your average social circle and mostly an excuse to play tennis or go skiing under the guise of "travel". We had a few dozen members and organized trips for the whole group, as well as small group tours. Five or six core members often put together short itineraries with very specific objectives. Tours to see listed cultural assets, or early Showa period buildings – that kind of thing. I enjoyed a ramble, so I often joined them. Makiko Saiga was also in that crowd.

My impressions of her? Well now, she was very mature. Composed, one might say. Which is not to imply she was passive or anything. I had the impression that she simply stood back and observed people. She seemed slightly aloof, which I interpreted as stand-offish in the beginning because she never initiated conversations or conversed in order to keep other people entertained. But once we spoke I realized that she was surprisingly unaffected and straightforward. Another thing about her, which you wouldn't have expected from her distant manner, was that occasionally she would become so excited she would rattle away like a machine gun. This contrast with her usual manner always astonished me.

Is she in Tokyo?

I see, so she has a daughter. Whom did she marry?

Aha, that means she didn't marry the fellow she was going out with at university.

Her boyfriend as a student? Well now, I never met him, but the word was that he was at the same university as us. My guess is they were in the same tutor group. I heard she started going out with him in second year and became engaged as soon as she graduated, but that might have just been rumour. You know how rumours can take on a life of their own.

You're asking why she chose me as her assistant? Good question. Even now I couldn't tell you the answer.

It wasn't as if I was indispensable to her. I'm sure that I wasn't the only one who could have done the work. Perhaps she simply thought I had the time. My being from Niigata, which isn't so far away, might have been a factor, but in actual fact I'd never been to K— before then.

All I did mostly was carry equipment, which wasn't a particularly onerous task. There were also papers and so forth to transport, of course, but by equipment I mean a tape recorder, which was simply a Walkman with a recording function – yes, they were on the market by then. I also assisted with transcribing the tape recordings.

Yes, interview recordings. That was indeed a challenge. I was meant to write down everything verbatim, but it was damned hard to catch it all. Before I got an ear for the local accent – which took some time, I might add – I had great difficulty following older people's speech in particular. I was often confused. Although I was born and bred in the Hokuriku region, there is an enormous variety of local dialects, and vocabulary and expressions differ significantly over short distances. The older generation also never learned standard Japanese at school, which meant that they tended not to distinguish between dialect and standard language, and that added to the difficulty of my task.

It was hard work, yes indeed, but interesting nonetheless.

At the time, we were discussing a crime that had taken place more than a decade earlier. Hence with the passage of time... er, how do I put this... it had taken on an aspect of legend or myth.

Sorry, that's probably not the best choice of words – of course it was a terrible crime. The impact on the surviving family and everybody else in the community was immeasurable.

Nevertheless, the interview subjects appeared to have put it behind them over the course of time. It's my belief that talking about it often had helped them to digest the experience to a certain degree. And in the process of that they had, in my opinion, gradually created their own versions of the story in their memories. Which meant that they had their stories already rehearsed in their minds, and perhaps explains why they were so interesting to listen to.

Yes, it was most fascinating to hear versions of the same event from many different perspectives. Hearing those stories frequently gave me cause to ponder the nature of truth.

Every person spoke in the sincere belief that what they said was the absolute truth, but if one thinks about it, it's difficult to describe an actual event in words exactly as one sees it. More like impossible, in my opinion. Each person has their own idiosyncratic biases, visual impressions and tricks of memory that shape their perception, and when one also takes into consideration the individual knowledge, education and personality that influence each single viewpoint, one can see how infinite the possibilities are. Hence, when hearing about the same event from a number of people, one starts to notice that all the accounts are, without exception, slightly different.

That's how I came to believe that it's impossible to ever really know the truth behind events. Once one accepts this, it follows that everything written in newspapers or textbooks as "history" is actually an amalgam of the greatest common factors from all the information available. Who killed whom may be known, but the parties directly involved were probably not aware of all the facts, nor could they have interpreted a situation at the time and know everything that led up to the event. Only an all-seeing god – if there is such a thing – could ever possibly know the real truth.

I recall being very depressed when I reached this conclusion. You see, I was a law student at the time. It mattered a great deal to me to know what we base our judgements of others on, and it was shocking to realize how presumptuous it was to think that we could know the truth of anything.

I did have memories of the crime. However, I was in primary school when it occurred, so those memories were only to the extent of being aware that something terrible had happened, and that all the grown-ups were talking about it.

After I agreed to help Saiga with her interview research, I did some research of my own in newspapers and so forth from the period, in order to get a handle on the chain of events. However, she told me that it wasn't necessary as she preferred me to have no preconceptions, therefore I didn't invest a huge amount of time and effort in preparation. The terms she offered were transport and accommodation plus a daily allowance, so as far as I was concerned it was nothing more than a short trip combined with some casual work.

Saiga worked a couple of casual jobs to fund her research, correcting homework for a correspondence course and serving in a shop that sold bento boxed lunches. She was very impressive in the way she set about executing a plan once she'd decided on it. She even calculated how much time was necessary to allocate to part-time work in order to raise the exact amount she estimated necessary to cover her research costs.

We stayed at a guest house near the station. In separate rooms, of course. I went with her to K— several times and we always stayed in the same lodgings. We also spent almost every night in the same way, with the two of us transcribing interviews. The people who ran the place apparently thought that we were budding folklorist researchers.

Yes, transcribing those tapes was painstaking work indeed. An hour or two can go by in no time during an interview. But when it comes to listening to tapes of those conversations over and over again in order to get them down in writing, however, it's extremely demanding work. We interviewed several people a day, hence the stack of tapes kept growing. We had to make at least a rough start on transcribing each conversation every day, or it only became harder when going back to find the necessary places the next time. It was intensive labour, similar to cramming for exams with a study partner. Yes, come to think of it, that's exactly what it was like – I was always reminded of the days I spent going back and forth to Tokyo to take my university entrance exams. I used to come up to the capital and study with one eye on the clock right up until it was time for an examination to start.

Saiga was always very economical with words. I don't recall her ever chattering unnecessarily. When the day's work was done, we would open a can of beer, talk a little to unwind, and then go to bed. That's how it always was.

III

Yes, I may as well confess. I did have feelings for her at the time.

It wasn't a romantic attachment exactly. I simply wondered what she thought about, what kind of person she was, and I wanted to get to know her better.

She wasn't a particular beauty, but she did have a distinctive quality about her – she was a person one noticed. I'm reasonably sure other men were very aware of her.

Female friends? Well now, she hardly had any as far as I knew. I suppose, from a woman's point of view, her demeanour was off-putting. She had a tendency to be dismissive of other girls, and whenever she had a request or needed to do something in a group, it was always the male students she approached first. She found men more efficient and straightforward to deal with. I remember her saying something to that effect.

However, I didn't have the impression that she simply fancied men. She wasn't the type to get annoyed if she thought they weren't paying enough attention to her.

Nor was she one of those lively, active girls who have had male friends since childhood. The kind who say other girls are boring and wishy-washy and that boys are simpler and easier to get along with. Deep down, that type of girl is actually a lot more "girly" than other girls.

That wasn't Saiga, either. She was very dry. That's why the other girls didn't think of her as someone who preferred men. If anything, she was regarded as a masculine sort, someone whose values were slightly different.

My impressions of her? She didn't trust anybody.

Yes, and she seemed to have no patience for all the intricate exchanges and games that went on between girls. She disliked that groupthink consciousness, of everybody having to do everything together all the time. From my observations of her, I formed the impression that she trusted nobody, and that when it came to the formalities of social interactions she would always choose men over women as her partner in any activity. If she ever asked something of you, it was never as a favour. It was give and take with her, she always made sure things were square.

Maybe that's why I was useful to her. I was someone she could be comfortable with, but I was also a safe choice because she knew it wouldn't go any further.

When we were transcribing the interviews, I used to wonder about the fellow she was going out with, what he was like and why she hadn't asked him to help. It might have been a simple reason, like the timing wasn't good for him, but she also might have wanted to keep her private life separate. From the beginning I could never picture what she was like in private. She never, ever let her guard down – to anyone.

When the two of us were alone together, she was no different from usual.

I didn't tell anyone I was assisting her, and I don't think she let it be known either. She wasn't the sort to open up about her activities to others, and since she was in her final year, she wasn't involved in the club any more. None of the acquaintances we had in common noticed the coincidence of us both being away from Tokyo at the same times.

When her thesis was made into a book, she asked if she could credit me as a collaborator, but I refused. For some reason, I didn't want anyone to know that I had helped her. I wanted that experience to stay a fond memory for myself alone. That was sufficient for me. In the end, however, my initials were amongst the acknowledgements, but nobody appeared to put two and two together.

IV

I only discovered after we began interviewing people that Saiga was connected with the case and had been at the scene on the day. She gave nothing away; I found out only in passing during the course of an interview. Imagine how astonished I was. It was all I could do to contain my surprise and maintain composure.

I'd read in a newspaper article about the neighbourhood children who had been at the scene but hadn't imbibed the poisoned drink. Never in my wildest dreams, however, had it occurred to me that she had been one of them! I'd assumed she was from Tokyo, and had no inkling she'd lived here as a child. In her student days her home was definitely in Tokyo.

Actually, until then I'd had my secret doubts about how effective the interviews would be. What would people think when a pair of students from Tokyo turned up and, apropos of nothing, started asking for their thoughts on a mass murder that had happened a long time ago. How would they respond? But when Saiga started speaking people opened up to her. Her surname jogged memories, and generally they remembered her. I was taken by surprise the first time it happened and asked her if she had prior acquaintance with that person. Then, to my astonishment, she informed me she'd been at the crime scene. The scales fell from my eyes. What I had anticipated to be a bit of casual work over the summer suddenly, and unexpectedly, became very direct and real. It cast her in a different light and caused me to reassess the situation. Up until then I'd considered her to be very cool and collected, so it was startling that she would decide to investigate a crime she had been connected with as a child. The thought crossed my mind that maybe this had been a defining period for her. Maybe it had shaped her personality. Maybe she had been dragging it around all her life.

It's not far from here, is it, the house where it happened?

Yes, it was the road along the river, I believe.

I went with her, just once, to the house. Yes, only the once. But I think she went there on her own a number of times.

It was a historic old stone house, with round stained-glass windows at the front. By then it was rather decrepit and had an air of having been forgotten by the world. To be frank, it was completely run-down. In spite of any preconceptions I had because of the murders, it didn't make a particularly ominous impression on me.

A crepe myrtle tree? Next to the front entrance?

Well, I can't really say. I don't recall it.

White flowers? I don't have any recollection as such. I saw the house in August, but don't remember a flowering tree. I might have simply forgotten, however.

I accompanied her to almost all the interviews.

The only one I didn't go to was at that house. When Saiga met Hisako Aosawa I didn't go with her. She told me my company wouldn't be necessary. That's why I only ever saw the house once. Which was also on the last day, when all the other interviews were done and we were about to leave.

The last thing I saw was that house. Saiga kept staring at it, right up until it was time to go and catch the train.

V

My word, the wind off the river is strong, isn't it? These gusts are unpredictable.

The wind blows from unexpected directions because of that hill, I presume.

Cities with a river through the centre aren't uncommon, but a city like this, with hilly terrain at its heart and surrounded by two rivers, is unusual. Defence was clearly the ruling principle of town planning here.

One can keep walking along here for quite a long way. Riverside paths like this, where there's no traffic allowed, give me a great deal of pleasure. Maybe this space is the reason this city has produced several world-famous philosophers. Isn't something similar said of Kyoto? And walking is supposed to be a source of inspiration, isn't it?

It's surprising how much a stroll along here jogs the memory.

I remember being in a dark house with lots of different people, and her sitting slightly apart from everybody else, operating the tape recorder.

Yes, people are indeed a mystery. The way they present themselves changes according to the place and person they are with. Everybody does that to some degree. However, I was astonished on a very deep level when I listened to Saiga conduct her interviews. It was as if she became an utterly different person. I knew she was intelligent, but I was unaware of this other talent.

From the moment she asked me to help her I was curious to know how she planned to go about conducting the interviews. I'd never seen her try to reach out to other people before, which is the kind of action that reveals what a person is really like.

I imagined that she would ask questions matter-of-factly, completely logically and with detachment.

But she wasn't like that at all. She presented herself completely differently, every time, according to whom she was speaking with.

I can't express it very precisely, but it was as if she became the kind of interviewer that the other person wanted her to be. She'd make the adjustment in an instant, changing her personality just like that. Even her expressions and vocabulary would vary. I might be expecting a timid, unsophisticated student, but she'd say something straight out and come across as an arch, with-it college girl. I don't really know if it's a good thing or not for an interviewer to be like that... it might be more desirable to present a consistent face.

Before then, I'd never seen her focus all her attention and energy on the person in front of her, so I was utterly taken aback by this aspect of her. It was quite discomfiting, actually, because she herself didn't appear to be aware of what she was doing.

I asked her once after an interview why she changed her persona so much.

That was in the beginning, when I still wasn't used to her drastic adjustments for each interviewee.

She was completely perplexed. "What do you mean?" she said.

I thought she must be teasing me, so I laughed and said, "You were incredible. When do you decide how you're going to present yourself with each person?"

She only looked at me more suspiciously. "What are you talking about?"

"But you were completely different with the person just now – the way you talked, your expressions and everything. Just like an actress."

She simply looked at me with a blank expression.

I realized then she had no idea she was doing it.

For some reason that sent a chill down my spine. At the same time, I was taken aback to realize just how deep the level of her concentration was in these interviews.

Why did I feel a chill down my spine? Well... probably because I realized she was capable of using any means to achieve something she'd set her sights on. Also, because I understood she would achieve that goal no matter what.

I was also uneasy about why she was going to such lengths. What exactly did she hope to discover?

She'd been at the scene of a heinous crime as a child. However, the perpetrator had been identified and for all intents and purposes the crime was solved. What drove her, then? It did cross my mind that I might unwittingly be involved in something significant. But maybe I was reading too much into it.

Please don't get the wrong idea. My intention isn't to level any criticism at her. There's a part of me that still admires her.

My abiding impression of Saiga is that she's a deep enigma, someone I will never be able to understand. You might say that in some respects I feel I failed.

That's also why, perversely, I wasn't much interested in the actual content of the book, despite the sensation it caused. For a time everybody who knew her was talking about it.

She came in for some strong criticism because of the title and subject matter, but I wasn't worried for her as I believed she was resilient enough to take it.

I also had an instinctive feeling that she'd achieved her goal the moment the book came out.

Yes, that's when she accomplished her objective. And it's why she lost all interest in it after publication. That was my sense of it, anyway.

When was it finished? Well now, I can't say I really know. But I do believe that the actual process of writing was significant to her.

VI

Hisako Aosawa? I never did get to meet her.

Saiga almost never mentioned her either, though I had the impression she wasn't inclined to share information about Hisako with me. Hisako Aosawa was very special to Saiga.

Hisako also seemed to be an unusual character. People reacted visibly when her name came up in interviews. A change seemed to come over them. Apparently she held quite a sway over people, despite her relative youth at the time of the murders. She seemed to be adored, respected and feared alike. Everybody we spoke to had a strong feeling of some kind about her.

What?

Ah, ha ha, you've seen through me yet again.

I'm no match for you. I never was any good at lying.

Yes, to tell the truth I did see her once, from a distance. This is just between you and me, you understand.

When one hears a great deal about a person, it's natural to be curious and want to see them in the flesh. I'd heard she was very beautiful and was desperate for a glimpse of her. She sounded like a heroine of tragedy or legend. I suppose it was natural for a young man to think as I did, though anybody might have felt the same.

When I realized Saiga wasn't going to permit me to meet Hisako, I became even more curious.

So one day when Saiga went out by herself I decided to follow. She sometimes went out on her own, and while she was away I would spend the time transcribing, or wander around the city sightseeing. On that particular occasion I pretended I was going out to see the sights by myself.

I had a rough idea where the house was, and managed to follow her there.

I saw Saiga walk briskly through the gate. But before she could press the doorbell the door opened, as if someone had been waiting for her.

Then I saw a slim young woman with short hair. She wasn't tall but seemed poised and dainty. I couldn't tell her age, but I did have the impression that she wasn't too far advanced in years.

I couldn't tell that she was blind. That's why I didn't realize at first she was Hisako Aosawa. If her eyes had been shut I might have known, but they were wide open. At first glance she looked like someone who could see.

So how did I know it was her? Strange, isn't it. But the moment she looked at Saiga and smiled sweetly, I knew.

Aha, so this is her, I thought.

And that was it. The first and last time I ever saw Hisako Aosawa.

My impression? Well, she certainly did seem special in some way.

Why? Well... I suppose because, hmm... I'm slightly uncomfortable talking about impressions. And I also regret using expressions like "uneasy" and "chill down my spine" about Saiga before. I hope you understand that truth is nothing more than one view of a subject seen from a particular perspective.

Perhaps it was my imagination, but when the door opened, she was looking at me.

Yes, she looked directly at the spot where I was standing.

I realize what I'm saying sounds contradictory. Of course she couldn't have seen me. But I firmly believe that in that moment, she was clearly aware of me.

Maybe it was just coincidence. Maybe she simply happened to turn her face in my direction. In all truth, I think that's probably what happened.

However, I know what I sensed. Hisako Aosawa knew I was there, and she knew I was looking at her.

Where was I? Well, I was standing in the shade of a tree on the other side of the street, which was very narrow, I might add.

Being summer, the tree was thick with leaves. I was in the shadows, and it would have been difficult to see me even from the other side of the road.

That's why I said to you that the truth is nothing more than a subject seen from a certain perspective. However, I was convinced at the time that she had seen me.

A crepe myrtle tree?

In front of the house?

At that time? No, I don't recall it. Is it significant?

After that? Well, I was rather shaken and went straight back to the guest house. I felt as if I'd done something very wrong.

Naturally I didn't mention any of this to Saiga.

VII

You'll recall my saying that whenever we came to K— we always stayed in the same guest house.

Well, Saiga also chose the same room every time.

Yes, it was an upstairs corner room at the end of the corridor. Occasionally I had a different room, but hers was always the same one.

I asked her once why she always stayed in the same room, and she answered that it was because she felt more relaxed. However, I suspected another reason.

We did the transcriptions in her room. We never spoke when transcribing, but as I said before we used to spend an hour or so winding down over a beer and snacks after finishing up at midnight. It was a time to review the day.

As I also mentioned earlier, we didn't speak a lot, but a few points have stuck in my mind, one of them concerning that room.

Saiga had a habit of staring up at a certain place on the ceiling whenever she was deep in thought. She would do it in the middle of transcribing, and sometimes in the course of conversation too, when she was considering what to say next. In moments of concentration, that's where she focused.

The guest house was Japanese-style with knotted wooden ceilings. You must know the type. As a child didn't you ever look at the ceiling and scare yourself silly imagining all kinds of ominous meanings in those marks? One never sees ceilings like that in modern homes, so children don't know what it's like to be afraid of a ceiling any more.

Anyway, when I looked up to see what she was staring at, I noticed a roughly oval-shaped gnarl in the ceiling.

She saw that I'd noticed and asked, "What do you think it looks like?"

"An amoeba, maybe," I replied. "What does it look like to you?" I asked in return.

"I don't know," she said. "A kettle maybe." Then she added, "A house I used to live in had a knot in the ceiling just like that."

That's why I concluded that the mark in the ceiling was the reason she always chose that particular room. I had no other evidence to support that, of course.

She asked me something else once: "What would you do if you wanted to send a message to one particular person when everybody is looking?"

I didn't understand her point exactly, but answered, "Isn't that the purpose of those three-line advertisements in the newspaper? Everybody sees them, but only the people they're intended for understand what they mean."

"Oh, I see," she responded.

Then, sometime later, she asked me again, "What if you planned to leave a note on the table at home or in a club-room to communicate something to one particular person only, what would you do then? And of course you didn't want anyone else who might see it to know who it's meant for. What would you do?"

I thought about that for a while. "If I could consult with that person in advance," I told her, "I'd decide a code or some kind of password to draw their attention."

Then she said, "What if you couldn't discuss it in advance?"

My response to that was, "The only thing you could do is write something which only that person could know about. It wasn't much of an answer."

But she repeated what I'd said – "something which only that person could know about" – then sank into thought for a long time, with a serious look on her face. I continued with transcribing and didn't give the matter much more thought. I still don't know if it's significant in any way.

VIII

I was aware that a strange letter had been left at the scene of the crime, but I never knew what it said. Saiga seemed familiar with it though.

After our conversation about the note, I thought it might be relevant and did some research in newspapers and magazines, but I couldn't find any reference to its content. The police apparently treated it as a clue to the murderer's identity. Yet although the murderer was identified, the police still don't know if that note was written by him or not.

I can't help feeling there's something inexplicable about this crime. I don't know how to express it precisely, but there's something incoherent or indefinable about it, something the human mind isn't equipped to engage with.

IX

Shall we turn back now? I think the rain has finally arrived.

The two rivers either side of the hill at this city's centre have very different characters. Although much the same in size, one is said to be masculine and the other feminine. The feminine river has a gentle, graceful ambience, while this masculine river has a certain wildness. Interesting, isn't it, how similar rivers can project such different personalities.

Well, this has been a most enjoyable stroll. I do like to take the occasional detour.

What kind of trip is this? Well now, I'd have to say it's slightly out of the ordinary.

I'm not here for the purpose of seeing a particular sight. This journey is one in search of something that exists only in my memory.

No, I don't have any desire to see Saiga again. My memories of her are sufficient. Besides, I still have a copy of *The Forgotten Festival.*

Yes, I did read it when I first received it. I wanted to know if Saiga's interest lay in the murderer's identity, or in the crime itself.

In the end, I couldn't decide. As I said earlier, I'd already come to the conclusion that her object was to have the book published.

Sorry, what was that?

Did she suspect that the real criminal was someone else? Are you referring to back then, or something she said recently?

Not clear?

Hmm, that surprises me. Perhaps she thought that all along. It could explain why she was so keen.

If that's the case, then that might have been significant too. By that I mean of course the title, *The Forgotten Festival.*

X

There was another reason I didn't want my name printed in the book as a collaborator. I kept it to myself, but it was in fact the real reason.

After hearing what you just told me, however, I'm inclined to think that Saiga may also have had her reasons. I had a feeling there was something she intended.

Well no, they were merely small things.

I don't think they were crucial.

But who knows?

I was with Saiga during almost all the interviews, and I transcribed them into writing. I remembered most of what had been said them.

Which is why when I read the proofs of *The Forgotten Festival*, I was surprised to find a number of perplexing discrepancies. Details that were different to the testimony we had heard.

Small things, not relevant to the main thread of speech. But unmistakably different to what had been said. To rephrase, I'd say they weren't the kind of mistakes you would expect as the result of oversight or carelessness.

When I began reading, I felt there was something strange about the text. At first I thought they were misprints, but there were too many for that.

Saiga had tremendous powers of concentration and was meticulous about double-checking, therefore I don't believe she overlooked these errors in the process of reviewing and correcting. I couldn't fathom how she had made such mistakes. But since they didn't affect the main narrative directly, I didn't dwell on it too much.

Is it conceivable she did it on purpose? Did she perhaps deliberately change the testimony when she wrote the manuscript? She did say it was neither fiction nor non-fiction, didn't she?

When the book came out, that's the position she took. It was neither, and she didn't mind which way it was taken. Which of course only exasperated the mass media even more. The media like to paint everything as black or white. Make a comment such as "I don't know", "either way" or "it's a grey area", and they come down on a person like they've committed a crime.

It's common to deliberately change identifying factors such as setting or appearance when actual people are the subject of a novel, but that theory didn't fit either. The persons involved could still be identified, and if the altered details were removed it wouldn't have changed anything.

Besides, the only parts that were altered were details that didn't matter in the least.

But they must have meant something to her.

In that case, however, it must follow that those words have some other significance.

She did ask me what one could do if one wanted to send a particular message when everyone was looking, if you recall.

I took it for granted she was referring to the letter left on the table at the crime scene. Up until this moment that's what I've always thought.

But what if? What if at the time she was doing her research, she already anticipated it becoming the book *The Forgotten Festival*?

Do you think that's a possibility? It's something that everybody sees, and through it she could send a message to one specific person while everyone was looking.

That bestselling book would be a way to do it. A message to a specific person... Someone connected with the crime who would be likely to pick up that book...

Someone she couldn't consult in advance or share a code with.

All she could do was write something which only that person would recognize.

Do you think it's relevant that she thought over what I said to her for a long time?

The parts she deliberately changed could be a message to a particular person, written so that only that person would understand, don't you think?

But if that's the case, there's one thing I don't understand.

Her attitude after the book came out. After it was published, she appeared to lose all interest in it. If that book really were a message for someone, wouldn't she care about their reaction? It's incomprehensible that she could lose interest in it entirely, just like that.

Or was she simply satisfied that she had made her charge and sent out her message? Was it all up to the other party, then, the one receiving the message, to interpret it and take action?

XI

It's getting dark.

I've got a train to catch, so I should be going soon.

Yes, I took over the family business back in my home town. We have an old traditional inn serving speciality high-quality cuisine. It's important for a place like that to have a reliable mistress for the front-of-house business, which is why I was able to come out today.

Yes, it's my wife – I'm not equal to her, I'm afraid.

Today was a journey in search of memories.

I never thought I'd come back here again, but it hasn't done me any good coming here today.

This journey has brought me face to face with something else in my memory, which wasn't part of the plan. Something I shouldn't have seen, and which I didn't want to see. I understand now that the temptation to see things you shouldn't see is much greater than the temptation to travel to see something you *want* to see.

Yes indeed, that's today's lesson from this city with its male and female rivers flowing through the centre. Its protectors.

What do you suppose those two rivers protect? Do you think they're conspiring? I'm starting to get that feeling.

Saiga didn't need me or anyone else to help her with the interviews. The Walkman and gifts for the interviewees that I carried for her weren't so heavy that she couldn't have managed alone.

But she had me accompany her on purpose.

She had me go with her to the interviews, do the transcriptions with her at night, and she made sure I remembered it all.

Was one river not enough? Was another river necessary for protection?

What was I doing there? What was it she had me help her with?

Is it possible I was there as her witness? Did she require an observer for some reason? Did I satisfactorily fulfil the role she expected of me, I wonder? Or did her calculations miss the mark?

I can see myself in future taking a leisurely stroll along this river bank. Coming here often to visit after I retire and hand the business over to my son. Coming in search of something in my memory, something I ought not to have seen, and dragging my old bones down to the river to stroll along here in the evening with a gentle breeze blowing off the water.

Ah... I just realized something else important.

The changes she made intentionally... the message to a specific person.

Could it be, by any chance, that the message was meant for me?

I was the person most likely to read the book and notice any irregularities. After spending every night with her working on the testimonies, I was the only one qualified to find all the discrepancies in the finished manuscript. Apart from her, the only other person in the world who would know is me.

It would follow then, of course, that she would lose interest in the book once it was published.

If her object was to have me read the finished book, then it had to have been written for one reader alone – me. There was a message in it for me. Her goal would be accomplished at the point I received the book and read it. Hence it didn't matter what happened next.

Ah yes, I'm well aware this is no more than wild conjecture on my part.

After all, the truth is nothing more than a subject seen from a certain perspective. I understand that.

But she's the kind of person who will stop at nothing once she's decided on a course of action.

I have no doubt she's already achieved her objective.

3

THE EMISSARY FROM A DEEP, FAR COUNTRY

An excerpt from* The Forgotten Festival *by Makiko Saiga, published eleven years after the murders

For the longest time the young girl did not know what to call the crepe myrtle tree, because although she had seen the name written down, she could not pronounce it. But as she grew older and her attention became focused away from the earth, the flowers of this tree, which bloomed between seasons, came to mean no more to her than a pattern vividly inscribed on the fringes of her world.

All human beings are alike at the beginning of their lives in that they live in close proximity to the earth and propel themselves on hands and knees along the ground until mobile enough to stand up and be liberated from the dirt, thus becoming more distant from it in the process. As they begin to become aware of objects at eye level and higher, so begins an estrangement from such novel delights closer to the ground as moss roses, dandelions, ants and rhinoceros beetles.

On this particular day, however, the girl's attention was drawn by the profusion of red that enswathed the tree. The evenly coloured cloud of red blooms reminded her of the folded paper flowers draped around classroom blackboards to welcome new students on their very first day of primary school. The girl had helped make these by folding layers of pink tissue paper into accordion creases and slipping a rubber band over the centre to hold them in place before opening them out to form a flower. She had folded one after another, flinging each completed flower into a cardboard box, until this bored her and she had begun to play volleyball with the folded paper flowers, sending them lightly through the air before they dropped to the floor.

But these look more like paper balloons than paper flowers, she thought, as she gazed at the tree on this particular day. The blooms were the same colour as toy paper balloons that make a dry, rustling sound when picked up and give a satisfying pop when smacked against the palm.

That day the sky was leaden with dark clouds. They crawled across her vision, blocking the sun, which had not once made an appearance since she had risen that morning. The world appeared drained of colour, and the flowers less vivid than usual. The girl did not like this hot weather, especially the humidity, which made her feel vulnerable and oppressed by a sense of silent malice.

On summer mornings, the air hung heavy.

The temperature remained constant overnight as the machinery of the city continued to function ceaselessly, generating even more heat to add to the already high humidity. The city was like an unventilated factory, and the shrill keening of cicadas that switched on early in the morning like the buzz of idling engines assaulted the girl's ears as she walked to the park for her early-morning exercises.

The uncomfortable heat constantly generated by this relentless factory sucked moisture from its workers until they were ready to drop with fatigue. As the end of the summer holidays drew near, however, the arrival of a low-pressure system heralding the approach of the typhoon season promised a respite from the heat.

An augury of rain was not the only thing out of the ordinary that day. The young girl was aware of the excitement in the air, unique to a special occasion, which had begun to pervade her neighbourhood early that morning. The air of anticipation that hung over the streets infected everybody, and the grown-ups, instead of keeping to themselves indoors, as normal, were outside rushing to and fro energetically, with more lightness of heart than usual.

Something's happening at the house with the porthole windows, the girl thought as she stared out at the garden from the dark interior of her home. She should have been finishing her summer holiday homework, but did not feel inclined to do anything as only her least favourite subjects remained. The situation was not yet urgent, but she did not have time to waste. It was the same every summer; there was always a period when the days slipped idly by before she was prompted to exert herself for the final spurt to finish her homework on time.

The girl shared a room with the younger of her two older brothers, who was three years her senior. Their room fronted on to the eastern side of a courtyard garden, roughly three square yards in size. Directly outside the room an old fig tree thick with amoeba-shaped leaves cast a spooky silhouette when evening fell. One night, not long after they had moved to this house, the girl had been frightened to tears by her brother suddenly raising his voice to yell melodramatically, "Look! Something's moving under that tree!" It was a very old tree and produced a great deal of fruit, which attracted flocks of birds when it ripened.

Even without the tree, however, the old wooden house that her father's company had rented for them was a gloomy place. There was a mark in a corner of her bedroom ceiling that looked to the girl like a face, and made her feel so uneasy that she could not bear to sleep there alone whenever her brother was away at school camp or elsewhere. She was not a particularly nervous child, but she was unusually imaginative. All the dark shadowy corners in the corridors, stairs and cupboards, and even the patterned paper covering the grime on the screen doors and door shutter box appeared sinister in her eyes and sowed the seeds of occasional nightmares.

Which is why the girl suspected she had had a visitation of another one of her nightmares. She had returned from early-morning exercises in the park, exhausted by the oppressive humidity of an approaching low front. She ate a hurried breakfast then went upstairs and flopped onto the lower bunk, where for some time she hovered in the borderland between reality and dreams. Though her body was all but asleep, one corner of her mind remained vigilant and alert.

Then, all of a sudden, she became aware of some kind of presence. A shiver of fear ran through her. What could it be? she thought. Naturally, the fig tree in the courtyard was the first thing to spring to mind. Two sliding doors separated the bedroom from the garden, each with four glass panes fitted in wooden frames, the lower two of which were frosted glass. All that could be seen through the panes was a blurred outline that cast indistinct shadows.

Someone's there, outside the glass door... No, not someone – something!

The girl was convinced of it. Tension slowly built as an internal struggle between drowsiness and fear played out. The fear won. She froze, paralysed in fright by whatever it was that she truly believed was out there. What was it? She wanted to see, knew she should see, but at the same time was desperately afraid of seeing.

Suddenly, her neck moved, but not of her own volition; something had made it move. Now she was able to look up and see the glass door as she lay on her bed.

On the other side of the frosted glass she saw a white shadow.

What on earth could it be? A cat, perhaps?

More than anything, however, it looked like a large, white cocoon.

A white cocoon?

The garden could be entered without passing through the front entrance, as the girl knew, because she had sometimes seen neighbourhood cats stroll along the top of the breeze-block fence and slip inside. But this cocoon-like object was too big for a cat; and besides, it moved in the upper reaches of her vision rather than along the ground.

She pictured a trembling white cocoon floating through the garden. Whether it was real or not was another question.

The girl could not have said how long she was in this state, but when at last she felt anchored in reality once again, she saw that the cocoon was no longer there. That presence of which she had been so keenly aware, so intensely that it almost hurt, had also vanished without a trace. Confused, the girl dozed off again. When next she awoke, everything that she had seen was gone from her memory, and she passed the rest of the morning listlessly as usual. It was to be a long time before any memory of this incident came back to her.

She had a feeling that the front door had been left open that day. In memory she sees herself sitting in the front hallway, looking out at the scene framed by the open door; she sees the crepe myrtle tree next to it, and people coming and going along the street.

Where were her brothers at the time? Junji was probably racing about the neighbourhood and would undoubtedly have been in and out of the house with the porthole windows since early morning. He was a sociable boy who could never stay still in one place for long. He slipped in and out of other people's houses without a second thought, and had mastered the art of doing so unnoticed.

Sei-ichi's voice still resounded in her head. The elder of her two older brothers was about to sit his high-school entrance exams. He had been in a foul mood that morning, however, because he was behind in the revision timetable he had set himself for the latter half of the summer holidays. His was the single room upstairs and he was now yelling angrily from the top of the stairs at his younger brother, who had apparently been in the room messing around with Sei-ichi's things out of boredom.

An image of Junji, trampling over all the canvas shoes lined up in the entrance hall as he beat a lightning retreat out of the front door, imprinted itself in the girl's mind.

After an outburst like that from Sei-ichi her mother would normally have been the first to admonish him, but the girl had no memory of that happening. Which meant that her mother must have been out at the time, calling at that *house to offer congratulations on the occasion. As newcomers to the district, the girl's parents could not very well neglect the social obligation to pay their respects to a family who were pillars of the community.*

The girl was sitting in the front entrance hall whiling away the time by reading a book about the life of Beethoven. It was one of a collected set of volumes for children about the lives of the great and famous. She had read this volume over and over because of one episode that particularly intrigued her. The episode that she could not erase from her mind was not part of the events leading up to the creation of Beethoven's masterpieces, nor his continuing to compose magnificent works despite his hearing loss, rather, it was an incident that had taken place just before he died.

One day, Beethoven had received a visit from a stranger; a young man dressed in black. They exchanged a few words, and shortly afterwards Beethoven died.

The man who had come to him was a messenger of death.

What did they say to each other?

The girl liked to imagine what the messenger might have said to Beethoven. Presumably the announcement had not been expressed directly; it would have to have been an enigmatic comment, something that was puzzling at the time yet made sense to Beethoven on his deathbed. What could he have said?

She tried to picture the face of the man in black. He would not be threatening or fearsome in appearance; if anything, she fancied him as a refined young man with noble features, whose expression hinted at his regard for the person to whom he was conveying the message and who had a sensitive insight into the nature of his mission. After the mission was accomplished, he would remove himself quietly.

To a distant place, deep in the bowels of the earth: the land of the dead.

The girl was fascinated by this image. She imagined a mountain at the edge of a wilderness, with an ancient cave at its base and a long staircase inside leading down into the depths. The man would disappear down it mounted on a horse.

Little did she know then that very soon she was to see a real emissary from the land of the dead, but for now she was still absorbed in her own make-believe image of a man who had returned below.

While lost in thought the wind had gradually picked up and the sky had become dark and overcast, though the girl had not yet noticed it.

However, upon hearing an immediately recognizable clacking sound outside, she lifted her head from the pages to see a stick searching the ground in the space framed by the doorway.

"Hisa!" The girl threw her book down and raced outside.

"Maki?"

Hisayo turned her head to look at the girl. It was not as if Hisa could really see, but that was how it appeared. As always, that moment gave the girl a start. The visitor's bobbed hair swung lightly, and she looked fresh in a dress patterned with pale-blue polka dots on a white background.

"Hisa, are you going somewhere?"

"I'm on an errand to collect the sweets for my great-grandmother's birthday celebration."

"How old is she?"

"Eighty-eight by the traditional count. It's a very auspicious number."

The young girl did not understand what was meant by traditional count, though she had often heard grown-ups use the expression.

"May I come in for a bit?" said Hisayo, registering the younger girl's uncertainty.

The girl happily took Hisayo's hand and together they sat down on the edge of the raised floor in the entrance hall, the boundary between indoors and outdoors. Hisayo laid her white cane on the floor. It seemed to the young girl that the visitor's presence had brought a cool breeze inside.

"When's your birthday, Maki?" Hisayo asked.

"The fourteenth of July."

"Oh, Bastille Day," Hisayo promptly responded. "On the day you're born you're zero years old," she continued, "but after a year passes you become one full year old. You understand that, don't you? So every year on the fourteenth of July you become one year older. But in the traditional way of counting, the year in which you are born counts as one, and every time New Year comes your age increases by a year."

The girl was confused. "Why count like that?"

Hisayo smiled gently. "In the past it meant a lot to people that they had lived to see in another year. Both adults and children recognized that a long life is a precious gift for which to be grateful. That's why every year we age is a happy occasion, so maybe people wanted a method of counting that gave them the most years possible. Not so long ago it was common for babies to die soon after birth, and many children died of illness even after they reached school age."

"Is today your great-grandmother's eighty-eighth birthday?"

"Yes. We've had visitors coming all morning, and it's so busy at home. I got tired of greeting everybody and having to be polite all the time, so I came out for a walk."

Hisayo poked out her tongue charmingly. It was pale pink, like a cat's. The young girl's heart pounded. To be sitting here next to Hisayo, just the two of them talking, was a momentous occasion for her. Sei-ichi and Junji were bound to be jealous when they found out. All the children in the neighbourhood idolized Hisayo.

"It's so hot and humid, isn't it? It smells like rain. There'll be a heavy shower before too long." Hisayo pulled a cotton handkerchief from her purse-shaped lace handbag and fanned her neck. A pleasant scent wafted from it.

"What do you mean, it smells like rain?"

"Gosh... it's the smell of rain clouds in the distance coming closer." Hisayo tilted her head slightly to one side. Perhaps it was due to her having to compensate for her lost sight ever since she was small, but Hisayo's senses were in a class of their own. The smells, sounds and feel of things that other people took for granted or gave little thought to seemed fresh and new when she gave comment on them.

Hisayo appeared to be listening intently. After a while she turned to the girl and said, "Is your mother out?"

"Yes. How did you know?"

"Because I can't hear any of the sounds a woman usually makes when she's at home. The small rhythmic sounds of somebody at work. Women make them when they move about in their own home, feeling safe and relaxed."

Hisayo's voice sounded like beautiful music to the young girl. She had once heard somebody say that Hisayo could see with her hands and face. Apparently there were people in foreign countries who could read print with the tips of their fingers. Not Braille. They really had cells in the fingertips that functioned like optic nerves. Maybe she had the same kind of cells in her body, one of the girl's classmates had said in all seriousness.

The girl had once witnessed Hisayo and Sei-ichi playing shogi *together. "It's easy if you remember the position of the pieces on the board. You can tell what each* shogi *piece is by touching it. Chess pieces too, that's why it's easy," Hisayo had said, but anyone could see that she had an extraordinary memory in addition to her rare ability to recreate a three-dimensional world inside her head from very few clues. Sei-ichi had lost that match, no doubt because he was too self-conscious in Hisayo's presence.*

The young girl wished that she could see inside the older girl's head. What did the world look *like to her? How did she* see *other people and the neighbourhood in her mind? The girl was sure it must be a boundless mysterious world that no one else could ever imagine or share. She stared at Hisayo's head; it was so small, yet it contained so much.*

"Oh, by the way, Jun was just at our house. I heard him at the back door." Hisayo spoke as if she had just remembered something.

"I knew it." The girl's voice was resentful. If Jun was at the house with the porthole windows, she wanted to be there with him. Her brother always went off by himself, leaving his little sister behind while he cheekily contrived his way into where all the fun was.

The girl felt the faint prickle of goosebumps rising, as if the temperature had dropped all of a sudden, and she sensed Hisayo's expression turning serious in that moment.

"Maki, I think it's best if you don't come to our house today," Hisa said sternly.

"What?" The young girl looked up at Hisayo, who sat facing straight ahead, staring outside with her unseeing eyes. From side-on her profile looked like a marble statue. "Why not?" the girl asked. Hisayo had never spoken so severely to her before.

"Just a feeling," Hisayo said matter-of-factly, in much the same tone as she might say it smelled like rain. "Tell Jun and anyone else too. The house is full of grown-ups from all over today, and some of them aren't keen on children, so it won't be any fun. The three of you can come over another time. I'll buy a log cake when you do."

The local cake shop's popular chocolate log cakes were delicious and also fun to share.

The girl nodded reluctantly. "All right."

"Don't come near our house today. Promise me," Hisayo reiterated, grasping her cane to stand up.

"Why not?" the girl persisted.

Hisayo went still, a thoughtful expression on her face. "It's just a feeling. But I think bats might come." And with this enigmatic comment, she quietly departed through the front door. Once outside she abruptly turned her face up towards the red crepe myrtle flowers. Apparently she knew the tree was in bloom. Hisayo's senses were so keen that without the cane few would have noticed that she was blind.

I think bats might come.

Hisayo often said this to express a sense of foreboding. She had a number of idiosyncratic sayings that she never attempted to explain, probably because she did not expect anybody to understand. These were baffling upon first hearing, but people would gradually become used to her manner of speaking and imagine that they were vaguely able to picture what she meant. It can only be supposed, however, that they actually did understand; for all anyone knew, what Hisayo pictured in her mind could have been wildly different. It was undeniable, however, that Hisayo's sayings added a certain mystique to her attraction.

Having lost her sight when she was small, could she have ever really seen bats? The young girl pictured bats with wings like a black umbrella. There were lots of bats in this area that came out in swarms in the evenings. For some reason the sight of them flapping about made the girl think of picture books showing star constellations. Perhaps it was their flight path as they wheeled and turned that reminded her of the lines connecting the stars.

The young girl remained sitting in the entrance hall, watching Hisayo's retreating back as she digested the older girl's parting words and recent presence beside her.

A cool scented breeze gently brushed her cheeks.

"Maki! What are you doing sitting here in the dark reading? You'll ruin your eyes!" It was the girl's mother, who had arrived home holding a small box in her hands. When the girl saw the traditional celebratory wrapping on it she realized that her mother had been to the birthday celebrations at Hisayo's house. The fact that her mother was dressed more smartly than usual in a white blouse and tight navy skirt also lent weight to this impression.

All of a sudden, the tempo of the house adjusted to her mother's presence. The girl lost interest in reading her book and went inside.

She opened up the small box on the table while her mother went about putting the kettle on to boil. Inside were two compact, neatly packaged sweet manju *buns filled with bean paste, one pink and one white.*

"Don't eat them, Maki," the girl's mother cautioned when she turned around and saw the open box. "That's from Dr Aizawa's house, and I want to show your father first. It's times like this I wish we had a family altar to put it on."

"I didn't eat anything." The girl replaced the lid. She had only wanted to look inside.

At that moment, Junji came hurtling through the front door. "Wow, you should see – it's amazing! There's loads of sweets," he said in a breathless rush to his sister. His eyes shone with excitement.

She knew immediately he was talking about that *house.*

"They said to come over. There are cakes and tea at the back door. Bring everyone, they said."

"Jun, don't go making a nuisance of yourself there today when they're so busy."

"Don't worry, Mum. All the adults are out the front but us kids are out the back. Everybody's there. Tasuku asked me to go back again. Otherwise it's too boring with just the grown-ups."

Junji spoke in a rush. He loved festive occasions, and big gatherings of people even more. Tasuku was the youngest boy in the Aizawa house.

Bitterness welled up in the girl. She had promised not to go near that house today. Hisayo's words weighed heavily on her, but she was in a quandary: should she mention it to Junji or not? Conflicting emotions smouldered in her breast; she wanted to boast about talking with Hisayo all by herself and nursed a strong desire to visit the house today, but at the same time felt obliged to keep her promise. While Junji continued to chatter away excitedly, the girl absent-mindedly made her way to the entrance hall, put on her shoes and wandered out the door.

"Promise me." Hisayo's voice echoing in the girl's head did not prevent her feet from pointing themselves in the direction of that house. She felt sweat break out on her skin. She would simply take a peep from a distance; that would be all. She would not go in; that would not be breaking her promise to Hisayo. Or so the young girl told herself.

Along the way, she passed elderly people carrying the same small box as her mother had brought home. Everybody was going to that house. The girl felt left out; she was the only one who had not yet been there.

She walked at a steady pace in the opposite direction to the flow of human traffic. The wind was gradually picking up, bending the roadside tree branches, and she felt occasional spots of rain. She saw people clutching boxes of manju *buns to their chests as they hurried home to beat the rain.*

When she arrived at the house with the porthole windows she saw that many people were still there, with the elderly guests sitting conversing on stools that had been set out for them. The white crepe myrtle in front of the clinic also caught her attention through the crowd. The gay atmosphere sent a thrill of pleasure through the girl, but at the same time it made her nervous. It was in every way an adults' world, with the men dressed formally in suits and women in kimonos.

In trepidation, the girl made her way around towards the back entrance. The house was bordered on three sides by roads, with the back entrance leading off a lane that separated it from the neighbour's house. The sound of children's voices coming from that direction made her relax slightly.

She saw children playing hopscotch in the lane on a grid marked in chalk, and stood at the entrance to the alley, hiding from sight as she watched them. The voices of other children floated out through the open roof-covered gateway. Women in aprons stood about chatting near stacks of beer cases, and she could see bananas and packets of thin-sliced rice cake laid out on a table covered with plastic cloth. Those must be the treats that Junji had mentioned.

"Promise me."

Hisayo's voice echoed in her head. What if she were seen loitering here? The girl's heart pounded. A fair-complexioned boy poked his head through the gate, glanced her way and spotted her almost at once. Startled, she prepared to flee, but he came bursting through the gate.

"Maki, come on in, there's loads to eat," he said with a smile, gesturing in invitation for her to enter.

The boy wore a white short-sleeved shirt and grey trousers held up by braces. This was Tasuku, the youngest Aizawa child. The Aizawa siblings were all fair-skinned with refined features. In addition, Tasuku exuded an air of well-bred good humour that set him apart from the other local children.

"Mm, but —" she mumbled.

"On a day of celebration such as this we have to share with others," said Tasuku, sounding very grown-up. He must have picked up this phrase from the adults.

"Well, just for a little while." The girl looked about nervously as she followed him, trying to be inconspicuous.

As they passed through the threshold of the gate she felt something underfoot. Looking down, she saw an old red toy car on the ground. Someone must have lost it.

"Tasuku, is this yours?" asked the girl, picking up the dirt-covered toy. She showed it to him.

"No, it's not mine. Somebody must have dropped it. Who does this belong to?" Tasuku called out in his limpid voice. Four or five children gathered near the back door all shook their heads when they saw the toy car.

"Not mine."

"Nah, never seen it."

"I'll keep it then. If you hear anyone's lost it, say I've got it." Tasuku brushed the dirt off the car and put it into his pocket with a responsible, grown-up air.

"Oh look, it's Maki. Hello, dear," said one of the women when she noticed the girl. "Jun was here just a little while ago."

The speaker was Kimi, an ample, welcoming woman in her fifties who had been coming to clean at the Aizawa house for many years. The neighbourhood children were all fond of her.

"He's home now."

"What a funny lad. Only a short time ago he was here for a spell, chatting away and having a great time. He certainly is busy." Kimi chuckled. She pulled a cellophane packet of lemonade-flavoured Ramune sweets from her apron pocket and put it in the young girl's hand.

"Me too. I want Ramune sweets too." Tasuku put out his hand for some as well.

"You already ate plenty," Kimi said sternly.

"Isn't this supposed to be a day for sharing?" Tasuku jiggled impatiently.

"Well, just one more then," Kimi said, putting another in his hand. She could never resist spoiling Tasuku. He was obviously aware of this and knew he could get his way.

"Come on, Maki. Let's eat."

"Okay."

The pair squatted at the back door and opened their packets. They thrust a handful of sweets into their mouths and the small pill-shaped candy stuck to their tongues, dissolving in the back of their throats with a sweet-sour fizz.

"Wow, there are lots of people here today."

"Yeah. Some city councillors came before, and they were bowing like crazy to Grandpa."

"What about Hisa?"

"She went out and hasn't come back yet."

The girl relaxed slightly. She resolved to be careful not to run into Hisayo on her way home.

"Oh!" An abrupt gust of strong wind snatched the cellophane packet from the girl's hand.

Hastily they jumped to their feet, but the packet had already disappeared over the fence.

"It's going to rain soon. I wish it wouldn't."

"Everything will be spoiled."

The two stood staring up in the direction the cellophane wrapper had disappeared. Swirls of inky clouds rolled furiously across the sky, rapidly changing shape before their eyes.

In the alley a motorbike engine sputtered and came to a stop. "Flower delivery," said the middle-aged man who dismounted, dripping with sweat and holding a bunch of lilies wrapped in white paper. "Delivery for the elder doctor, from Dr Terada of the Citizen's Hospital."

"Thank you very much." Kimi had put on sandals and come out to receive him.

The man removed his helmet and nodded in greeting. "Congratulations of the day."

"Thank you."

"You must have been busy all morning."

"Yes, we certainly have been. I'm run off my feet."

"Must be a happy occasion for the doctor to be blessed with them children. But his mother celebratin' her eighty-eighth at the same time is really summin' special. That makes 'er special. And a son and grandchild with the same birthday... well, that does make 'em different from ordinary folks."

"How's your mother doing?"

"Oh, she has 'er ups and downs. It's this weather, you know. 'Ard on the old folks, it is."

"Well, give your wife my respects. And thank you."

"I'll be off then."

The engine roared to life again, then faded into the distance.

"It's been like this all day, people bringing flowers and sake," Tasuku muttered, with just a tiny hint of pride.

"Wow."

Child as she was, the girl nevertheless grasped the tremendous influence and power of the Aizawa family, not to mention the gap between herself, an outsider, and Tasuku on the inside.

The last remaining sweet on her tongue grew bitter.

Kimi shook the water from the bunch of flowers and placed them in a bucket next to the back door. There were already three full buckets of flowers.

"Maki, take some flowers home with you later, dear. The house is overflowing with them," Kimi said, holding the lily stems over a burner.

"Are you cooking the flowers?" the girl asked in surprise.

Kimi looked at her quizzically, then smiled kindly. "No, dear. Scorching stems on cut flowers makes them last longer."

"Oh."

Peeking through the window, the girl saw several women in long-sleeved aprons bustling about the kitchen. A row of ceramic sake decanters testified to the numerous visitors. There was also a line of several stem vases on the table, waiting for flowers to be arranged in them. The girl's eyes were drawn to a beautiful blue glass vase that sparkled more radiantly than all the others beneath the fluorescent light.

I want that. She was seized with an abrupt, powerful desire to possess it.

"Here comes my sister."

The girl started at the sound of Tasuku's voice. She turned to see him craning his neck in the direction of the road. Moving to his side, she saw Hisayo come through the front entrance by the clinic and smilingly greet visitors. The girl observed how they responded with broad smiles in return and surrounded her. Although still a teenager and closer in age to their grandchildren, Hisayo was poised enough to hold her own with any adult. She had a mysterious presence that seemed to compel people to treat her with veneration, like a shrine maiden. She in turn received this treatment with the appropriate dignity.

The young girl was puzzled to notice that Hisayo was empty-handed. She held nothing except the lace handbag. Hadn't Hisayo said she had gone out to collect the sweets? Or had that just been an excuse?

"Tasuku, I'm going home."

"Hah? Already?"

"Don't tell Hisa I was here, okay?"

"Why not?"

"Please?"

Tasuku looked put out, but the girl ignored him and left smartly through the back gate. Though logically she knew that Hisayo would not be able to find her at such a distance, the girl could not help feeling uneasy. Being Hisayo, she was bound to notice. Here in her own home, she would surely pick up signs of the young girl's furtive visit, even from afar. The girl set off in the direction of home and sighed with relief once the festive atmosphere of the Aizawa house was behind her.

Then the rain came down.

No sooner had she noticed a few wet drops borne on the wind than they turned into a drenching torrent. The girl began to run. In no time at all her canvas shoes were soaking wet and the landscape was transformed. Passers-by bent over and scurried along, shopkeepers hurried to cover up displays outside their stores with plastic sheets, and people shifted their bicycles out of the rain. The girl ran as fast as she could through the monochrome scene.

"Maki!"

She looked up at the sound of her name and the rain instantly soaked her face. Junji was coming towards her with an open umbrella.

"Where did you go? Mum's looking for you."

"Where are you *going?"*

"Dr Aizawa's house."

"Again?"

"They said to come back later."

Junji was holding the umbrella, but she could not stand about chatting. Let him do as he likes, she thought with irritation. For no reason, she suddenly felt exasperated and ran off angrily towards home. It was no great distance, but avoiding the puddles made progress difficult and her breath quickened with the effort.

In the midst of all this, with everybody rushing frantically about, the girl's eye was suddenly caught by the sight of a young man standing on the street corner with a map in his hand, looking all around him as if he was confused.

He wore a black baseball cap and bright-yellow raincoat. Drops of rain trickled from the visor of his cap as he stood next to a motorbike stopped on the shoulder of the road, a case of drinks strapped to the back.

He seemed to be looking for signs that showed addresses, for she saw him hurry over to look at one with a street number on it. He compared the map with the sign, but was apparently not satisfied. Reaching his hand to scratch the back of his neck, the man seemed to realize for the first time that there was a hood on the raincoat, and pulled it over to cover the baseball cap.

The girl did not quite understand why the man had attracted her attention. Maybe it was because he was stopped in his tracks while everyone else about was running around in a panic. Or perhaps it was the bright-yellow raincoat that stood out in a landscape drained of colour.

Later, she was to replay this moment over and over in her mind.

With head cocked to one side, the man went to mount the motorbike. A clinking of glass sounded from the case on the back that held soft drink, beer and a large bottle of sake. He was about to grasp the handlebars of the bike when he noticed the girl looking at him and stopped to stare at her.

In that instant it seemed to the girl as if the world was enveloped in silence.

Instead of riding off, the man dismounted and walked briskly over to her.

"Pardon me, could you tell me if the Aizawa Clinic is near here?"

His voice was measured and clear. Beneath the baseball cap she saw a distinct five o'clock shadow. Unexpectedly, the Beethoven biography she had been reading in the hallway flashed into her mind.

"Are you going to the celebrations?" the girl asked.

The man looked at her in surprise. "Ah, I heard something's going on there today. I've never been to this part of town before, but I was asked to make a delivery."

He nodded and looked around him; left, right and left. She noticed his chiselled profile.

"It's over there. Go straight along this road, turn at that light, keep going and you'll see a stone house and the sign. That's the place." The girl turned behind her and pointed.

"Turn at that light? Thanks, you've been a big help."

The man nodded and gave her a smile. He lifted his hand in a small wave and flung his leg across the motorbike, then rode off with a rev of the engine, leaving the sound of clinking bottles in his wake.

Though thoroughly soaked by now, the girl remained standing there as she watched him disappear from sight. She satisfied herself that the yellow-raincoated figure had turned the corner, and once he had disappeared from the black-and-white landscape, the reality of the abysmal weather besetting the city streets returned to her.

Back home once again, the girl realized at last why the sight of the man had stopped her in her tracks.

The Beethoven biography.

The man who had paid a visit just before Beethoven's death.

This man, whom she had met on the street, was the very image of the man she had imagined as a messenger of death. A composed, clean-cut young man. An emissary from a far-off country, deep under the earth. She could not rid herself of the feeling that he had materialized here, in this present-day city, wearing a black baseball cap and yellow raincoat.

It can't be. It's just a coincidence.

The girl puzzled over it while her mother towelled her hair dry. And then she forgot all about him. When half an hour later Junji came back to ask her to go and get a soft drink with him at that house, her mind had already turned again to the homework that she had not yet finished.

4
THE TELEPHONE AND A TOY

The housekeeper's daughter

1

Yes, Mum passed away. Going on three years now, poor dear. Over twenty years after those murders.

She had a few minor strokes, but the last one left her unconscious in hospital for two months before she passed on.

Well, she did mumble to herself sometimes. Always the same thing. Like she was desperately calling out to someone. But we never knew who, though we always asked: "Who are you calling, Mum? What do you want us to say?" We never found out in the end.

Most of the time she looked like she was asleep, but sometimes a look of pain would come over her face. It used to give me a right start, make me think she was conscious again. It was like seeing a complete stranger take over my own mother's face. I always jumped and held my breath when it happened.

No, it wasn't because of the illness, she was stable by then. It was the past, coming back to torment her, that's what. She had terrible memories. More than anyone should have to bear. The thought of them made her twist her face in agony.

She lived those murders in her mind, over and over, I'm sure of it. The thought of her still trapped by the past as she lay on her deathbed breaks my heart, it does. Time stopped for Mum the day of those murders. She was still a prisoner of the past when she left us.

II

Yes, it's all very much over and done with now.

Mum's no longer with us. It's been some years since she passed. But to be honest, I still find it hard to talk about things. Even now I get a sick sinking feeling in my gut just thinking about that time. I know the pain's still there, stuck inside me like a splinter. That period of my life weighs heavy, it does. It's like a lump of foul, black jelly stuck somewhere deep inside me, but the last thing I want is to stir up the muck. I do my best to keep a lid on it, but never know when it'll come back… the slightest thing sets it off. It was evil we experienced then, you know, evil. The stench still hangs about. Nothing changes… the evil filth keeps pouring out and polluting everything.

I know people were scared out of their wits at the time, they had their suspicions to be sure, but my goodness, they said some terrible things… Unbelievable, it was.

I mean to say… Mum drank the poison herself, for goodness' sake! She was in and out of consciousness for nearly a week before she came out of the woods, and then it was another three months before she could leave the hospital. It was only coincidence she just took a sip of the poison. But that didn't stop people talking, did it? Dreadful, the rumours were. People said she knew the drinks were poison, that's why she only had a sip. They called her the poisoner, or an accomplice at the very least. Our whole family was under suspicion for a time.

It was criminal they way we got treated! Still upsets me to

think how the newspapers and gossip magazines hounded us… not to mention the tone they took! We got silent nuisance calls, and one day someone threw a stone into the garden, wrapped in an anonymous poison pen letter. Having to put up with that sort of thing on top of everything else was just rubbing salt in our wounds. It was a dreadful crime, I know, and everybody was caught up in the storm, but even so…

I can still hear Dad's voice when he went to the front door after that stone was thrown. I was holding the baby and stood behind him in the passageway, where no one could see me. I watched him deal with it.

Yes, he was. He sounded calm enough, but I could see his hands shaking. He must have been fit to blow his top.

Still, for all that, we managed to keep our heads low. It wouldn't happen that way now, with the media like it is. They're all over people in the news like a swarm of locusts. Nowadays they'd circulate photos of the family and before you know it you wouldn't be able to leave the house. Yes, it's mob justice for the criminal *and* the victims now… before the truth's known! But I believe the only ones with the right to criticize are the victims. I don't understand this behaviour nowadays… why is it okay to have a go at complete strangers? I really can't understand that.

III

At the time I'd just given birth, so I wasn't up the day of the murders. My first son was no problem, but for some reason the second was difficult, and I had a hard time recovering. I hardly ate, and didn't get up for two weeks. And I had dreadful black rings under my eyes for ages. My oldest burst into tears when he saw me, which just goes to show how different I looked.

That's right, my family's in the wholesale metal parts business. My husband's from a family of stonemasons, but being a third son he couldn't inherit the family business so he came to work for us instead. The understanding was he'd take over from my dad, who had no boys. When we married we lived with my parents.

Like I was saying, I was still in my bed, so my sister, a newly-wed at the time, saw to Mum in the hospital. She used to drop in on the way back to tell me how it was all going. I remember her crying and carrying on something dreadful as she told me how awful it was to see Mum like that. My sister's an emotional type. Always one to let her feelings get the better of her. When we were girls she used to cry whenever she was angry, and cry when she couldn't put her feelings into words. The tears would come rolling down... Anyway, that's what went on every single day when Mum was in hospital.

Yes, imagine how on edge we were, wondering what people were saying about us. If we'd had any more stone-throwing incidents I think it might have broken us.

But Dad was a rock, truly amazing he was. Told us to walk tall and not do anything that would give people cause to take advantage of us. There's always someone waiting for an opportunity to jump on others for their own amusement, he used to say. We did our best to stay calm and keep our heads down, just like he said. That's why we never had any direct run-ins over the rumours, though we knew what people were saying behind our backs.

Some people changed their tune quickly enough though, buttering us up and becoming ever so friendly and kind after police discovered who did it... though he was dead by then, of course. Maybe they felt guilty. We got given a heap of condolence gifts. To see all those boxes of sweets and fruit piling up made me very bitter, it did. Why pretend now, I used to say to myself. But we knew the ones who had changed their tune, and didn't touch any gifts from those people. Instead we shared them with families we got to know at the hospital. It was the least we could do to get our own back. Felt good, it did. Of course, even those people did the right thing by bringing a gift to mark Mum's leaving hospital.

Mum always was a hard worker, and cheerful too, never one to stand still. But after that day she was never the same again. She aged twenty years almost overnight. When I first saw her in hospital I was so shocked by the change I was lost for words.

She suffered after-effects from the poison of course, but I think the overall shock was just too much for her... she seemed to lose her will to get better. Part of it was seeing the youngest Aosawa child, a boy she thought of like a grandchild, die in agony right before her eyes. I don't think she ever got over it. Too cruel, it was. Mum herself experienced pain like nothing else on earth... that was another memory she had to live with... and, well, it was all too much to bear, I think.

Even now I wish I could kill that murderer. I can't forgive him committing suicide. The coward's way out. So unfair. A quick death is too kind. I'd like to drip-feed him his own poison, drop by drop, until he vomited and rolled on the ground covered in his own puke and poo. I'd make it last for days, too, so he knew what it was like to feel the same pain as his victims. That's what I wish.

IV

You want to know when my mother started working for the Aosawas?

She had always worked there, as far as I can remember.

Her family were gardeners, had been for generations. They had a small landscaping business and had been in charge of the Aosawa garden since the time of Mum's grandfather. She'd been going to the house with her father and grandfather ever since she was little. The Aosawas had a soft spot for her. Even gave her a fancy wedding gift when she married.

The younger doctor's wife was Christian. A fine woman, Mum used to say. Always gentle, never once did she hear the mistress speak impatiently or in anger. When the daughter lost her sight they did everything to try and get it fixed, but nothing worked. The master, the younger doctor that is, was very down about it, but apparently the mistress comforted him by saying it was God's will.

When the mistress started her volunteer welfare work they needed someone to help with housework, and that's when Mum's name came up. She'd known the family since she was small and liked being useful, so she was happy to take it on. I guess she'd been there twenty years or so when the murders happened. Like I said, she was always cheerful and spared no effort, so I'm sure they thought her a treasure, even if I do say so myself as her daughter. The children of the house were very attached to her. The youngest boy in particular... it almost made me jealous at times, even though I was an adult. Mum was awfully fond of that boy... he was her special pet.

I think you get the picture of how well she knew the family. The daughter, Hisako, and eldest boy, Nozomu, were both outstanding children, very self-possessed for their age and no trouble at all, so I understand why she might have wanted to spoil the youngest boy... he was a bit of a monkey.

V

Whatever else you might say about it, that house had a very particular atmosphere.

All the really good old houses are like that.

It was very tasteful. A lovely blend of Japanese and Western style, with high ceilings, a lace-covered three-piece suite and heavy curtains in the windows – just like a film set.

They always had music playing in the background. Classical, English songs, things like that – cheerful, classy sort of music. The master liked music, but that wasn't the main reason. People said the radio was always on for Hisako's sake. Apparently it's easier for the blind to find their way round with sound to guide them.

I used to go there a few times a year, whenever Mum asked me to take something over or I had to go and fetch her. But I never felt comfortable in that house, not like Mum and my sister.

I suppose because it was too different. Not real, somehow. Like a house in a play.

For one thing, visitors were always coming and going. You'd hear them talking, speaking so la-di-da like they were onstage. It always gave me a strange feeling to hear them. My sister liked hanging around there, but I never could bear being in the house more than ten minutes. They had imported clocks, and music boxes, and dolls we'd never seen the like of before, and any number of fancy, beautiful things. My sister loved to look at them, that's why she was always trying to get in there.

But me... I just didn't like it. Only a few minutes inside and the atmosphere of the place made me so tense I'd be itching to get out. So I always went to the back entrance if

I had to call Mum, and scooted off as soon as I was done with my errand. To avoid seeing anyone. If I ever ran into someone from the house I did a quick bow and kept going. They took me for shy, and used to say I wasn't at all like my mother. Mum used to ask me rather than my sister to run the errands there because she knew I wouldn't hang round. She could depend on me to leave straight away and never say anything more than I had to.

The smell used to bother me too.

I thought it smelled of disinfectant, because of the clinic.

But Mum and my sister said flat out there was no smell. Mum said the clinic and living quarters were completely separate, and that there wasn't any disinfectant in the house. She said I probably imagined it because I knew the clinic was there.

But it always smelled. Every time the back door opened that smell hit me. It was like a… how can I describe it… a cold, tart kind of smell. Made me feel like I wasn't wanted in there.

What I'm trying to say is, that smell might have had something to do with my feelings about that house. You know what a hospital's like, no matter how done up or how much the nurses smile, one sniff and you know where you are… in a hospital… a border zone between life and death. That's how I felt inside that house. I knew I had to watch myself, pay attention and be proper… be on my guard. That's the kind of feeling I had about the place, and I was always keen to get away soon as possible.

Of course, not everybody felt that way. Don't get me wrong about that.

They were a well-respected family in the community, known and admired for their good works. That house was a magnet for young people.

Once when there was a cholera outbreak before the war, the whole house pitched in day and night to care for huge numbers of patients free of charge. When I was a girl many people still remembered that with gratitude. I'm not sure if I'm making myself clear, but in any case that house was special.

Oh, by the way, I say the Aosawa house for convenience, but nobody really calls it that. I didn't even know for the longest time that the Aosawas were the family who lived there.

What people actually called it, if you must know, was "Round Windows". So-and-so of Round Windows, or at Round Windows, they'd say.

Round Windows. Yes, because it really did have round windows.

It was a nice-looking place. Built of stone, with three round windows in a row that made it look like a picture of an old-fashioned submarine. The architect was German. One of the doctors in the family got to know him while studying medicine in Germany. But the house was actually built by local workmen, so it sort of looks Japanese. You can tell that in places like the tiles around the windows, where the plasterers obviously used Japanese techniques to set them. Or the way the blue-green frosted glass was set in place.

I had a quick look once at the windows from inside. Each one's in a tiny room a few square feet in size. The middle room was a washroom with a deep sink, big enough to put a bucket in and fill with water to work with. The rooms either side both had wooden doors. On the right was a telephone room, but the one on the left had a shelf in it, that's all. The day I saw it, there was a single vase of flowers on the shelf. Strange, I thought, but when I asked Mum about it she was cagey for some reason. "It's the mistress's room," was all she'd say.

Nobody told me as such, but I know that's where the mistress said her prayers. I don't know if that was the room's original purpose. You know those foreign films where a priest goes into a tiny room like a telephone booth to hear confessions, so he can't see people's faces? Well, it looked something like that.

You could see the rooms lit up from a long way off in the street.

My friends and I used to play silly games on the way home from school in winter. We made bets on how many windows would be lit when we went past. It was dark, even in daytime when it snowed, which made the house look like a ship floating on a white sea of snow.

Everybody knew that house. It was the centre of our neighbourhood.

VI

Yes, no doubt about it, Hisako and Nozomu were the prince and princess of the Aosawa house.

They were slim, with fair skin and beautiful features. They'd have stood out anywhere. It wasn't so much that they stood out but that you couldn't help looking at them, your eyes just seemed to go in their direction. They looked like something from a fairy tale. Almost too perfect. Every time I saw them I used to think, *Those two aren't from the same world I live in.*

They were a mystery pair, all right.

I've met other people from so-called well-bred backgrounds, but those two had something special, something that put them beyond the understanding of ordinary folk like me. Children from that sort of background usually grow up a bit self-centred and naive, or perfect, or rebellious.

However they turn out, though, it makes sense because you can imagine that's how a person might well turn out if they grew up spoiled and wanting for nothing. Well, those two were both like that… set apart from the real world… but not in a way that made you understand them, if you see what I mean.

I can't explain it… they were both perfect. Good-looking, confident, clever, smiling, good manners, never naughty or above themselves. I don't think anyone ever said a bad word about them.

It must be hard to always be admired, always have people looking up to you.

It's tough to play a starring role. To always be the centre of attention. If a movie star ever goes off the rails, ever so slightly, there's a flood of criticism and they immediately get put in their place. Self-made stars can at least retire but those two were born to it, weren't they, born into a social system going back generations. There was no retirement for them. They were in it for life. That's what they faced.

Something about them made me think they'd given up on it all. Their situation in life, that is. I sensed… and this might be overstating things… that they had given up on their world. Because it was hopeless, you might say. They were kind and faultless because their situation was so hopeless… that was my sense of it, anyway.

Especially Hisako.

VII

I can't tell you anything about the day of the murders. I don't actually know any more than what was in the papers.

No, I never asked Mum about it directly. If she'd given the slightest sign she wanted to talk, I would have listened gladly, but I didn't want to bring it up unless she wanted, and she seemed to want to forget more than anything. In the end, I never heard a thing about that day from her.

The detectives who interviewed her were decent people. There were always the two of them, a man of about fifty and a policewoman. She was a bit on the plump side. They were so patient... the man wasn't like a detective at all. He was clumsy and awkward in some ways, but very gentle and kind... you might have taken him for a schoolteacher rather than a detective.

He was good with his hands too. I saw him in the hospital one day, fiddling about with something. I wondered what he was doing. Then I saw he was folding a tiny paper crane. He noticed me gawking and smiled. Told me he used to be a heavy smoker but gave up on doctor's orders, and ever since, whenever he craved a cigarette, he folded a paper crane instead. He was a bit embarrassed about it, and said it was his habit to fold a crane whenever he wanted to think.

I didn't know before that, but there's a kind of origami called Connected Cranes, and lots of other origami techniques for making cranes. Apparently a monk from the Ise region wrote a book about the traditional secrets of origami during the Edo period. The detective folded a few cranes from that book to show me right there and then, on the spot. He made a big crane with a small crane sitting on its tail, lots of cranes joined together in a circle, and two cranes joined at the stomach like they were attached to their reflection in water. It was magic the way he did it, using tiny scissors sometimes to make cuts. They all had fancy namcs. I still wasn't well at the time, and must have looked it because when I was sitting in the corridor the nurses spoke to me like I was a patient. That detective was always very kind. Oh, that's right, I remember the name of the crane that looks like it's reflected in water – it's the only one I remember. Dream Path it's called, apparently. Pretty name, isn't it?

The two detectives had permission from the doctors to visit every day.

Mum didn't say much at first, but she came to trust them, and I remember their little talks gradually got longer and longer. I don't think she ever said anything that gave them a clue as to who did it, though. They got on well enough with her, but the detectives always looked disappointed when they left.

It was painful to read the newspapers and magazines at the time. I wanted to know what had happened, so at first I bought up all the papers to read, but when rumours about Mum started going round I was too scared to read them any more. I'd open one up and all I'd see were the headlines. It felt like they were going to jump out at me and stab me in the chest. Sometimes I tried to open a newspaper but couldn't move for half an hour. I had to get my husband to look first and give me the all-clear.

That went on nearly two months. Time dragged because nothing was happening with the investigation by then. It had completely hit the rocks. The detectives didn't visit so much any more, and when I saw them again after a long while they looked dreadful… so tired and worn out. The minute I saw their faces I felt angry and hopeless all over again. Those people worked like slaves… how long would this go on for? While taxpayers' money got used up in the process… how long would the nightmare last? We were in agony having to wait so long, not knowing who to blame or who to complain to.

VIII

When news of the murderer's death came it was a bolt from the blue.

I'd never heard or seen that name before. It lit a fire under the media all right… they went into a frenzy, but we were left high and dry. Yes, the ones at the centre of the case were just simply tossed aside.

Straight away the papers and magazines started raking over the life of the man said to be the murderer, but for some reason it all felt remote to us. We were worn out by then. Even Mum barely batted an eyelid when she read about him being charged.

Then we all started to feel sort of uneasy. Was this the end? we asked ourselves. Could it really end this way? What would happen now… was this how we had to go on?

It was despair, I guess you might say… despair born of fear that this was how it would end. It was so disappointing the way it all ended. The murderer was already dead, so at least the media soon got over their excitement. Compared to how they'd been when the news of the murders first broke, that is. Before we knew it everything was over and done with, and the whole thing was all but forgotten. Just like that, we were out of the public eye again.

It's strange, but ever since the day the murderer's name came out, I lost my fear of the papers and magazines. Like I was set free of my demons… nothing scared me any more. I could read about the crime in the papers and not feel a thing.

The detective visited us to give a final report on the investigation. When I saw him in his warm dark-grey suit it gave me quite a start to realize how much time had moved on. It was autumn by then.

He looked calm enough, but there was something in his face that suggested he wasn't quite convinced. We felt the same, so it was a bit awkward all of us sitting there squirming in our seats.

He told us they were positive the man they had charged was the one delivered the poisoned sake.

From the way he said it, though, it sounded like he suspected someone else was involved. The real culprit. But he didn't tell us anything more.

"I followed a different line, I suppose," I remember him mumbling to himself just before he left.

"What's that then?" I asked him. He just laughed and said, "Oh, nothing." Then he seemed to remember something and pulled a Dream Path crane from his pocket to give to Mum.

It was made from lovely paper. Not his usual cheap stuff, but a fancy piece with flakes of beaten gold leaf in it. He told Mum to take care of herself, and said she had nothing to feel bad about. The way he said it was almost like a prayer.

But the moment Mum took that crane in her hands she burst into tears and nearly collapsed. Took us completely by surprise. The detective and I held her up between us, but she couldn't stop weeping for a long time.

"No, no, it wasn't like that, I wasn't supposed to survive," she cried. I was crying too. I asked what she meant by that. She just kept shaking her head and saying "No, no", over and over. I told her she didn't have anything to blame herself for.

The detective left without another word.

Mum and I went outside to see him off, and we both stood there crying for a bit.

To the end of her days she never mentioned another word about her outburst then, and what she meant by it.

That paper crane sits on my mother's memorial tablet even now.

IX

I was scared of Hisako.

I don't know why. I can't explain it in words.

I suppose I was jealous. She couldn't see, but she had everything. Or maybe everything came to her because she was blind. I know blind people might not like me saying that. But Hisako wasn't just anyone. You couldn't compare her to anyone, not by my standards, or by anyone else's.

It's my belief that she gave her sight in return for the world. Not the world that we know, but something different. I can't help feeling she made a deal when she was born into this world. *I'll give you my eyes if you give me the world in return.* At least that's what I think. That's why I was afraid of her.

I saw her on the swing once.

A small swing in a local park.

She was never afraid of swings, even though she lost her sight falling off one when she was little.

It gave me quite a shock to see her sitting on the swing at dusk one evening.

She was pumping her legs to make it go as high as she could, and looked almost desperate, actually. She went so high it worried me to watch her.

Then I saw the expression on her face.

She had a great big smile from ear to ear.

Looking like the cat that got the cream.

I've never seen a look like that on her or anyone else's face, before or since. I almost felt guilty, like I'd seen something I wasn't supposed to.

I was fair stuck to the spot… couldn't move.

Because for one moment, I had a vision… just a tiny peep… of the same world she was seeing from that swing.

Pure white, it was. White in all directions, a pure white world of nothingness. And the only thing moving in that pure white world without end was the swing.

It was like a revelation, I tell you, a real eye-opener.

I felt like… in that moment, I understood.

I understood the deal she made when she was on the swing that day. She was pumping her legs, making herself go higher and higher, and somebody said to her, *I'll give you the world if you give me something in exchange.*

So she said yes, and the next moment she took her hands off the swing.

x

I hardly know a thing about Makiko Saiga.

I saw her at that house a few times when she was a girl, but that's all. I had the impression she was quiet but sensible, and no fool. The sort of child who was always on her own, quietly watching while other kids played noisy games. My sister was also the curious sort, always staring at everything, but not in the same way as Makiko. Makiko was steady as a rock. Like she'd come into the world fully formed and nothing could ever shake her. That's the kind of girl she was.

When she came to see Mum I didn't realize she was the same Makiko I knew as a child.

They exchanged letters, and I knew Mum had agreed to talk to someone, but I didn't know until I asked that it was someone who used to live in the neighbourhood.

Mum had fond memories of her.

At the time Mum seemed to be on the mend, finally managing to shake off the effects of the murders. I think she might have felt like talking to somebody just at the time that Makiko contacted her.

I thought it would be good for her. She needed to draw a line somewhere, and I believed talking about it would help her work through things in her mind… that it would be a good thing for her to come to terms with events. Dad was against it from the start, but Mum told him she'd be fine, so he gave in.

Makiko came over once a month and spoke to Mum for several hours each time. She'd grown into a serious and responsible young lady. Every time I saw her, and remembered what she was like as a girl, I couldn't help feeling she hadn't changed a bit.

No, she was always by herself. Nobody ever came with her.

It worried me when I heard Mum crying sometimes while Makiko was there, but she always looked so relieved afterwards, like she'd got a load off her shoulders, so I didn't think too much of it. I can see now it might have been like counselling for her to talk about the past and say things she couldn't tell us or anyone else. Even Dad said he thought it was going well.

But when the book came out and there was all that fuss, Mum shut herself up inside the house again.

We were on edge too, because of talk about opening up the murder case again, and I wasn't too happy with Makiko Saiga then, I can tell you. She hadn't told us she was going to write a book, had she… all she'd said was that she was collecting material for her graduation thesis. Dad and I were both furious.

We wanted to have it out with her, but Mum dug her heels in and refused to let us.

"Don't worry, it's all right," she said.

She said that over and over again. Almost like she was trying to convince herself. So Dad and I had to leave it.

It was true Mum kept to the house during all the fuss over the book, but it wasn't like she was hiding from the world or was hollowed out and empty like at the time of the murders. She seemed to be concentrating very hard on something and lost in her own world for a long time. She was calm... yes, that's the best way to describe her... and spent every day, morning till night, looking through all the letters and old photo albums she put together for her talks with Makiko. She also had this air about her, like she wasn't going to be beaten. She used to get so deep in her thoughts I don't think she heard anything around her. So we just left her to it. Then all the fuss died down, like it usually does if you ignore it, and the papers moved on to the next big story of the day. Then Mum was left in peace again.

I can still see her now, sitting at the low reading desk on the floor of the tatami room, going through the photographs in that book ever so carefully.

I haven't seen Makiko once since then.

I wonder what she's up to now. I didn't hear of her writing any more books after that.

XI

Good heavens no, I never read that book.

After you got in touch I picked it up to flick through for the first time, that's about all. It was a slap in the face to our family. But we couldn't very well get rid of it.

Like I said, to her dying day Mum never mentioned a word about the murders to any of our family.

I don't know why she went on that day, saying "No, no, it wasn't like that" to the detective. We never found out.

But while she was reading that book, I could see in her face she was starting to remember things, bit by bit.

She never told us the whole story, no, but sometimes she dropped comments in passing. After Makiko had been at the house, and Mum was still upset. Times like that she talked to herself.

One day she came out and said, "Oh, there was a phone call."

Just like that. So I asked her, "From who?"

She just said, "On that day." But she had this faraway look and her eyes had a spark in them.

"That's right, there was a phone call, just when everyone was lifting their glasses for a toast. I'd just picked mine up and had only had the one sip, but when I heard the phone make a clicking sound I knew it would ring any second, so I rushed to pick it up. My ears were good, you see, and it was my job to answer the phone. It used to make such an awful racket I was afraid it would spoil the party. But already, in the back of my mind, I was thinking that something in that drink tasted funny."

Well, I thought that was very interesting, so I asked her who this phone call was from. Mum was unusually chatty that day.

"A woman… it was a young woman," she told me. "She didn't give her name. She said something strange… what was it… like she was nervous. 'Er, is everybody well?' and 'what's new?' – that kind of thing. 'Who's speaking, please?' I asked, and 'Who would you like to speak to?' Then she said something queer: 'Have you seen a thin dog?' I thought maybe it was a prank call, but all of a sudden I came over sick and dizzy. The house seemed to go dark. *What's happening?* I thought, then I heard the person on the other end of the phone say 'Ah!' and hang up. So I put the receiver down around the same time, because everything was going dark and I suddenly felt like throwing up violently."

I don't know if she ever told the police about this phone call.

To me it sounded like that was the first she remembered of it. I guess she'd had a memory blackout up to then.

But, you know, it makes me wonder how that changes things. If this woman on the phone said things like "is everybody well" and "what's new", well, doesn't that sound like she knew what was happening? She could have been calling to check if everyone had drunk the poison! Maybe the thin dog was a code word for the man who delivered the drinks.

So maybe there really was an accomplice. Maybe the woman who made that phone call was the real murderer. I couldn't stop worrying about it in bed at night after she told me this, I tell you. Maybe I should find that detective, I thought, and tell him about it. But when daylight came I always changed my mind. That detective was long retired, and the case was officially closed. There didn't seem to be anything I could do, so in the end I did nothing.

I remember Mum saying one more interesting thing.

One of the women helping out that day had stepped on something and almost tripped when she was carrying in the tray of sake and soft drinks.

Mum said she looked down and saw a red toy car on the floor.

It wasn't Tasuku's, because he didn't like getting his toys dirty. He had a big collection of model cars that he kept in a special case and only played with inside. That car was covered in mud. It was already dry but looked like it had been left outside and maybe someone – Tasuku perhaps – had taken it inside. Mum wondered who it belonged to. It doesn't matter now. But she did wonder about it.

Mum said it was a downright pity she didn't fall over. If she had, maybe not so many would have drunk the poison. She was very regretful about that.

You see why this story bothers me a lot?

What if someone in that house knew what was going to happen?

I can't say how much they knew, or if they were involved. But my feeling is that somebody knew the drinks were poisoned and tried to stop it happening. One toy car on its own can't do much, but put it on the wooden floorboards of the passage, where someone wearing slippers might tread on it, and it could be downright slippery and dangerous.

Mind you, this is just my guess.

But I don't know. Recently a lot of things have been preying on me.

I feel like Mum left me homework to finish off. Me… at this age! What am I to do?

Lately I have the same dream over and over, just before I wake up.

I'm walking across the surface of a white lake, like a ninja. I know Mum's supposed to be waiting for me, way up ahead. In front me is the Dream Path, and in my dream I know if I go along it I will see Mum.

I keep my mind on trying to walk across the water. It's misty all around and I can't see, but I know for sure Mum is up there ahead of me.

I hurry. Then I happen to look down and see a reflection of myself walking on the surface of the lake.

Me upside down… walking along underneath.

I look at my face.

But when I look closer, I see it's not me after all.

It's Hisako.

Hisako is walking upside down right underneath me.

I scream. Then I run, desperate to get away from her.

But Hisako runs too, keeping up with me no matter how fast I go.

I'm scared out of my wits.

I run and run and run. It feels like my heart will burst if I run any more.

Then I wake up.

XII

Mum used to visit the Aosawa family grave every year, on the anniversary of the murders. She always went by herself, none of us family ever went with her.

After she died none of us went either.

But I think I might go this year. Like Mum did, on the anniversary of the murders.

She wanted some of her ashes scattered in the sea, you know. It's because she grew up by the sea. The house she lived in as a girl had a sea view, and her primary school was set one street back from the beach. She used to say she always had the sound of waves in her ears. I kept back some of her ashes like she wanted, to scatter there, but haven't been able to actually bring myself to do it, so they've been in the house all this time.

But I think that this year I'll visit the Aosawa grave, then go to the beach near her old school and scatter the ashes there. Another thing I'm thinking about doing is reading this book through properly from the beginning. It might help clear my mind a bit.

It's a hot summer this year, isn't it?

That year was a hot one, too.

I think it's a good time to scatter Mum's ashes, at the end of summer.

Lately, I get an odd picture in my mind whenever I look at the sea.

I see a swing hanging down from the sky, over the water.

I can't see where the swing ropes start. They're hanging from high up in the clouds, like beams of light.

The swing rocks slowly over the water.

She's on the swing, of course.

Just like she was that day I saw her.

Pumping that swing with a smile so bright it's like she's not of this world.

I squint my eyes and watch her for a long while, swinging above the horizon.

Nobody else sees her. Only me.

Just like that day I saw her in the park... when was it?

Oh yes, the day of the joint memorial service for the victims. They held it after the murderer's suicide brought the case to a close. Anyway, I was coming back home around dusk when I saw her sitting on the swing, with a great big smile on her face.

5
THE DREAM PATH: PART ONE

The detective

I

It was because of ants that he chose his profession. The moment he saw them swarming all over a melted purple ice cream lying in the gutter, he had a feeling it was the right thing for him.

Since he was a serious boy who got good marks at school, his mother dearly wished for him to find employment as an office worker in a bank, or a trading company, or something similar that would pay a regular monthly salary, as she found it a struggle to raise four children on the unreliable income from her husband's earnings as a joiner. His parents pinned their hopes on their capable eldest son and made every sacrifice they could to ensure he received a good high-school education. He in turn had every intention of meeting their expectations, and had wished for nothing more since he was a young boy than to become independent in order to contribute to the family's income.

In the spring term of his last year at high school he began to discuss and explore his options with as many people as possible. Naturally, his first preference was to become an office worker in accordance with his parents' wishes, and after consulting an acquaintance who proudly gave him an introduction to a medium-sized trading firm, he went to visit an office for the first time. What he discovered when he went there, however, was that he felt very out of place in that environment. At first he could not identify the nature of this emotion, because he had never visited a company or seen the inside of an office before, and assumed it was simply connected with the novelty and surprise of it.

The scene that he encountered in the office was one of men briskly answering the telephone and office girls in dazzling white blouses, the energy and smartness of it all radiating promise of a bright future. If he had been like other youths his age the blood would have rushed to his head at the thought of being accepted as one of them, and his chest would have swelled with pride and hope. He might have imagined himself eventually joining the ranks of those men, making important phone calls, drawing up documents and bantering light-heartedly with the young women.

However, the only sensation in his chest was unease, and every attempt he made at picturing himself working there failed miserably. He was nonplussed by this emotion. What was it? Why couldn't he picture himself there? Why didn't it feel right?

The acquaintance who had given him the introduction assured him that these qualms were nothing more than a general symptom of anxiety about finding employment. "It'll be fine," the acquaintance told him breezily. "Everyone's nervous when they first start work. You'll have no trouble, Teru, you'll see. You'll get the hang of it in no time. And with your head for numbers, they might let you into accounting and you'll be promoted quickly."

Though he nodded vaguely in agreement, he did not find this reassuring. His uneasiness continued to grow. It was impossible for him to explain why he felt this way. He already had considerable work experience in a variety of casual jobs – delivering newspapers, labouring on construction sites and sorting invoices – which all went to show that his unease was not an allergy to hard work as such, nor could it be put down to anxiety about job insecurity, as that was not the case in the life of an office worker. Whichever way he looked at it, he simply could not picture himself in that environment.

After a great deal of thought he came to the conclusion that it might be due to lack of life experience, so with this thought in mind he asked his teacher to arrange for him to see other companies that accepted intakes of high-school graduates. This, however, did not make any difference, and wherever he went, he still experienced the same sense of unease.

If he had tried to express it in words he might have said it was the insincerity he sensed in that environment, the treachery he sensed in the cosmetic atmosphere of an office, which seemed superficial in comparison to his experience of life and the world.

In the impoverished neighbourhood where he grew up he was often derided for being a "goody-goody", or "aloof", or "looking down" on other people. He never denied that he felt different, and nor did he deny that he wanted an escape from there to help better his family's situation. He could not abide their cramped, squalid life with its complete lack of privacy, although he never expressed this sentiment openly. However, he did not feel comfortable with the world that awaited him when it was time to leave school and nor, in all honesty, did it hold any attraction.

By the time the summer holidays of his last year in high school rolled around he was still unable to open up about his feelings to anybody. In the holidays he took a job carting ice, conscious of the absurdity of hauling cold ice under a blazing sun while drenched in sweat.

One evening, as he was on his way home from the ice factory after a day of heavy labour, he noticed a commotion on the corner of a backstreet factory. Police rushed busily about, shooing away curious spectators.

He stood among the throng watching from a distance, and heard the whispers in the crowd around him.

"What's going on?"

"Woman stabbed her husband, apparently."

"She really stuck it to him – there's blood everywhere."

"Them two were always fighting. Husband's a real tomcat. Always heard 'em screaming they were gonna kill each other."

"He sneaked some pussy home in broad daylight when the missus was out."

"Blew her top when she came back and found 'em."

"Didn't think she'd really have the guts to do it."

He saw a policeman speaking to a middle-aged woman standing in a daze near the factory gate. There was a blank look on her face, and she gave no reaction whatsoever to anything that was said to her. Upon looking more closely, he noticed that her purple work smock and hands were covered in blood that was beginning to blacken. It was a weird contrast to the orderly row of morning glory vines in planters lining the alleyway.

Separately, he observed a young woman crying as she leaned against the railing of the entrance to the factory housing. Her white cotton kimono was open from the knees down, starkly exposing naked calves that trembled and twitched like the limbs of a dying frog.

He straightened up. A shiver coursed through his body. An entirely unfamiliar emotion rose in his breast and bared its fangs, his heart beat fast and hard. *What is this feeling?* he thought in wonder.

Perplexed, he cast his eyes restlessly about him for no specific reason and caught sight of a black lump in the corner of his field of vision. He bent down nimbly to examine it and discovered ants crawling all over some kind of object. His first reaction was to automatically recoil, but then he leaned in again for a closer look.

A white paper bag lay dropped in the shallow gutter. Inside, he saw two sticks of melted adzuki ice cream, dotted with exposed beans and stuck firmly to the paper. The swarm of ants that had appeared, as if from nowhere, was busily traversing the surface of the now shapeless ice cream.

It was just a hunch, but he had the feeling that this paper bag belonged to the woman standing by the factory gateway.

The evening was oppressively hot. Perhaps the woman had spontaneously bought ice cream for herself and her husband, wanting something sweet and cool after her labours were over for the day. But then she had seen the young woman in her disordered kimono come out of the house and something inside her had snapped. She hadn't been aware of herself breaking into a run and dropping the ice cream.

In that moment of insight, he had a vision.

He saw a man lying on a tatami floor covered in blood, the sobbing woman with trembling legs, the woman in the blood-covered smock standing rooted to the spot, and all the curious bystanders gathered outside. And then there was a youth, standing alone, apart from the crowd.

He had divined the nature of events while gazing at the object in the gutter, and that was when he knew it: *This is where I belong.* He was certain. From then on, he had no more doubts about his future.

The following year, after graduating from high school, he joined the police force.

II

Although he became a detective by choice, he was still something of a misfit in the workplace. Whether it was temperament that set him apart or an unconscious deep-seated rejection of something, he never became completely assimilated into the organization. While his colleagues in the force kept their distance, pegging him as an intellectual who was somehow different to them, they nevertheless respected him since he was affable, level-headed, carried out drudge work assiduously and did not rush into hasty, needless action.

Though he would never have actually said that he had found the perfect job, he was in no doubt that this was where he belonged. The work suited him, irrespective of the organization.

He liked a drink or two but drank mostly on his own, apart from with a few select colleagues. The bars he chose to patronize were places where he could enjoy a quiet drink in peace, for he never talked much about himself, and at his regular bar the other customers and staff assumed he was a teacher or researcher.

At thirty-two he married a woman who was introduced to him by an old high-school friend. By then his father had passed away and his siblings were all independent, which lightened his responsibilities somewhat. From the first he hit it off with his wife, a girlish, easy-going woman with no special ambition. Her outward demeanour, however, belied an inner strength that sustained her as she patiently nursed his mother through a long illness until death, and bore him two sons. Because of her, he was able to make a home and family.

His job was a busy one, but he was fascinated by the work. When attending a crime scene he always experienced the same vivid sensation that had come over him the summer he had seen the ants. Whenever he felt that thrill run through him he always felt guilty, as if he must be a deeply sinful man to experience such emotion. But essentially it was born of his curiosity about the true nature of human beings and a desire to understand them, which said much about the sort of person he was.

He used to ponder this and other such existential questions regarding human nature over a cigarette at the counter of his regular bar: *Who am I? Would I kill someone in an extreme situation if I were cornered? Are all humans the same? Is reason ultimately no kind of restraint?*

Shortly after turning forty-two, he was sitting at the counter drinking as usual one weekend when he felt an unaccustomed pain in his chest; the bar owner, noticing that something was amiss, called an ambulance that carried him off to hospital. There he was told by the doctors to stop smoking or there was no guarantee he would live. After this warning he felt compelled to quit. His cigarette consumption had increased since joining the force to the point where he was smoking close to two packs a day.

Cigarettes, however, had long been his constant companion and therefore giving them up turned out to be far more difficult than he had anticipated. Lollies or caramels were ineffective as a substitute as he did not have much of a sweet tooth to begin with, not to mention that they made him feel thirsty and left an unpleasant stickiness in his mouth.

One day, while in a highly edgy state brought on by the intense craving to smoke, he ran into an old school friend he had not seen in a long while. At the time he was working on a difficult case that had reached an impasse, which may have had something to do with what happened next. Unable to concentrate on the conversation, he unconsciously reached his hands out for a cigarette; then, realizing what he had done, he tried to cover up by taking hold of the sake cup.

The friend could not let this pass. He picked up the paper envelope for disposable chopsticks from the table and opened it out into a long rectangular piece. Then, without haste, he began folding it.

The detective's attention was captured, and he watched as in almost no time his friend folded it into a three-dimensional accordion. This impressed him so much he forgot all about cigarettes.

"Whoa, how did you do that?"

"Origami's all maths, you know. Maths was your forte, wasn't it?"

This friend had found a job after leaving high school but had then struggled to return to study at university; he now worked in a research laboratory. The detective recalled that his friend had always been deft with his fingers and good at origami as a boy. In addition to folding standard pieces such as cranes and beetles, he also used to make original creations that he designed himself.

From that day on the detective took to carrying paper about with him. In his pocket he kept square sheets of advertising flyers creased into four, which he opened up to fold any time he needed to think, or felt the desire to put something in his mouth, or needed something to fill time while drinking.

For an origami piece to turn out well the paper should be equal in length on all four sides. In the beginning he used to purchase paper sold for the purpose, but it wasn't always cut evenly, and so he began to prepare the paper himself, which also helped to economize a little. It became his habit on days off to use a carpenter's steel right-angled ruler to measure and cut squares from loose leaflets that came with the newspaper. His wife also collected flyers and decorative wrapping paper from cake and sweet boxes for him to use.

He rapidly became adept and moved on to trying his hand at more elaborate origami. Making original pieces and geometric designs in three-dimensional forms interested him too, but in the end he always came back to the most basic pattern, and the one that is also the ultimate in origami: the crane.

Cranes have been auspicious symbols since ancient times. Origami cranes were folded originally as part of Shinto rituals, and in fact the art of paper folding itself was believed to be a pathway to the gods. It was so highly regarded as an art that ancient documents record the importance of pouring heart and soul into every bird folded. Tradition has it that the first origami crane was folded at the Ise Grand Shrine, one of the most sacred of Shinto sites, which perhaps explains why priests from the Ise region were responsible for the invention of various crane designs during the Edo period.

The detective obtained copies of the ancient documents, and he liked to puzzle over pictures of completed pieces to work out how to fold them without referring to the explanatory diagrams.

With connected cranes – a series of large and small cranes joined together, requiring the use of scissors – he enjoyed trying to figure out where to make the cuts. He realized that once he had fathomed a set pattern it was all a question of application, but if he became fixated on the pattern it was impossible to do anything new.

In some ways this resembled his work. He had come to learn that people's actions were to a certain degree fixed patterns, a template for reading the train of their emotions, but he could not allow a pattern to solidify into assumption or prejudice, as that would prevent him from seeing anything else.

Three years had passed since he had taken to concealing origami paper in his jacket pocket, and he was now forty-six years old. It was at this point in his life that he encountered the most incomprehensible case of his career so far, one that failed to make any sense and was impossible to comprehend based on any of the other patterns he had met with so far. He was to remember it all his life: the case of the mass murder poisoning.

III

The detective acknowledged the existence of a faculty that humans call instinct, as well as intuition that could be honed by experience and professional knowledge. Although he would never dare express it in those words exactly, he had encountered many instances that led him to believe there could be no other explanation than these faculties at work.

There used to be a very popular American detective show that he watched with his wife in the evenings. It was one of those inverted mystery-type dramas that begins with a scene of the person committing the crime. In the show, the perpetrator is usually intelligent and someone of high social standing who at first glance appears to have committed the perfect murder. Then along comes a mediocre-looking detective in a shabby trench coat, catching the culprit off guard. The mediocre-looking detective is in fact outstanding; sharp and observant, he sticks close to the culprits, frustrating and annoying them at every turn, boxing them by slow degrees into a corner.

Some of the detective's colleagues dismissed the programme as unrealistic, but the detective was not averse to a police drama with a clear, comprehensible motive that wound up satisfactorily in under an hour.

Teru was watching this programme with his wife one evening when she said to him, "Can you tell the first time you meet a criminal whether or not that person is guilty?" The detective in this particular drama was always saying that he could tell the first time he met a guilty person because he had a nose for these things.

He didn't know how to respond to this. In almost all the murder cases he had handled it was obvious from the first who the murderer was, since he or she would either be at the scene of the crime standing next to the victim in a state of bewilderment, or would have fled in horror at their own actions but be easy enough to track down quickly. He had never seen a perpetrator like the ones on TV – a tuxedo-wearing, champagne-drinking schemer who lives in a mansion with a pool, has complicated interests at stake, is the type to say "call my lawyer" and commits a carefully thought-out crime requiring the preparation of an alibi and the planting of red herrings in advance – and nor did he ever expect to encounter one either.

"No, not at all," he answered his wife, but deep down he heard a voice inside: *You never know.*

It could happen. He did think it possible, but was doubtful that he would ever have the chance to test himself.

He was not to know that this very opportunity awaited him in the near future.

IV

That opportunity arrived towards the end of summer.

The day started out unbearably hot due to an approaching typhoon, with warnings of torrential rain forecast for the afternoon. As he left home in the morning the detective patted his pocket with a sigh. His usual sheets of folded paper were in there, but he knew that the heat and humidity would turn them damp with sweat and render them unusable. It would be impossible to fold anything in this weather. On previous occasions when he had been caught in heavy downpours, afterwards he had had to scrape a wet pulpy mess of soaked paper from his pocket with great difficulty. It crossed his mind that he might be better off leaving the paper at home today.

The misery of the endless, wearying heat was compounded by the prospect of having to spend the day on long-delayed paperwork. Much as the detective loved his job, even his feet dragged as he set out wearily for headquarters.

However, there was something else going on under the surface, another reason that he did not feel like going into work today: a hunch that something bad was going to happen. From the moment he had awoken he had been unable to shake this feeling. At first he hadn't identified it as a premonition. Perhaps he wasn't well, he thought, or maybe the weather had brought it on. But by the time he left home he was close to being convinced that something bad was going to happen that day.

He patted his jacket pocket again, still in two minds over whether or not to leave the paper behind, but thought that it might be better to avoid doing anything different from usual today, and so he left it in there.

The weather might have had something to do with the fact that headquarters was more crowded than usual with colleagues grimly tackling their paperwork. In the afternoon the rain arrived in a cycle of violent downpours that periodically beat against the windows, highlighting the quieter than normal atmosphere inside.

"Aargh, my brain's on strike today."

"Even my cigarettes are soggy."

Curses punctuated the silence between downpours.

The detective rose to fill his cup with weak, watery tea and pulled out the origami paper from his pocket as he walked back to his desk. Sure enough, it was damp and difficult to open up, let alone fold.

In weather like this he tried to stick to warm drinks as much as possible as lots of cool liquid made him feel drained, but his cup of tea was uncomfortably hot to hold. On the spur of the moment he put the piece of folded paper down to use as a coaster, then went back to his paperwork while waiting for the tea to cool. But it was taking a long time, and he was thirsty.

Inwardly cursing, he persisted with his pen. The irritation mounted, threatening to spill over: *the heat… this blasted paperwork… something bad is bound to happen…* He could not take in the words on the paper.

He sighed and unconsciously his hand sought his pocket, but then he remembered that the paper was under his cup. At last the drink was cool enough to sip, but his face screwed up in reaction to the unappetizing taste of the weak, insipid tea. He'd be better off with plain hot boiled water.

The detective was about to wearily put the cup down again when his glance fell on the paper he had used as a coaster. Where the cup's base had touched the paper was a wet ring, through which the print on the layer underneath was visible. Two words inside the ring leapt out at him, one in the upper left and the other in the lower left. Taken together they read `woman trouble`.

He was startled. Though it was still hot and he was dripping with sweat, a chill swept through him. He stared at the two words. Why these words? Uneasily he peeled away the top layer of paper to reveal an advertisement for a pharmacy below:

> `For the woman who suffers from cold or hot flushes, joint pain, knee or back trouble.`

He smiled wryly. *So that's it.* Just a coincidence, that was all. He felt foolish, but nonetheless relieved. Still, the chill did not go away.

Something very bad was going to happen today.

This thought was in his mind when he heard the harsh, loud ring of a telephone.

V

The detective and his colleagues were reeling with disbelief as they made their way to the crime scene through driving rain and strong wind after receiving the first report. How could this have happened? And in such awful weather? The wind was steadily picking up and the rain, which was already bucketing down, was only getting worse. Ferocious gusts rocked the car as they stopped at an intersection. The detective wondered briefly whether the weather might have been a factor in the perpetrator's choosing this day to commit the crime. Rain shutters on houses were firmly closed, umbrellas were useless, and it was difficult even to open your eyes. People were staying indoors, which meant that inevitably there would be fewer witnesses and no one would have heard anything. Any evidence such as footprints would also be washed away. It was possible that the weather had been a deciding factor in the timing of the crime, he concluded, but his prevailing mood was still one of disbelief.

Unusually for such extreme weather, upon arrival at the scene they were met by a large crowd of people in raincoats standing motionless in the rain. The police, who had arrived first, were controlling traffic on the other side of the crowd. Water streamed from the voluminous waterproofs that shrouded them like filmy white membranes and their voices were drowned out by the rain, making the scene look like something from a silent film.

A sense of reality returned when the detective saw parked patrol cars and ambulances blocking off the road. Despite being prepared for it, the roar and onslaught of rain and wind that whipped his body when he opened the door still took him by surprise. He hurried over to the huddle of police officers, and by the time he reached the entrance of the house he was as drenched as if he'd been in a swimming pool. With the driving rain limiting his vision he had not been able to get an overall view of the house until now, but once ushered inside he was at last able to look around and absorb its grandeur. The place was huge. These were rich people. He thought of a tuxedo-wearing, champagne-drinking villain. That thought, however, was instantly driven from his mind by the overwhelming stench that assailed his nostrils.

"Ugh!"

The sour-bitter, metallic smell was overpowering and prompted everybody entering with him to automatically cover their noses.

He noticed a woman collapsed in the corridor, lying in an unnatural, contorted position, and his first impression was that she must be terribly uncomfortable.

Ambulance personnel reacted in horror to the smell, despite the masks they wore. They emerged from the interior waving their hands. One of them spoke to him. "Don't go in. There might still be poison in the vomit and excrement. We need to get fresh air in, but I can't open the windows in this weather." The man sounded desperate.

"Police. Are they all dead?"

"We took the ones still breathing to hospital. The rest are gone."

"How many went to hospital?"

"Five."

"What about the doctor?"

"Not here yet."

"Was it poison?"

"More than likely. Looks like they drank a toast and all went down together. Even Dr Aosawa," the paramedic gasped. His face was pale. "There are glasses lying all around. I'd like to prohibit entry if possible."

"Hey, are you all right? Do you feel okay? Maybe you absorbed some of the poison too."

"Yeah, I'm okay. I —" The paramedic staggered and reached out for support. A strange sound came from the back of his throat and the detective realized that he was about to vomit. He rushed over to the man. "Hey, not in here. Somebody help!"

After escorting the paramedic outside and getting him assistance, the detective went back and returned to his examination of the corridor. Peering cautiously along it, he saw that there were in fact two prostrate human forms, and it was clear that both were lifeless. He swallowed hard, pulled out a handkerchief to cover his mouth and cautiously ventured along the corridor. The floor was wet with liquid spilled from dropped glasses. He tried to touch as little as possible as he stepped gingerly, determined to commit everything he saw to memory. Outside the raging wind roared, but inside the house was heavy with the silence of death.

It was literally deathly silent. Light spilled from a room at the rear of the house, accentuating the darkness of the corridor. The bodies belonged to two women who both wore aprons. Household help, he thought. One appeared to be in her forties or thereabouts, and the other was perhaps about sixty. At the moment of their deaths their bodies had twisted into unnatural positions. Their throats bore scratch marks and their hairpieces were out of place. *Had they crawled this far?* he mused. The air reeked of vomit mingled with urine. He clutched the handkerchief he was holding over his mouth and drops of cold sweat formed on his temples.

Glancing down, his eyes lighted on a small red toy car lying at his feet. It gave him a jolt: so there were children in this house.

Reaching the doorway to a room, he peered inside. The sight that met his eyes struck him physically, like a blow to the face. He stood rooted to the spot.

It was a large room, with a high ceiling, and there were more – many more – people in there than he had anticipated. He ran his eyes over them all, carefully counting. Twelve in total.

His first impression was that they were all asleep, because the scene reminded him of sleeping together in the big hall at kendo club training camp. But that impression lasted only for an instant: in the next moment he took in the meaning of what his eyes were seeing and froze in horror. Every body bore testimony to the extreme suffering of the occupants of the room in their last moments. They lay twisted with their clothes in disarray as if, incongruously, they had been dancing, and their faces had contorted in expressions of agony as, covered in their own vomit and excrement, they had kicked against tables and chairs in their dying throes.

A woman wearing a kimono, an elderly man in a suit and a well-built man in his fifties were slumped on and behind the sofa. Another elderly man had died hugging his knees. It was pitiful to see the bitter realization of defeat writ large on their faces as the final moments of their lives ebbed away.

He felt something clutch at his heart and trembled violently at the sight of boys lying toppled on top of one another in the shadow of the table, boys who looked to be about the same age as his youngest child. They lay with limbs flung out like dolls, their defenceless, ashen faces turned to the ceiling and mouths hanging slackly open.

It was unspeakably tragic. The parents must be in here somewhere, too.

At the sight of a teenage boy in school uniform he felt another another stab of horror.

No, it can't be. Yukio…?

A fear that this was his own son impelled him to look closer at the face, but the soft brown hair and pale complexion of this youth soon confirmed that it was not. He shook with almost hysterical relief. And, close upon this reaction, a sudden comprehension of the full reality of the situation dawned – that he was in a room full of dead bodies – and made him want to scream out loud.

The paramedic with whom he had spoken earlier must have felt the same, he realized, and most likely have been overcome not by noxious fumes but by the sight of all these corpses.

Something in him broke as he felt overwhelmed by an intense, ominous sense of cold reality, the like of which he had never experienced before. The room seemed filled with ants crawling over ice cream mingled with the vomit scattered over the carpet. Chills coursed through his body and the ants crawled over his skin. He felt a suffocating, cold, otherworldly evil. An enormous, unshakeable evil that was capable of crushing his puny, insignificant self. For a moment, the horror overpowered him.

Two conflicting voices clashed in his head.

Run. Escape. Get out of here as fast as you can – now!

Look. Imprint this in your brain. Comb the murder scene with your eyes!

He sighed deeply into his handkerchief and made a determined effort to focus his mind. But his feet would not move. He didn't know what stopped them from moving. Pale-faced, he forced himself to stand in the centre of the room and look all around. He saw a barely touched feast. Overturned glasses scattered here and there.

Abruptly, a jarring sense of something out of place prompted him to turn and look behind him. He recoiled. Yet all that met his eyes was an empty rattan chair: a light-brown, comfortable, single-seat rattan chair with an indigo dyed cushion on it. What was so strange about that?

Feeling a shade more composed, he turned this over in his mind and soon realized what had triggered his reaction. While all the other furniture in the room had been knocked out of place by the agonized death throes of the occupants, that seat alone was in the right position. Amid the chaos which had engulfed the room, only that seat remained untouched. Did this mean that the person who had been sitting in that chair was unharmed? With so many people in the room, somebody must have sat there. Had that person stood up immediately after sipping the poison drink and moved away from the seat?

`Woman trouble`. The words underneath his teacup. For no reason they flashed into his mind. The memory startled him. And then he realized that he had unconsciously assumed that the person who had sat in this chair was a woman.

He ran his eyes over the room once more, then gently withdrew. Out in the dim corridor he took a moment to compose himself before continuing his exploration of the house, casting his gaze all about him as he trod carefully. When he reached what he guessed must be the kitchen he peered in and saw plates of food covered in plastic wrap, a stack of sushi bowls, bottles of beer and soft drinks, and ceramic serving bottles of sake neatly arranged on the table. Obviously this was where everything was prepared before being carried to the other room.

Then something on the table caught his eye, a sheet of plain, white notepaper held down by a vase holding a single withered Asiatic day flower. Something was written on the paper in unremarkable handwriting. He read it. *What the hell is this?* he wondered.

VI

Outside, the noise level had ratcheted up with the arrival of the medical and crime scene units. With more and more people arriving, the cacophony of voices drowned out the clamour of rain. His instincts told him that the media were there too. Now things would get complicated.

Crime scene staff streamed noisily into the house, amongst them a colleague, also soaking wet, who whispered into his ear, "It's no good. Three died on the way to the hospital."

"Any survivors?"

"One might pull through. Still unconscious, though."

"No chance of an interview, then. Who raised the alarm first?"

"A nearby police box put the call through. There was a party on today and some of the neighbourhood kids were here. One came late, saw what had happened and ran to get help."

A neighbourhood kid. He felt an ache in his chest. Several dead children were in there.

"Any suspects?"

"There was a young guy wearing a yellow raincoat who delivered sake and soft drinks. Someone saw him bring them. Never been seen here before, apparently. Their deliveries usually came from a local liquor shop." His younger colleague looked troubled. "This is going to be a shitstorm," he said in a low voice.

"Certainly looks that way."

"This is the Aosawa Clinic."

"The Aosawa Clinic?" So far the detective hadn't paid much attention to the name of the place.

"Yep," the colleague continued, "old medical family. The founder was a graduate of the Fourth High School at the Imperial University. Used to be head of the Prefectural Medical Association too. The son took over a long time ago, though."

"I see. Then all these people…"

"Yep. The wife, son, his wife, grandchildren – all dead. The whole family was killed. Ambulance guys knew their faces."

The detective frowned. People of social standing. He knew what that would mean, all the extra attention it would attract. After what he had seen inside he also had a sense of the complexity of the case, the tangled, nerve-fraying reality of it, and could foresee the enormous workload it was going to bring down on him. Already he felt tired at the thought.

Something else occurred to him. "Hey," he said, looking his colleague in the face.

"Yeah?"

"You said three died, didn't you? And one was unconscious, likely to survive."

"Yeah."

"What about the other person?"

"Other person?"

"Five people were taken to hospital."

"Huh, really? I didn't hear that."

At that point another older, veteran detective came through the front door. He too was wet through, and his thinning comb-over was in a tragic state.

"The TV and newspapers are already here. Their ears are sharp," he complained in place of a greeting.

"Taro, do you know anything about the victims taken to hospital?" the younger detective asked. Taro was short for Taromaru, the man's full family name.

"Three dead. Two survivors, but no visitors allowed."

"Two? Two survived? Both unconscious?" he asked eagerly.

Taromaru shot him a bleak look. "One's unconscious. The other's physically unharmed, but is under sedation due to severe shock."

The younger detective's heart pounded. Survivors. There were survivors who had seen what had happened from the very beginning.

Taromaru looked at him pityingly, as if he'd divined

this thought. "It was the granddaughter. Hisako Aosawa. A middle-school student, I think."

"Aosawa. A grandchild? She survived?" His heart rent with pity. Her grandparents, parents and siblings had all been in there.

"But I doubt we'll get any testimony from her." Taromaru looked glum.

"Why not?" he asked, puzzled. "She was there the whole time – she must have witnessed it."

Taromaru shook his head. "Ah, but you see, Hisako Aosawa is blind."

VII

The typhoon had passed on, but overnight a storm of another kind had descended. A peculiar atmosphere pervaded the streets of the city as a steady stream of journalists from Tokyo began converging on it.

Early information about the crime had been so confused that a full picture had only emerged late the previous night. The general gist being reported in various newspapers was that a mass murder by poisoning had occurred at a party held to celebrate the birthdays of three generations of the Aosawas, a well-known medical family in K— city. Police had begun to search for a man aged around thirty who they believed may have information of interest. The man had delivered sake and soft drinks to the house at approximately 1 p.m. on the day, wearing a black baseball cap and yellow raincoat. Seventeen people in the house that day died from what was thought to be a cyanide-based compound. One person was unconscious and in a critical condition. Six of the dead were from the Aosawa family, four were relatives, and the remainder were local residents.

Prefectural police had established an investigation headquarters and announced their intention to make a swift arrest due to the heinous nature of the highly unusual and serious crime. More than fifty officers were assigned to the case. The deaths in such a prominent local family had sent shock waves through the medical fraternity and given rise to much speculation.

Against the backdrop of this maelstrom, the detective and his colleague set out with anticipation for the hospital. They sat in the car in silence, arms folded, stomachs churning with pressure and anxiety. The Prefectural Medical Association had issued a statement calling for the crime to be solved as quickly as possible. There had been many calls from the public offering information, but the majority had been to simply express fear of an invisible poisoner in their midst.

After a while his colleague spoke.

"Come to think of it, those people's birthdays became their date of death too," the colleague said.

"Yes, that's right."

"What are the chances of three generations having a birthday on the same day?"

"Me, my youngest brother and cousin have the same birthday. It can't be that uncommon."

"But *three* generations? That has to be unusual," the colleague continued desultorily, still looking out of the window.

One full day after the incident, Hisako Aosawa was now awake and calm enough for doctors to grant permission to interview her. Although the detective had been disappointed to learn she was blind, she had undeniably been present at the scene and so he clung to the hope that there was some kind of lead to be obtained from that. Something that would lead to the arrest of the killer.

"Teru, what would you do if everybody in your family died, everybody except you, all at once?" his colleague asked, still with her face averted.

"Hmm... I can't say," he hedged. He didn't even want to think about it.

"Me, I'd be lost. To be the sole survivor... I couldn't handle it. I'd follow them."

The detective glanced over at his colleague in the seat next to him. He couldn't see her expression, nor could he tell if she was in earnest or simply speaking to fill the silence.

In the corridor of the hospital the nurse cautioned them repeatedly. "She looks calm enough, but don't put too much store by that." Her voice was filled with emotion. "Please don't forget this patient's circumstances. That child was in the same room, from beginning to end, while her whole family died in agony around her and she heard it all. She's been through a horrific experience."

They stood in a cool, white corridor. In tandem with the rise of an inward tension at the prospect of meeting the surviving witness, the detective was also experiencing something else, a sudden stir of agitation at the memory of the enormous, indifferent malice that he had perceived fleetingly in the party room the previous day. Something hitherto unknown to him, beyond anything he had ever imagined or encountered before.

That's right. It was like there was something in there beyond the realm of human understanding. But immediately he dismissed this thought as foolish.

The detective stood before a white door at the end of the corridor. The nurse opened it with a click, and he and his colleague nodded as they entered the room behind her. He saw the girl sitting up in bed, and somewhere in the back of his mind he heard his wife's voice: *Can you tell the first time you meet a criminal whether or not that person is guilty?*

He stared at the girl before him. The interview began, and he confirmed from her that she had been sitting in the rattan chair in the party room, the chair that was not out of place. Then, in his head, he silently answered his wife: *It's never happened before, but in this case, yes. I knew immediately that the girl in front of me was the culprit.*

6

INVISIBLE PEOPLE

Sei-ichi, the author's eldest brother

I

You don't mind if I help myself to a drink, do you? Have one too if you like. You must be thirsty after coming all that way in this heat.

Yes, I'm more relaxed like this. Don't stand on ceremony.

Would you like a glass?

Sure? It's a bit rough, but let's drink like this.

I make sure we never run out of canned beer. It's my one pleasure, you might say. I like a quiet drink during the day when I'm not working.

The wife's at a friend's house. She knows I'm happier left to my own devices, so she goes out to do her quilting and leaves me to it. Her friend is some kind of textile artist. I went to one of her solo exhibitions once with the wife – social obligation and all that – and it curdled my blood to see the amount of work she puts into it. Made me think of a girl I knew in high school who once gave me a sweater she made. I wasn't interested in her at all. If I was I might have been touched, you know, going to all that trouble to make something specially for me, but that wasn't the case. When someone devotes all that time to you for their own pleasure, all it does is make you wary.

I've watched them work on the quilts, and it's beyond me how they can be so absorbed by such fiddly, tiring work. To be honest, I prefer to rattle around alone on my days off, so I'm grateful to my wife for going out. The kids have left home too.

I never drink much except at home. Everyone at work thinks I'm a teetotaller, even though I'm quite partial to a glass or two. I have a couple of close friends I drink with outside the house, but that's all, and they have nothing to do with work.

Coffee shops? I'm not one for those much, either. If I couldn't avoid going to one in my student days, I'd order something but not touch it. The staff never liked that, of course. And friends thought it was strange, too. But nowadays there are more places where they pour the drinks right in front of you, so I'm a bit more relaxed about it.

Why?

This may sound foolish, but in a bar or coffee shop there are any number of opportunities for someone to slip poison into a drink while it's being brought to you. That's why.

II

Ah, what can I say? That may have had something to do with it. I don't know for sure. I had a slight germ phobia to begin with and might have turned out like this in any case. As a boy I never ate rice crackers or *manju* buns that had been touched by anyone. I couldn't share drinks with friends, and I couldn't abide using the same hand towels as the rest of the family.

My brother couldn't touch soft drinks either for a long time afterwards, but he got over that once we moved away. He had no qualms then about accepting food or drink from other people if what was on offer tempted him. So to come back to your question, I don't think the murders were a turning point for me in that respect.

The way I see it now is that it's a natural form of self-defence.

You hear of lots of food and drink tampering incidents these days. They're on the increase. You never know what people will do. Even in the office kitchen, anyone could do anything. You never know who's holding a grudge or is unhinged and waiting to spring.

Men are particularly at risk. They're so used to having their mothers do everything for them, they're under the illusion drinks appear whenever they want – just like that. They don't realize that every single thing that goes into their mouths has been handled by any number of nameless people first. Many women might be just as vulnerable too these days.

I have a bit to do with foreign executives through work and, let me tell you, those people are surrounded by invisible servants. They don't think twice about letting maids or tradesmen from residential management services into their homes while they're out.

No, it's not because they have absolute trust. It's because they're like kings with underlings to do everything for them, even down to changing their clothes, so they're completely unembarrassed about being seen in the nude by the people who wait on them. It's the same thing. To someone like that, other people are invisible.

III

Ah, I barely remember the murders. After all, it was decades ago.

I was busy studying for my high-school entrance exams at the time, and only went to that house reluctantly because my brother and his friends made so much fuss about it. And yes, I admit, probably because the parents also told me to put in an appearance. I was in a foul mood because the weather was so damn hot and I couldn't concentrate.

It was insanely hot and humid – very strange weather.

I remember that some key or other didn't work.

You know how difficult it can be to turn a key in extreme humidity? Because the metal shrinks and expands. And the humidity that day must have been off the scale. The foehn winds were blowing and the temperature was way up as well.

Ah, now I remember – it was the key to my school satchel. As I said, I was very sensitive about my things being touched by strangers, so I had a lot of locks in my room. Obviously I didn't have much of value, only being at middle school at the time. A strongbox for my toys and my school satchel, that was about all.

My satchel had a tiny, cheap lock, and I couldn't get the key to turn at all that day. So I was even more irritated because of that. I don't remember if I managed to lock it in the end.

Anyway, I was still fuming over it when we arrived at that house.

The minute we got there I could tell *something* was wrong.

I don't know how else to express it – *something* wrong.

All hell had broken loose? No, it wasn't like that. When I picture it now, I see people lying on the floor, like black amoebas. I can't recall their faces or facial expressions. The thing that sticks in my mind is black amoebas writhing about on the floor.

I don't remember hearing any screaming or groaning, either. There was noise, of course, but it sounded more like the house rumbling than voices. I use the word *rumbling*, but that's because I don't know how else to describe it. The whole house sounded like it was wailing and shaking. Maybe it's a trick of memory, but that's how I remember it. It was like my bones were vibrating, and I just knew that *something* very bad had happened.

I think I might have yelled at my brother and sister to stay put. Told them not to move.

Then I ran. All I could think was I had to get help.

Ah, the nearest police box was about ten minutes away, I guess.

But truth be told, I simply wanted to get out of there as quickly as possible. Put as much distance as I could between that place and me, even if it meant abandoning my brother and sister.

When I got to the police box I'm pretty sure I said something terrible had happened at the Aosawa house, and that people were lying on the ground in pain. The officer on duty was confused at first, but soon caught on when I repeated myself. He leapt into action, made lots of phone calls, people started appearing, and in no time a huge commotion had started.

The thing I remember most is the anxiety I felt. I was the one who had pushed the switch to set all that in motion. A train of action suddenly moving at high speed. If anything, that frightened me more than when I had entered the house. Whatever had happened in there became acknowledged fact, and the world was reacting to it because of me. The way I see it, it was like a merry-go-round had started, spinning faster and faster, and though I was the one who had started it, I was instantly left behind. I'm not someone who ordinarily initiates action. I'm an opportunist, you could say, someone who always looks to see what other people are thinking before taking any action myself. That way of thinking is so ingrained in me that when I started running for the police I was already having doubts in a corner of my mind about whether it was a wise thing to do.

The one thing I remember is that the young policeman had been drinking instant coffee and had left the spoon standing in the cup. I can't abide spoons left in cups. But when all hell broke loose there was no time for drinking coffee.

The cup with the spoon? It was left sitting on the desk.

I felt like that was me in some way. As if that cup and I were the only still things in the room while everyone and everything else was moving at high speed.

Of course the police questioned me repeatedly, but I was only inside the house very briefly before I went to get help, so there wasn't much I could tell them. They interviewed my brother and sister a lot – especially my brother, because he'd been in and out of there all that day – but I don't think they had much to add in the way of testimony either. I couldn't believe we were asked the same questions over and over.

Yes, that's all I remember.

IV

That's right. It was a terrible crime – everybody was shaking in their boots because of it – but I took a very cool view.

You have to understand I was an adolescent at the time. And doesn't everyone go through a cynical phase during puberty? Thinks the whole world's against them, treats adults with contempt, behaves with hostility to everyone and everything. I was going through that phase. I didn't care about public opinion, didn't have the time for it.

But I did have one thought about the whole affair.

The way I see it is, it was *inevitable.*

Yes, that's the sum of my thoughts on it.

Inevitable.

That word kept going through my mind, from the moment I ran to get the police.

Let me see… how shall I put this?

I've always been very sensitive to power dynamics, ever since I was a child. Probably the result of changing schools many times and having two younger siblings. I realized at a very early age that strength lies in numbers – two is better than one, three more than two. Intuitively I understood that there are far more potential connections when the numbers are on your side.

Power dynamics are important in the classroom, too. You have to know which kids not to get too close to and which kids not to cross in order to survive. With experience, you learn to read the lie of the land. Every place has an established hierarchy, and there are certain things you have to put up with accordingly. To rise up in the world, you have to follow the right path but not stand out too much. I think I learned that lesson very early on in life.

So, to come back to what I said about this crime being inevitable, well, it leads you back to the invisible people I mentioned before.

We understand instinctively that invisibility is the best strategy for survival. The new kid at school knows he or she mustn't stick out. They should act as though they've been there all along, and not do anything to attract attention. Because being *visible* carries appalling risk. Conversely, however, those who want to set themselves apart from others actively seek to become visible.

That house was *visible.* And so were the people who lived in it.

Yes, that family had authority. The kind that infiltrates and puts down roots in every corner of the local community. Naturally they also had the aristocrats' sense of duty and virtue to go with it, and it was a fact that the community accepted and respected this.

But there's a fine line between respect and contempt, admiration and jealousy.

Over the years the numbers of the *invisible* would have grown.

At some point the family started to take the service and loyalty of invisible people for granted. I'm certain of it.

They stopped keeping track of the numbers of the invisible, and what *they* might think or feel.

Hisako Aosawa, I suspect, was the epitome of this.

Which was deeply ironic, since she couldn't actually see.

She acted like a queen and was treated like one in return. Of course, she was dependent on help, and it was natural that people helped her because she was blind.

But the way I see it, is that she was symbolic of that family at the time, because the people who waited on her were *literally* invisible, in all senses of the word.

I'm well aware that my analysis may come across as sour grapes.

But think about it. The person who carried out that crime was a virtually anonymous social dropout. He was nothing if not invisible. And a total stranger to the Aosawas as well, someone whose existence they weren't even aware of.

Don't you think it's an odd coincidence that the family was brought to grief by a person like that? Does that not seem like the revenge of the invisible to you?

I've played chess with Hisako Aosawa.

Of course I admired her. You'd walk on air too if you could play chess with such a beauty. She was bewitching – intelligent and graceful. Simply being in her presence put you under her spell. Everybody was her servant. You couldn't help but marvel at the existence of a person like that. To sit down opposite her made me as happy as I'd ever been.

But I was also conscious of another deep-seated emotion. An awareness that people like her, who are waited on hand and foot, gradually accrue even more power and fortune that in turn leads to even more people serving under them, and feeding off the energy of society in this way brings success to only the very few.

I know. People want to be exploited, and they want to serve. The Aosawa family was a product of invisible people who desired its existence.

Which is exactly why this was *inevitable*. Nothing in this world is as we would wish it to be.

V

Sibling relationships are an odd phenomenon.

Siblings spend years together in childhood, then suddenly they're cast out in the world and become estranged, just like that. Like seeds that burst out of a seed pod, scattering in all directions after long years of being nursed inside the parental pod.

My siblings and I weren't especially close. But perhaps that's normal.

We associated with each other because we lived in the same house, but once we went our separate ways that wasn't necessary any more.

I knew kids who were good friends with their brothers or sisters, but I never understood it. Why choose to hang out with your siblings when being with other kids was so much better? I thought it was strange.

The three of us all had completely different personalities. I know some people get along because of their differences, but it wasn't like that with us. We each did our own thing only because we didn't understand each other. Our mother must have had a hard time. We had absolutely no sense of group camaraderie or unity.

My brother was resourceful and friendly, but from my perspective that was an unfortunate compulsion. He constantly needed validation from others and was therefore never satisfied, which meant he was always moving on to the next new thing and never sticking with anything for long. On the surface it looked like he had many friends, but they were all shallow relationships. I don't think any of those friendships lasted long. It was natural that he went to the Aosawa house often, because if he could be accepted by them his inner peace was guaranteed. He was good at finding people like that – the ones whose acceptance counted. He wanted to get in with them and be their hanger-on. That's what being a second son will do to you.

And my sister… to tell the truth, I don't understand her even now.

I never understood her when we were children. Any contact I had with her was almost always through my brother – I have few memories of direct contact with her. I always had a vague notion that she was a complete mystery.

I never knew what she was thinking to begin with. The girls at school or in the office were far easier to figure out.

She seemed emotionally stable enough. She liked to play by herself, but at the same time observed what other people were doing. Whenever my brother and I were working on a craft project or homework, she'd watch from a distance then quietly start copying us. She wouldn't ask us anything. And yet her projects turned out better than ours. Sometimes my brother used to explain to her what to do, then got her to make something and submitted it as his own work.

You know those demonstrations you sometimes see in department stores, when they have artisans demonstrating various traditional crafts? It's a kind of sales technique. My sister, she used to watch them for half an hour or more without getting bored. The artisans were always impressed and used to say what a patient kid she was.

I can't remember when exactly, but once when she was in high school I told her she ought to become an artisan, only half joking.

She's persistent, and could pick up everything she needed to know by watching and learning from a master craftsman.

But she shook her head and told me, "No, I'm not cut out for that kind of work."

She was absolutely serious. I thought she was being modest, and told her so.

But she just shook her head again and said in all seriousness, "All I do is imitate. I haven't got any originality."

I took issue with that. I told her that everybody starts out by imitating, and anyone who can't make a good copy has no hope of making anything original, so for her to say she could only imitate was conceited. Or something along those lines.

But she just shook her head again. "No," she said, "you've got it wrong. I don't imitate techniques, I imitate people. All I did was imitate that person's actions, not the technique. I only want to imitate the person." She really meant it.

I must have looked puzzled because she added, "Don't you ever want to be someone else?"

That was quite a leap. *Don't you ever want to be someone else?* Why on earth would she ask that?

Then she said, "I can only ever be myself for the rest of my life – I can't be you, or Mother. I'll never know my whole life what other people are thinking, only what I think – don't you think that's boring?"

Can you believe it? And she meant every word of it. I was dumbstruck, as you might imagine.

"Yeah, that's true, but what do you expect?" I replied. "Think what it would be like if you did know what other people were thinking. I doubt any good would come of it."

She thought that over for a while, then said, "I suppose, maybe you're right."

That was the end of the conversation at the time.

Then there was another incident that gave me a bit of a shock, though I had heard rumours.

I can't remember when it was exactly, but my sister had brought some friends home, and for some reason one of them said to me, "Maki does amazing impersonations." Hah? My sister? I thought – I couldn't get my head around that. For one thing, she hardly ever spoke at home – she was Miss Aloof, never said anything more than necessary. When we watched TV together she hardly ever laughed. I would never have guessed she was capable of doing impersonations.

But there was something else... What was it?... Oh, I know. The spring she graduated from high school she had some kind of part-time job doing telephone sales. One day she had to leave work early before finishing her quota of calls for the day, so when she came home she told us she was going to use the phone for a while, to call ten more people, and began ringing them.

What an eye-opener that was.

Her voice... it wasn't the voice of the sister I knew. Of course, people use different voices inside and outside the home. But it wasn't as simple as that. She literally became someone else. And, what's more, she changed her personality every time she called another customer.

Apparently these weren't cold calls. She was ringing customers with a history of purchasing from this company, so it was a well-targeted group who weren't going to hang up on her immediately. I think she might have been explaining a product to people who had expressed interest in buying it, something like that. Anyway, she had a list of names and information.

Before each call she looked at this list, thought for a few moments, then calmly made the call. It was obvious she changed her approach with each person. One minute she was a brazen middle-aged woman, next a timid but basically decent person, then a pushy salesperson with hard logic – you would have thought a completely different person was speaking each time.

Only Mother and I were home at the time, and we couldn't believe our ears. Neither of us had ever heard her speak like this before. I remember Mother looking at me and saying, "Well, this is a surprise."

When she finished I said to her, "Hey, aren't you something. Where did you pick up those voice techniques?" But she just looked mystified. So I pointed out that she'd used a different voice and personality each time.

"Ah," she mumbled, "I just imitated Aunt in Takasaki, and then the girl behind the counter in the cake shop, and the lady in the office at high school."

That's when it all started to make sense to me at last.

I remembered what she'd said in the past about wanting to become other people. She genuinely wanted that.

What we'd overheard wasn't her changing the sales pitch each time, it was her identifying completely with another person.

"So that's how you do it," Mother said. I think she was rather naive. "I thought she reminded me of somebody and now I know who – my sister!" She was laughing about it.

Once Mother had pointed the resemblance out, I saw it. She had sounded just like our mother's sister who lived in Takasaki. The aunt who had been selling insurance for many years and could be quite pushy.

That call in our aunt's voice had given me a real start. It was essentially a faultless imitation.

I was a bit disturbed by this. Mother laughed about it, but I couldn't. Ever since then I've kept in mind that my sister has peculiar ambitions.

Maybe it's not unusual. Probably everybody secretly wants to be someone else. Actors have the clearest outlet for that desire in their profession.

But my sister didn't quite fit that category either.

She wanted to *be* someone else. Literally. That gave me an uncomfortable feeling.

VI

When the book came out?

Floored. In a word.

I had no idea she was so obsessed by the affair. We'd all forgotten about it. My brother and I had both left home by then, and the three of us didn't see each other any more, so it seemed surreal that the person who wrote that book was *family*.

The content, too. Yes. Whenever I tried to read it I became agitated by the thought that one of my own family had written it, I kept seeing her face.

After my sister went to university we became even more distant. Same thing happened with my brother. I was working by then, and we led very different lives.

The book sold well but I didn't tell anyone close the author was my sister. My brother told his friends he was in the book, which was a rather low-key reaction for him, so perhaps he too was still uncomfortable about being associated with the murders. Or perhaps deep down we both doubted that our sister really had written it.

To tell the truth, I was more concerned about what she did with all the money that she made out of it. But I heard later from Mother that a large part went towards gratuities for all the interviewees, and after taxes she gave the rest to Mother. She sent us some too, for having used us in it.

My brother and I were both glad she'd given the remainder to Mother.

Mother had had a hard time after the divorce.

Yes, after the murders my father was transferred to Nagano, and then some time after that my parents divorced.

VII

Their relationship had been strained for quite a while before the murders, that was true.

It was the usual story – another woman. Father had been seeing this woman before we moved there, and my parents used to argue over that. But he declared he was going to make a clean break, so moving to the city was meant to be a turning point for the family. I think he really did mean it at first.

Things seemed to go well when we moved. I was relieved that the home situation looked like it might settle down at last.

As it turned out, though, he hadn't ended it after all.

That fact came out shortly before the murders. It turned out the woman had been coming there to see him and staying in a hotel. It wasn't such a big city, so eventually they were seen and the news reached Mother.

The atmosphere at home immediately soured, and it stayed that way. There were a lot of tears, which made things worse as it was an old Japanese-style house with thin walls and we could hear everything that went on.

I mentioned before that I was going through a cynical stage at that time. That was due in large part to my parents' relationship. I threw myself into study as a way of escaping the conflict.

The reason Mother insisted I go to the Aosawa house that day was because Father was expected home early and she planned to talk with him. I was vaguely aware it was some kind of important discussion – nothing that would affect us immediately, but preparation for when the time came, apparently.

Father was never home much as he was always either busy with work or spending time with the other woman when she was in town. Mother had asked to have this discussion many times, and finally it was going to happen – on that day. That's why I couldn't refuse her when she asked me to take the other two to that house. But you know how the day turned out, so I don't know what happened with their discussion.

Secretly I hoped the murders might be an opportunity for them to patch things up. I thought it might make them see how lucky we were to all be together as a family, compared to what happened to the Aosawas.

Though it did bring us together temporarily, in retrospect I can see that the murders were just the final straw.

When it came to the crunch, it wasn't Mother that Father wanted to be with, but the other woman. It was obvious in the end that he preferred her.

Oddly enough, Mother kept hoping they could patch things up, but I had the feeling she gave up once the case was solved. I remember hearing her say to herself *No chance now* when it was announced that the perpetrator had committed suicide. I still don't understand what that was supposed to mean.

Father dutifully sent living and education expenses, but I think Mother was never sure how much she could count on him for. With three children to look after, there was always some kind of expense cropping up, and it didn't seem as if she could turn to him for those. We knew other single-parent families like us who had difficulties when childcare money ran out. Mother started working. I suppose she had to, but it must have been awfully hard for her after being a housewife for so long. Anyway, she had a hard time getting by and we were all witness to it, so I was very relieved that Maki had given her some money from the book. On that point, I have to say, I'm grateful to her.

VIII

I seem to have gone on and on about nothing much at all, haven't I?

I didn't keep in touch with my siblings a great deal after leaving home, and a long time went by before I realized it. Come to think of it, the day of the murders was the last time the three of us ever all played together. I know that can't actually be right, but setting out for that house is the only memory that comes to mind of the three of us doing something together. Siblings really are a mystery.

Won't you have another beer? I'm having one. There's nothing like a drink in the daytime on days off to relax. Though the alcohol certainly does go to the head faster during the day. I wonder why that is. Maybe the metabolism functions more efficiently in daylight. It slows down at night, which means it's better to take medicine in the evening for the effects to last longer.

I think about things sometimes.

Is it a sin to not understand?

There are some people who you can never understand, even if they are relatives, like parents, or children, or brothers and sisters. Is that wrong? Isn't acknowledging that lack of understanding, and giving up, one kind of understanding? That's the kind of thing I think about.

But in this day and age, society doesn't forgive those it doesn't understand. To not be understood leaves you open to bullying, or gets you labelled suspicious. If you're not convincing in the eyes of society it makes you vulnerable to attack. Everything has to be by the book – reduced and standardized. The reason for anger is, more often than not, simply lack of understanding.

In fact, the people we truly understand are far and away in the minority. To say you understand doesn't solve anything. That's why it's a mistake to believe it's realistic to think about surviving in a world that can't be understood.

I think about it sometimes.

What was it my sister wanted to understand so much she was willing to go to such lengths?

Why did she want to become someone else to that degree?

I remember the last time we all ate together as a family. It was when my parents divorced and Father was about to leave the house for good.

Father was really a very ordinary man. Hard-working, basically a good person, loved his children. So it didn't even enter our heads to blame him when we heard he was leaving. We were sad and resigned more than anything. There was a time when I was miserable about his abandoning us, but – how can I put it? – it was complicated because he seemed more depressed than me, even though he was the one leaving. I think he felt very guilty about us. But that didn't carry enough weight to stop him leaving.

It was fine, warm weather the day he left.

On the surface of it we looked like any normal happy family. The three of us were playing around. Somehow it felt like that was what we ought to do.

Mother and Maki started cooking a beef stew early in the morning.

We sat at the table chatting and eating. It was excellent, so we all had seconds.

But as time went by, I began to feel queasy and started getting shivery. It wasn't just me either. Mother, Father and my brother looked pale as well. We were all looking at each other oddly.

"Is everybody all right?" Mother asked.

I remember Mother and Father looking at each other.

And then it happened. We all began to race out of the room and vomit. We didn't have the time to wait for the toilet to become free so we had to vomit into paper and plastic bags. The whole house reeked.

When Father asked if it might be food poisoning, Mother told him, "There's nothing in the stew that would do this. It's been cooking for hours."

I remember thinking their faces looked like wet rags.

We were all so busy vomiting there wasn't even time to think about calling an ambulance. The situation was rough for a while.

But once our stomachs emptied we felt better, and it showed on all our faces. There didn't seem to be any other symptoms such as numbness or fever. We all drank gallons of water and felt much more ourselves.

"What on earth caused that? We should get checked out by a doctor," Father said.

Mother said that was a good idea as it was a worry to not know what caused it. They still looked like a couple. The atmosphere had been tense all morning, but this incident had taken the edge off a bit.

Then suddenly we all fell silent.

Literally, all at the same time. And for some reason we all looked at Maki.

She was sitting there, steady as anything, not blinking an eye. None of us had noticed up to then, but she was the only one not affected. All the time we'd been running out to be sick, she'd sat there observing us.

So when this suddenly hit us all at the same time, we just looked at her, not comprehending.

And she just stared right back at us.

I noticed she'd barely touched her food.

"What's wrong? Why didn't you eat?" Mother asked.

"It's this," she said, and held out her hand to show us something in her palm. She was holding some kind of grass with serrated leaves.

"What's that?" Mother asked her.

"I picked it on a school excursion the other day," Maki said. She said this quite coolly, not showing any emotion.

Mother looked like a ghost.

"I put it in the pot," Maki told her.

"In the pot? Into the stew?" Mother's voice went screechy. Maki only nodded in reply and didn't look sorry at all.

So Mother ripped the plant from Maki's hand and asked, "What is it?"

Maki was surprised and tried to pull it back, but Mother held her hand up high so she couldn't get it.

"Ah... it's something that brings on vomiting," she told us.

Mother looked scared and fit to explode by turns. I'm sure you can imagine. She put her face up close to Maki's and demanded to know if it was poisonous.

Maki shook her head and said the teacher had told her it only brought on vomiting, and that animals chew it to empty their stomachs after eating something bad.

Mother really lost it then. She started screaming at Maki, asking what she was thinking of, putting that in the stew.

And it was only then that Maki started to look unsure of herself. As if she didn't know whether to answer or not.

Then Father butted in and pushed Mother away by the shoulders. He told her to leave it be, because it was his fault.

He looked very upset, and I'm sure he thought it was some kind of revenge on him. That it was the least his children, who had no say in anything, could do to make a stand against a father who was leaving them.

But Father didn't get it. He didn't understand Maki or any of the rest of us in the slightest. The same way I didn't understand Maki either.

The table went quiet then. I knew Mother thought the same as Father. I wanted to tell them that they'd got it wrong, but I couldn't say anything.

Maki looked at Father and said to him, "I wanted to know."

"Know what?" he asked her. But with some hesitation, as if he didn't really want to know.

"What it felt like to poison people," she answered.

We were all stunned. Even Father. He looked at her open-mouthed.

Nobody said anything for a while, then we all turned to look at Maki.

I asked her if she'd found the answer. Purely out of curiosity.

She put her head to one side, with a mixed expression of anger and exasperation.

"Nope. I still don't know."

And she sighed.

IX

Would you like another can of beer?

This is when I'm most relaxed, having a drink on my own. Beer cans aren't easy to doctor. It would be easy to spot if they had been tampered with.

There are many things and many people in this world that I don't understand.

Some people want to understand everything, and others only want to understand certain things.

My sister wanted to understand one person alone. When she said she wanted to become someone else, she meant a specific person. The only person who committed the crime. The murderer who sent the poisoned drink and indiscriminately killed so many people.

I imagine that Maki wanted to understand the killer's mind. I wonder if she was ever able to become that person. Even after reading the book, I still don't have the slightest idea.

7

PORTRAIT OF A GHOST

The Young Master from the stationery shop

I

Rumour had it that the hanging scroll in the window case of the soba noodle restaurant was a portrait of a ghost. Nobody knew when this story first began, but anyone familiar with the neighbourhood was aware of it.

Schoolchildren who walked past the shop on the way to school were aware of it because older students routinely repeated the story to the younger ones. And in summer, when it was the custom to tell scary ghost stories, children would come by on purpose during the long summer holiday to stare at the scroll in delighted terror.

The restaurant, which was situated on a corner in the middle of the shopping district, was much like any other noodle shop in the area. All that set it apart was the modest hanging scroll and bamboo vase in the window case at the shop front, where usually customers might expect to see a display of plastic models of dishes on the menu. This could have been interpreted as a sign of refinement were it not for the fact that the window case was only dusted twice a year, meaning that the scroll had turned a dusty, grimy colour that made it barely indistinguishable from the wall, and the petals of the artificial bellflower in the vase set in front of the scroll were quite faded. In consequence, the majority of customers who passed through the restaurant door barely gave the window display a second look.

Occasionally it occurred to regular customers to enquire about the origins of this scroll; however, the proprietor, who was gruff at the best of times, would simply reply with an air of weariness that he had been ordered by his father never to remove it, and there the conversation would end. Those customers who were curious enough to persist over the years in asking, however, succeeded in learning that the proprietor's grandfather had acquired the scroll on his travels and subsequently experienced such a run of good fortune that he had come to believe the scroll brought luck. He had therefore given strict instructions for it to be kept permanently on display in the family business, and the current proprietor was simply obeying this injunction inherited from his father.

"Hard to believe a creepy thing like that could be lucky," the regulars whispered behind his back.

"But the restaurant does well."

"True, the noodles are good, and the other food."

"It's often the case that so-called lucky objects are actually quite bizarre."

"Ever seen Ebisu's face close up? For a god of good fortune he looks downright sinister, if you ask me."

"Maybe the scroll's got historical value."

"How can it? There's no signature, for one thing." The speaker shook his head. Commonly known in the neighbourhood as the Young Master from the stationery shop despite being well into his mid-forties, he fancied himself as something of a calligraphy expert.

He had happened to be present once when the scroll was taken out for dusting and had had an opportunity to examine it. The closer he had looked, the shabbier it had appeared. Kept as it was in an environment without humidity or temperature control, it was no wonder that age spots had speckled the canvas, the lines of the painting had blurred and the original colour had faded. Any historical value it might once have had would certainly not have been preserved. Not to mention that there was no artist's signature or seal that could verify its authenticity or add to its value. For all anyone knew, the painting could easily have been cut from a screen or some such thing and mounted on the scroll. The way it had been mounted suggested a lack of aesthetic sense, with no consideration given to showing the picture to its best advantage.

The point of the painting was also obscure, and no matter how hard the Young Master racked his brain he could not discern its meaning. What might the artist have intended it to convey? Its composition – a man standing vaguely in the centre – was not particularly artful, and it was not clear who the subject was. The painting might have made sense if he were a hermit or an elder, but his age was indeterminate, and although the face was smooth it somehow conveyed an impression of elderliness. There was also something peculiar and not quite human about it that was slightly repellent and no doubt gave credence to the ghost story. But the major contributing cause of the rumour, however, was undoubtedly the forehead. Though faint, the man unmistakably had a third eye high in the middle of his brow. If he were a buddha this might have been understandable, but a third eye on the forehead of a man who did not project a particularly virtuous image provoked a sense of uneasiness in anyone who noticed it. Children whispered solemnly to each other that it shone in the dark, and watched to catch people's eye as they walked by.

It was certainly a curious painting, but the third eye was not especially conspicuous, and appeared as no more than a blemish to the casual glance.

In short, the scroll had little to recommend it; there was nothing that appealed to the eye, nor anything in the lines that demanded attention. It was simply a piece of art for which the value of even hanging it on the wall was open to question. Give it another ten years in the window and it would probably fade away completely.

However, it had come to the attention of the Young Master recently that there was a young man who was interested in it, as he had seen this young man staring into the window at the scroll two or three times over the last few months.

In contrast to the painting, this young man made a positive impression. He was an almost painfully fresh-looking youth who dressed unremarkably in grey trousers with an open-neck, short-sleeved white shirt, and although the shirt was not new, it was always neatly ironed. His hair was trimmed very short, and his face was chiselled and spare, with finely drawn features. There was not a single excess ounce of flesh on the lean outline of his body, which evoked a recently carved statue. His face was handsome; lack of colour in the cheeks served to emphasize his features, not least the dark eyes set deep beneath a jutting, high brow.

On the sodden city streets at the height of the long, humid rainy season, he alone radiated an air of cool stillness.

How old is he? the Young Master wondered. Based on the young man's physical appearance, he would have taken a stab at mid-twenties, but there was something about his eyes, and an aura of maturity that made him seem older.

I've seen that face somewhere before, he thought, *a long time ago, when I was a kid, by a white roadside...* A face in profile wearing a cap with stars on it flickered in the Young Master's mind.

Toshi? Could it be him? The name came readily to mind, much to his relief. Of all his relatives, Uncle Toshi had been the most talented, advancing to the Imperial Japanese Army Academy from the prep school in Nagoya. His cool, handsome looks had drawn admiration from men and women alike, but he had been a quiet man who liked children and was at ease playing with them. "Toshi, Toshi," the children would call happily whenever he made an appearance, and they would stick to his feet like puppies (*Including me,* recalled the Young Master). A scene he had witnessed as a small boy – Toshi walking along the street before going off to war – was imprinted firmly in the Young Master's memory even now. In his mind's eye he could see Toshi's handsome profile, visible beneath the shade of his cap.

He was sure of it; his uncle's eyes were like this too: old beyond his years. Still eyes suffused with torment and uneasiness, as if he alone bore the weight of the whole world on his shoulders.

His uncle never came back from the war. All they ever knew was that he had lost his life on the Chinese mainland; his bones were never returned. Which meant that to the Young Master his uncle was forever young and handsome. And his was the face that overlapped in his mind with that of the young man who had taken to peering at the scroll at the entrance to the soba restaurant. He would stare at it, lost in thought before abruptly turning on his heel to leave, as if he were suddenly no longer interested.

It never occurred to the Young Master to speculate any more about him. The young man was simply an intriguing figure whom he occasionally caught sight of, that was all.

*

Then one day the Young Master came face to face with the young man utterly by chance. It was at a temple on the outskirts of the city, where he had gone with some old classmates to attend the memorial service for a former teacher.

Suddenly a familiar figure caught his attention. A man in a neatly ironed shirt was sitting on a bench in a corner of the temple grounds, among hydrangeas illuminated by subdued sunshine that had broken through between showers of rain.

There was a kindergarten in the temple grounds, and the clamour of children's voices rang through the air. The man was sitting in a cosy garden nook, surrounded by children at his feet.

The Young Master felt a sense of déjà vu. He might well be one of those children, and the tiny garden filled with soft sunshine a corner of heaven where he used to play with Uncle Toshi.

But unlike his uncle, this man did not appear to be especially engaged with the children. Though he smiled at them as they milled at his feet chattering among themselves, his expression was remote and hinted at sorrow. Unexpectedly, his appearance brought the word *saint* to the Young Master's mind.

"Is everything all right?" Noticing the Young Master rooted stiffly to the spot, the middle-aged abbot approached and spoke to him.

"That man over there – is he with the temple?"

The abbot glanced at the man and, sensing the unspoken questions, nodded with a sigh. "He comes here sometimes to worship," he replied politely, "and plays with the children before leaving. For one so young he's had a lot of misfortune in his life. Do you know him?"

The Young Master hesitated. "No, but I've seen him around the neighbourhood sometimes. I remember his face because he's so good-looking."

"Ah, I see. Near your home, you say. May I ask where that is?"

The address that the Young Master gave seemed to mean something to the monk, for he nodded several times and said, "He's still going for treatment, then."

"Treatment?"

The monk turned to look at the garden, avoiding the Young Master's eyes. "Three years ago there was a young couple murdered near the Asano River."

"Yes, I remember. They were out on a date. The gang that did it were caught, I believe."

"That couple were engaged to be married. They had no connection with the gang at all, but they were killed in an extremely cruel manner. Well, the girl was his younger sister."

Seeing the Young Master's expression of shock, the abbot continued.

"They were very close because the parents both died when the children were young, so they looked after each other," the monk told him. "He managed to put himself through university, get a job and save up for his sister's wedding, just as his parents would have wanted, but then tragedy struck and it nearly destroyed him. He became extremely despondent and depressed, and was hospitalized for quite a while."

"So that's his story." The Young Master felt a stab of pity. No wonder the young man looked old beyond his years.

"He's a born worrier with a sensitive temperament, but he managed to keep going and worked hard for his sister's sake. I heard from quite a few people that his parents were exactly the same, and that it probably helped send them to an early grave," the monk said evenly.

The Young Master wondered fleetingly if it was appropriate for him to hear such private information, but he was curious to hear more.

"In hospital he met a professor of Buddhist art, would you believe, who happened to be in the bed next to him," the monk continued. "He told me that's how he came to be interested in Buddha." The monk had a strong Kansai accent. Perhaps he had lived in Nara or Kyoto.

"I hope that Buddha can be of help to him," the Young Master said.

"He seems to be interested in Buddha statuary rather than Buddha's teachings. In particular the Urna. You know, the dot that represents a third eye on the forehead in Buddhist images? That's what seems to attract him most."

The Young Master was startled: the eye in the middle of the forehead. He remembered the young man standing outside the soba restaurant staring at the scroll.

In the same subdued tone, the monk proceeded to recount fragments from his conversations with the young man:

"What's this eye? Or maybe I should ask if it is *an eye."*

"It's not an eye exactly. That's hair growing between the eyebrows on a Buddhist saint. The curl to the right makes it look eye-shaped. Sculptors usually make it circular. Sometimes you see it as a grain-sized crystal inset. It's supposed to emanate sacred light."

"So it's not actually an eye then?"

"No. Some buddhas do have a third eye, like the horse-headed Kannon, or the Fudo Buddha, but you'll find it's mostly the wrathful buddhas that tend to have a third eye."

"Wrathful?"

"That's right. These third eyes are a mystery. Images with a third eye, or a spot that seems to give out heat, have been found in cultures and religions round the world since the dawn of time.

I learned about the phenomenon in my religious training. I'm not sure if it's relevant, but pictures of Francis Xavier and other monks you see in textbooks show them with a bald spot on top of the head. One theory is that building inner strength through spiritual training causes the energy circulating in the body to become self-regulating and produce intense heat at the top of the body, leading to the natural development of baldness. Which is why all the really virtuous monks have that hairstyle, or so the story goes. But it's the most common pattern of baldness in men, so I suspect an element of convenience in that explanation."

"By clocking up virtue? I wonder how everything would look with an extra eye."

"Beats me. I'm not one to know. But I expect you'd see the world differently, at another level."

The Young Master remembered gossip he had heard at a school reunion about the abbot at this temple. Apparently he had only recently inherited the position from his father. Before that he had been something of an adventurer, travelling around the world and getting involved with hippy culture in America. After this conversation, the Young Master could well believe it. He had a sense of something unconventional about this monk.

The abbot continued his reminiscences about his conversations with the young man:

"I really don't know what to do."

"Do about what?"

"I have to give an answer, but don't know how to answer."

"Give an answer to who?"

"Um... I don't know how to express this exactly, but an answer to the world."

"Revenge is not the answer. Revenge will always come back to bite you. It's a vicious circle. Nothing good comes of it. Your sister would never rest in peace."

"You're wrong. Don't get me wrong. I don't have a grudge against the world because of what happened to my sister. It upsets me that people think that, because I don't."

"What do you mean, then?"

"The world is asking me questions. It's like a heavy weight coming down on just one person – me. I've stayed quiet so far, but I can't stand it much longer. I have to answer somehow. That's why I feel a great sense of responsibility right now."

"Responsibility? Responsibility for what? Your sister's death wasn't your fault. Many people feel guilt after being caught up in terrible situations through no fault of their own. There's no reason at all for you to feel responsible."

"Really? But the reality is I was the one caught up in it. Nobody else – I was chosen. Don't you think there's a reason for that? I have to answer somehow."

"Aha, it's all becoming clear now."

"Huh?"

"Thanks to you."

"What do you mean?"

"I have a feeling this was meant to happen – that I come back here and meet you."

"Me?"

"My problems were trivial compared to what you've been put through, but I used to have similar questions about the world. I was born in this temple and had a Buddhist upbringing, but I rebelled and went off in search of answers. When I got tired of travelling I came back and dutifully took over from the old man and now I give sermons without blinking an eye, like I'm better than everyone else... but then I meet you – like this. And I think it's because you are meant to receive Buddha's teachings."

"I am?"

"Yes, you are. The professor of Buddhist art you met was also a

sign. If anyone is in need of the Buddha's teachings, it's you. The fact of you being here with me, now, says it too."

"Is that what you think? Well, I don't believe in destiny. Or signs."

"Call it what you like, but I think it's meant to be that I'm here now with you, for you to receive the teachings of Buddha."

"If you say so, maybe it was meant to be. In any case, I feel responsible, and I want this eye. A third eye. So I can look down on myself and see the world from a different level, somewhere way up high, and I won't have to suffer any more. That's all I hope for."

"Your friends are back." The monk broke off and pointed to the Young Master's companions signalling from the other end of the passageway. It was time for them to move on for lunch. They had a vegetarian meal waiting at a nearby restaurant, the kind of meal that might once have been unthinkable at these gatherings, but they were now all of an age to have various health issues to consider, and it was enough simply to see each other again.

The Young Master was about to move off when a photograph taped to a pillar in the passageway caught his eye. It showed a monk walking along, dressed in vivid yellow robes.

"Where was that taken?"

"Er... Sri Lanka, I think. I'm not sure any more. I'm embarrassed to say, but in my youth I bounced around quite a bit, not distinguishing much between one place and another." It was evident the monk had taken this photograph himself.

"I'd appreciate it if you'd keep what I just told you to yourself," the monk continued. "The only reason I mentioned it is because you seemed interested in him. Please don't cause him any trouble, or reveal what I said to anyone else, I beg of you." The monk solemnly bowed his head.

Naturally the Young Master had no intention of speaking directly to the young man or telling anyone else about him. He casually turned to look at the hydrangeas again and saw that the kindergarten yard was now empty. The sun had disappeared behind the clouds, no children's voices could be heard, and there was no trace of the man in the white shirt.

II

Although the monk's words left a sober impression on the Young Master, as the days went by the matter faded from his mind. Yet his connection with the young man was fated not to end there, it seemed, as he encountered him for a third time in the middle of a heavy downpour towards the end of the rainy season.

To be strictly accurate, they did not exactly meet. The Young Master had been on his way home from a business meeting when the bottom of his paper carry bag became soggy and dropped out, and so he had stopped at the shop of a tobacconist acquaintance along the way. While transferring his belongings from one bag to another he sensed someone outside, walking through the driving rain, and lifted his eyes to see a figure pass by on the other side of the frosted glass sliding door that fronted onto the lane separating the shop from the residences opposite. It was a young man. That much he could tell. He watched the figure continue up the road and eventually disappear.

The wife of the Young Master's acquaintance arrived bearing a cup of tea and found him staring with a puzzled expression at the glass door. "Oh, did you see the lodger next door?" she asked.

"It must have been. I didn't know there were flats there."

"Yes, just behind us. The hardware shop next door owns them," she said, glancing at the sliding door with a dark expression. "So young but he can't work. Health problems, apparently."

"Is that so?"

"When he's up to it he helps out with deliveries for the supermarket up on the main road, but these days we rarely see him come out. Shuts himself up in his room the whole time. It's a little worrying." She covered her mouth with her hand, as if she had said something inappropriate.

The Young Master made sympathetic noises.

"But he looks like a decent enough young man. He's nice-looking, quiet and well mannered. Always neatly dressed," she added hastily, as if she didn't want to be thought a malicious gossip.

Her description struck a chord in the Young Master. Surely not... it couldn't be him?

"Children do seem to like him a lot," she continued. "He seems to hold a mysterious attraction for them. My grandson often chats with him. I was quite surprised the way they got to know each other in no time."

Now he was sure: it had to be the same man. The Young Master could see him, sitting in the temple garden surrounded by children. Clearly he still wasn't back on his feet yet. It was heart-rending. He recalled the monk describing the tragic events in the young man's life, his despondency and illness.

"Grandma, where's Big Brother from next door? Is he back yet?"

As if on cue, a boy wearing long wellies came racing in. The Young Master guessed he was around eight or nine. The boy must have seen the young man turn into the lane from a distance.

His grandmother frowned. “He is, but he’s not looking too good. Don’t go disturbing him and making a nuisance of yourself,” she chided.

“But he promised to teach me how to build a radio.”

“Leave it until he’s feeling better. Besides, it’s raining cats and dogs.”

“But isn’t it better to be inside building a radio when it’s raining?”

A child’s logic is unbeatable, thought the Young Master as he listened to this exchange with amusement.

“And anyway, he don’t hardly come out now. He just sits in his room reading sutras all day, or goes out to find stuff… I dunno what. Now’s the time to catch him.”

The Young Master remembered the monk’s conviction that the young man was meant to receive the teachings of Buddha and was glad to hear that he appeared to be doing so. He thanked his friend’s wife for the tea and left her still chatting with her grandson. Outside, the rain fell unabated.

Connections to people are a curious thing, the Young Master thought as he grappled with how to describe this young man’s relationship to himself. There were countless people living in the same city with whom he never exchanged a word and whose existence he was not even aware of, yet for some reason he had become conscious of one particular person who had come to his notice by chance. Should he consider his connection with that person to be fate?

Despite having no place in the Young Master’s daily life or conscious awareness, thoughts of the young man would float into his mind at odd moments, stirring up an uneasy feeling.

Though the rainy season had ended, the torrid heat continued. Out on the streets, a sweltering, sauna-like humidity prompted pedestrians to seek out shade as they walked in order to escape the relentless sun. This was what drove the Young Master to dive into a sweet shop one day when he was on his way back from a meeting about a delivery of office supplies, and his attention was caught by a sign hanging outside that read ICE. Without hesitation he ordered a strawberry shaved ice, then took off his glasses and wiped his forehead. A soothing, gentle breeze flowed in through an open window and he breathed a sigh of relief. The breeze also carried with it a fragment of conversation taking place on the other side of the window, which sounded to the Young Master's ears like primary school students talking.

"Dunno what he goes on about now."

"He's gone cuckoo or something."

His ears pricked up; one of these voices was familiar. The Young Master swivelled to look out of the window and saw two young boys walking along the street. Could it be… yes, that was him.

"He doesn't *look* any different. When he teaches maths he's all right. He explains science and maths stuff heaps better than any teacher."

"So what's this third eye he's always on about?"

"Dunno. It's been bugging him for ages. Always going on about looking for a third eye. After somebody told him about one he started saying 'I found it, I found it' all the time. Sooo boring. I took off then."

"Freaky, hey?"

"Yeah."

"But hey, class two…"

The voices faded into the distance.

The Young Master was perturbed by this exchange. Obviously they were talking about the young man, and it was clear he had discovered the location of a third eye. What on earth did that mean? *This has to be some kind of omen,* he thought, pressing the cool shaved ice against his forehead. It was like walking out into the street with a particular question in mind and every overheard word taking on a special significance.

So, what had he just learned from these young boys' conversation? And why did mention of this young man so often reach his ears in this fashion?

What it boiled down to, he realized, was his own desire to know more about him. About the man whose name he still did not even know. In fact, come to think of it, the name did not even matter; he was simply curious to know what this young man, who so resembled his uncle, thought about, and how he was going to cope in future bearing the burden of terrible tragedy.

After finishing the strawberry ice the Young Master's overheated body felt cooler at last. The sun was finally lower, he noted, and so he ventured outside again and set off in the direction of a place it had not originally been his intention to visit: the tobacconist's, where he had received a new paper bag that day in the rain. This was where the young man lived, at the rear of the shop. A man who the Young Master had only ever seen by chance several times, whose name he did not know, and with whom he had never spoken.

Though the most intense heat of the day had passed, the earth continued to roast slowly under the sun's rays. In the hush that had descended on the city, the Young Master walked along the silent streets of this exposed world, and upon reaching the tobacconist's he guessed from the unattended street-front counter that whoever was watching the shop had retreated from the heat into the cool of the interior. It wasn't just this shop, he observed; the whole city almost looked as if had been left unattended.

He stood outside hesitating. The lane was only a few steps away. It would be easy enough to go down it, turn the corner, and finally meet the young man with the aura of a saint and a face old for his years.

What on earth am I doing here? he thought.

He remained there indecisively, conscious of the sweat dripping from his pores. Still he could not bring himself to move. Then, in a sudden moment of decision, he turned on his heel and went in search of a bus stop.

Summer dragged on interminably. The days were marked by the sound of empty beer bottles clinking as they were carted away by liquor stores, and an accumulation of debris from all those foods favoured in summer: hulled soybeans, sweetcorn cobs stripped of their kernels, white chewed-up watermelon rinds and wooden ice-cream sticks. Children who were scolded for upsetting their stomachs with too many cold drinks blenched at the bitter brown pills they were forced to swallow. City residents sweltering uncomfortably, and feeling as if summer would never end, realized that a change of season was imminent when a typhoon was forecast.

That morning the Young Master awoke to a close, heavy feeling in the air as a result of the rising humidity. For several days in a row the minimum overnight temperature had not dropped below seventy degrees Fahrenheit, a sure sign that a low-pressure system was closing in.

He had been sweating unpleasantly since first thing in the morning and was disgruntled, a feeling that was aggravated by the clatter of noise as his children prepared for school, but upon being hit by a wall of stifling-hot air when he opened the door of the shop, a mood of gloom descended upon him.

The weather looked to be turning ugly very early on in the day.

His mother, who had gone out to collect her medicine from the neighbourhood clinic, came back complaining.

"The clinic's closed today."

"Oh? Is Dr Takano all right?"

"It completely slipped my mind he had an engagement today. He did tell me. He's gone to a party given by an important doctor who was good to him at one time. I didn't remember until I reached the entrance, and could have kicked myself for being such a scatterbrain. If only I'd remembered sooner." She seemed more annoyed by her memory failure than the clinic being closed.

"The wind's picking up. You'd better get on with the deliveries early today," she said to him, smoothing down her hair.

The Young Master agreed, and decided to postpone the sorting he always did in the mornings so that he could do his rounds first.

Outside, people scurried about, busily preparing for the storm predicted to sweep through in the afternoon. Though it was not yet noon the sky was dark, and capricious gusts of wind buffeted the Young Master from all directions as he sat astride the delivery motorbike. Though it did not yet bring rain, the sticky, moisture-laden wind brought no relief, and if anything only seemed to increase the humidity. The Young Master's shirt, which he had changed into just before leaving the shop, already clung stickily to his skin. He cursed under his breath. Then, something caught his eye and made him pause.

A yellow robe.

He had a flashback to the photograph in the temple of a monk walking straight towards him. It was *him* – the young man. Walking directly towards the Young Master, dressed in a yellow robe.

Automatically the Young Master slowed his motorbike and watched as the young man came towards him, unaware of being observed. He wore a black baseball cap and strode along briskly, looking downwards. What the Young Master had taken to be a robe was, in fact, a yellow raincoat. The young man was pallid, but handsome as always, and the sculptured features stood out in sharp profile more than ever on his lean face, while his youth and maturity had melded to such a degree that it was impossible to tell if he were young or old.

He projected an aura of cool stillness amid the flurry of activity on the streets ahead of the impending storm. And he did resemble a monk swathed in yellow robes. But this was only the impression of a moment's observation. In less than no time the young man had disappeared behind the Young Master, from which point on his yellow swathed back grew smaller and more distant in the rear-view mirror.

The Young Master wondered where he was going as he followed the figure in the mirror. There was no time to think about turning around to give chase, however, as before he knew it the lights turned green, and he reluctantly continued with the deliveries.

By afternoon the wind had strengthened and was finally bringing rain. The Young Master paid close attention to warnings and weather updates on the radio. His wife and mother went outside to examine the shop front.

"Should we close the storm shutters now?"

"But it's so humid… and it'll be completely dark inside."

Customers were few, and the number of people on the streets was only decreasing. Some shops were already closing up early for the day.

The image of a yellow raincoat stayed in the Young Master's mind even as he busily sorted out delivery statements. In fact, it was true to say that the man in the yellow robe-like coat was the only thing on his mind.

Where was he going? Was he back in his flat by now? Maybe he was reading sutras in his room at this very moment.

"Ah, here comes the rain."

He looked up at the sound of his wife's voice to see the pavement outside the shop turn white as large drops of rain smashed against the ground.

"Goodness me, the windows are all shut, aren't they? Oh dear, I think I left the bathroom window open." The Young Master's wife jumped up in answer to her own question and rushed into the house at the back of the shop, followed by her mother-in-law, who went to check too.

It crossed the Young Master's mind that his father, who was out for the day with other retiree friends visiting the Yamanaka hot springs, would not be enjoying the hot outdoor spas in this weather.

The sound of the rain increased in volume until the radio next to the cash register became inaudible. All the while, however, there was a quiet, still space inside the Young Master's head, where that cool young man walked in tranquillity, moving steadily, all alone, caged in by the rain.

Returning with a start to reality after his thoughts had drifted, the Young Master noticed that the radio was audible again and the rain had decreased in intensity. No doubt the cycle of torrential and light downpours would continue for some time to come.

"That was a close thing," said the Young Master's wife upon her return. "Luckily the rain didn't blow inside. By the way, where's the torch?"

"On the shelf under the stairs, I expect."

"It's broken. I changed the batteries, but it still doesn't work. Remember the trouble we had after the blackout from that last lightning storm."

"That's right. I forgot. I suppose I'd better go and buy a new one now."

"In this weather? Are you serious?"

"The rain's eased off – it'll be all right. I'll get a bite of lunch while I'm at it. I've been rushing about since morning, and now I think of it, I haven't had a thing to eat."

"Don't be gone too long."

"It's all right, don't worry."

Outside, the wind blew so hard his umbrella was useless, and he had to hold his glasses against his face as he made a dash for the electrical goods shop nearby. While the assistant wrapped up his torch, the Young Master thought about where to go for lunch, and decided on the soba restaurant. He would get a quick plate of cold soba noodles and hurry back home again.

Tucking his purchase under his arm he ventured back out onto the street, whipped by the uncomfortably damp wind. The landscape was drained of all colour. In the distance he thought he heard a siren that sounded like fire engines.

The soba restaurant was empty as he dived through the door. Unlike many other food establishments, it did not close in the hours between lunch and dinner, and customers could always count on it being open late afternoon.

"Welcome. Awful weather, isn't it?" said the proprietor. A taciturn man by nature, this was an unusually loquacious greeting for him.

"The wind's atrocious. I was soaked through in no time."

"Here, use this," said the man, thrusting a cotton towel at the Young Master, who gratefully accepted it to wipe his head and shoulders.

"Cold soba and a beer, please."

"Everything okay?"

"We're shutting up shop for the day. There are no customers in this weather, and it'll only get worse."

As he watched the proprietor open the bottle of beer, the Young Master could not help feeling that something was missing. Then it struck him that it was the absence of sound; there was no satisfying *pop* as the cap was removed from the bottle because it had been drowned out by the rain, which now fell harder than ever, producing a deafening din on the corrugated iron roof. Both men turned to look at the ceiling with exclamations of astonishment; the noise was so loud it was impossible not to react.

While nibbling on slices of boiled fish paste dipped in wasabi and sipping on his beer, the Young Master noticed the sirens again. "I wonder what's happened?" he remarked. "The fire engines and ambulances are out in force today."

"Fire, maybe?"

"Would they need so many hoses in this rain?" He strained his ears, listening for the scream of sirens through the cacophony on the roof. There seemed to be no end; as soon as one faded into the distance, another could be heard following immediately behind. He wondered how many had been despatched. This evidence of others' misfortune made him feel uneasy.

"What on earth is going on?"

"Hmm. Very strange," said the proprietor, moving over to switch on a television that sat on a shelf close to the ceiling. He found no news, however, only a tedious repeat of an old drama series.

By the time the Young Master had eaten his noodles and drunk the tea to go with it, the rain had once again diminished in force. He glanced through the back window and saw the eight-fingered leaves of the paper plant outside bowing in the wind.

"Looks like the rain's eased up. I'll make the most of it to get home. Thanks."

"Best get moving. Always welcome."

The Young Master paid his bill and stepped out into the maelstrom again. He grimaced; though the rain had eased off slightly, it still had enough impetus when carried by the wind to pelt his face with stinging force. Then he froze as he became aware of the presence of someone else beside him, standing outside the restaurant. Turning his head, he saw the young man again staring at the scroll in the window case, the outline of his ash-grey silhouette etched in sharp profile as he stood there, oblivious to the rain beating down him. The Young Master felt a wave of déjà vu, as if a scene had been lifted from his imagination and made real.

How long had he been standing there? The yellow raincoat he had been wearing earlier was nowhere in sight. His slacks were black with wet and his white shirt was soaked through, with the lines of the undershirt beneath clearly visible. Rain streamed from the visor of his baseball cap.

He seemed unaware of being observed. *Why is it he never notices me?* the Young Master thought bitterly. *Why am I always a bystander who can never enter his world?* He felt a sudden, deep frustration.

The man gazed intently at the scroll, without moving a muscle, while the Young Master stood nearby, observing him side-on. He saw the young man's lips move as he mumbled to himself. His expression was different from before; there was something new in it, something that to the Young Master looked like satisfaction mingled with relief, and also exhaustion. He was consumed by curiosity: where had the young man been since this morning? There had been no sign of him when he entered the restaurant earlier. And what had he been doing – in this rain – that could be the cause of so much satisfaction? The Young Master racked his brains and strained his ears to hear what the man was saying, but could make out nothing.

"I have my answer at last. This is my answer," the young man mumbled under his breath, over and over.

8
THE FLOWER VOICE

The tobacconist's grandson

I

Fami-res is a weird term, don't you think?

No? I always do. Every time I hear it.

Uh, I know it's short for *family restaurant*, but I always hear *family-less*. You know, no family. Like people say *sex-less*.

Lots of people use family restaurants for work. They're handy for business meetings or lunches or whatever, because of their big tables and good lighting.

But you don't see real families eating here. I reckon real families only come to places like this at certain times. When it's late – like now – the only other people you see are loners, or parents and kids with something going on, or students, you know… the *family-less*. Only people with some kind of defect or families that don't make the grade as a regular family are here at this hour. Look around. See the distribution? Like dim spots under the bright lights.

Fami-res customers don't smile.

Uh, I noticed that a while ago. They know waiters smile because it's in the manual. It's not really for customers. Same way customers don't come here because they wanna be in a *fami-res*. They're killing time, or don't wanna be home alone, or just want a change of scene. This place isn't their first choice, but it'll do. Staff and customers go along with that, in their own way. Nobody tries to put on a different face, or pretend they're happy or whatever. Every person brings their life with them to the table.

But I suppose, if you look at it like that, maybe *fami-res* is the right term, strangely enough.

II

Yeah, I was married once.

If I'm honest, not because I thought it was necessary.

Nah, wasn't anything wrong with her. Wasn't her fault at all. In fact, she was a really great gal. Never made any fuss about compensation, though I was the one who ended it, and she had every right to. I guess deep down she wanted to finish it too.

But I don't know... I just couldn't see any reason for us to be together.

Uh, people have all sorts of reasons to live together. Someone to talk to every day, a roof over their head, social pressures, a carer for their old age. Loneliness. Wanting to be useful. None of that felt relevant.

Towards the end, I used to think *why is this woman here?* Every time I looked at her. She wasn't annoying, or a pain to be with – nothing like that. It was a straight question, simple as that. Why is this woman here? Why does she occupy the same space as me?

I think she cottoned on to it.

She told me she couldn't stand the way I looked at her. Said I had no idea how cruel I was, like I was denying her existence or something, and that's why it really hurt. But she knew I didn't mean it intentionally, and I think she thought that was even more inhuman.

That's what she told me when we separated, anyway. But I suspect she was glad to leave.

Yeah, I bet you're wondering why I got married in the first place. I think because everybody else was getting hitched too. I had this idea that I should try it once. And my married friends seemed to be having a good enough time. When all your buddies are doing it you start to panic about being left behind, don't you?

Housework doesn't bother me. If anything, it's easier to do it myself the way I like it done.

You know, at bottom, no offence, but I think women are insensitive and lack finesse. That's not discrimination. I mean, it's hard work to give birth and raise a kid, so women have to be like that – they're built to just push on with things, no matter what. Men are essentially more uptight about everything, in my opinion.

But hey, why discuss this now? Is that what you want? I'm sure you didn't come to hear me talk about this kind of thing.

Yeah, sadly I wasn't a roaring success as an engineer. I liked tinkering with machines and making stuff, but I didn't have any bright new ideas, or the drive and ambition to be an innovator. I'm in sales and planning now – generalist, comprehensive type of work. That pretty much suits me.

People say I lack ambition.

Uh, emotion, too. I have no delicacy, apparently.

It's a shame I didn't have more ambition as an engineer, or work for that matter. When I think about it, I'd still like to do that kind of work.

But as far as ambitions in life go, I still don't get it.

Why should living in a super-deluxe condo, owning several foreign cars or building a second house be called success? What's to be jealous of? The basic essentials of a house are the same for everybody. A bath, kitchen, toilet, place to sleep and place to relax. Sure, a garden or study increases the space or number of rooms slightly, but no matter how big a house or apartment, the basic format is the same. I really don't see why luxury condos and apartments should be so different in price, even taking difference in floor space into account. And speaking of not understanding, Americans have no idea either. Their idea of success is a mansion with a pool, a flash car, foxy women, and parties flowing with wine and champagne. No art or imagination in that.

Yeah, people often call me a cold fish. I don't understand that either. If I did, I might have made a better go of things, I suppose.

But anyone close to me who hangs around a while ends up dead. Is that my fault? I sometimes wonder. Am I so cold and hard it gets to them too? Does it build up inside them till they can't stand it any more?

Only six months after we split my ex-wife died. It was a car accident, but there were rumours it might have been suicide. I still don't know.

There was another friend, too, from university. We were in the same club and good buddies for four years, but after he got a job he couldn't get on with the people in the department he was assigned to. So he did himself in.

Thinking back though, the first person I ever knew who committed suicide was a guy I used to call Big Brother. When I was a kid, at the time of the murders.

I'd completely forgotten about that till you turned up.

III

Yeah, those murders. I still don't think Big Brother did it.

But that's because I was just a kid then, and even now I'm not perceptive about people, or good at saying the right thing.

I always felt uncomfortable when people spoke about him like he was a perverted evil killer and some kind of monster. It didn't fit the image of the Big Brother I knew.

Why the name Big Brother?

Uh, I never even thought about it. He was always Big Brother to me. I had a real big brother, four years older, but I didn't look up to him the same way. That guy was Big Brother, with a capital B. I couldn't call him anything else.

When we heard he was behind the murders, my mum went half crazy. Actually, gloating was more like it. She was so smug, jabbering on to all the neighbours and journalists who came to our tobacco store. Going on about how she'd always known there was something strange about him, and how he was bound to cause trouble one day. It was embarrassing – I couldn't stand it.

But she was also scared the media would get wind I was friendly with him, and chased me away whenever reporters came near. That was all right with me. I didn't like being given the third degree about him either, so whenever a journalist type turned up I took off quickly, pretending I was on my way out somewhere.

One day I couldn't stand it any more – her superior attitude and going on about it to customers all the time – so I piped up at dinner.

"Hey, looks like you're enjoying yourself Ma," I said. "How come you're so happy we had a murderer living next door? You're like the cat that got the cream, jabbering away non-stop about it."

Hell, did she go ballistic... it really shook me. I never saw her look so fit to kill. And the belting she gave me... I'll never forget it.

But, yeah, the fact was from then on she kept her mouth shut and avoided journalists, so what I said must have struck home.

I had a friend at the time, a kid from Osaka. Being around him had given me a bit of a Kansai accent. More than a bit, actually. You know how harsh it sounds. If a kid spoke to me now in the same sarcastic tone I used then, I might well lose it and be tempted to throttle him.

Uh, looking back, I do have some sympathy for the old lady. Out of the mouths of babes and all that. It's cruel what a kid so young could come out with.

When I think about it now, it's understandable she was worried. I mean, your son gets friendly with a stranger living in the neighbourhood, doesn't listen to a word you say, always argues back. There was nothing she could do. No wonder she was mad.

Especially since the stranger in question doesn't have a job but there's nothing she can object to about his behaviour or appearance, so she can't accuse him of anything. I think she was looking for a reason all along to get me away from him. Then the murders happened. And on top of that he commits suicide and disappears from the face of the earth.

Yeah, she must have been relieved all right. Her kid was safe now. Not to mention she'd been proved right. That's why she got so carried away.

In any case, single men always get a raw deal. Look how Big Brother was treated. His parents were dead, his sister murdered, and he was sick in hospital for ages. But he was labelled unreliable just because he couldn't work.

I come in for that kind of treatment too. But luckily people know I'm divorced, otherwise if anything happened all eyes would be pointed straight at me. People think I'm all right because I work for a company, that's all. Because it's true that unemployed young men do commit all kinds of crimes.

People with families have a lot of hostility towards singles. Where does that come from? I'm not especially jealous of married couples, but I don't put them down. I hope they're happy – I don't want to get in their way. But they're jealous and they pity us. It used to be a single person was just pitied. Now hatred and jealousy come into it too. Apparently we're the only ones who have it easy...

Uh, even an insensitive clod like me picks up on that vibe.

Even so, compared to what it used to be, I think there's more social acceptance of different family situations.

Big Brother must have been really alone back then.

IV

He was a quiet guy. I think he must have been really brainy.

Maths and science always made perfect sense when he explained it. I still remember it. It was thanks to him I became any kind of engineer.

Lots of people can make simple things complicated, but not many can make difficult ideas easy to understand.

Yeah, how can I put it... when Big Brother explained some concept, it was like you could see the logic being constructed, three-dimensionally, inside his head. Very precisely, with methodical structure. All the details firmly in place, so it didn't matter what angle you questioned him on, everything hung together and was easy to visualize.

Another thing about him was he didn't change his attitude just because you were a kid. Kids know instinctively when someone treats them as an equal. That's why he was popular with them.

Uh, most adults are stingy about their time with kids.

It's like this. If the sum of all their time is a hundred, they'll allocate ten parts to kids. Adults in the neighbourhood might use up two or three parts of that on a kid with no connection to them. You can see them doing the calculations in their head, deciding how much of their time you're worth. If a kid asks something and they think there might be a chance of having to use three parts instead of one, they'll panic and push the kid away.

Kids are very sensitive when adults begrudge them time. Which only makes them want more, so they try to steal as much of adults' time as they can. Usually it has the opposite effect and they fail. Gradually they learn to distrust adults and give up on them.

When something happens, though, those same parents and teachers who are usually stingy with their time say "Tell us everything, don't hold back."

Wouldn't give you the time of day, but will shamelessly ask a kid for theirs. It's no wonder kids push back against that.

Big Brother never resented spending his time with kids. Maybe it's cause he wasn't working, and did have the time.

Yeah, he was kind, you know.

He wasn't abnormal at all.

Sometimes he said some weird things, but he was never scary or twisted. He was more the dreamy type, off in his own world. The type to get hurt rather than hurt anybody else. More likely to be bullied than bully somebody.

When it came to science or study he was super clear and precise, but if the topic changed he immediately lost the thread, used to get this distant look on his face.

I almost never heard him talk about himself. He always dodged personal questions.

But it's true, you know, that all he seemed to do for a few weeks before the murders was recite sutras. He wouldn't see me.

Yeah, but I had thick skin, so I kept going back. I was in the habit of stopping by to say hello on my way home from school.

I'd whine and try to persuade him to let me in, but he'd just look at me with sad eyes. I couldn't say anything to those eyes, so I always gave up and left.

That's another thing – he often mentioned a third eye.

Uh, he used to mumble away about training. Said that if you made a breakthrough you could acquire it.

That didn't interest me, so when he started going on about it I used to think here he goes again, and let it wash over me without really listening. So I don't remember much.

What I remember most is the stuff about the voice.

Yeah, sometimes he'd be talking and suddenly jerk, then look at the ceiling or out the window for a moment.

If I asked what was up, he'd say, "There's a voice."

I told him he was hearing things, but he'd say no, and shake his head.

Then he'd say, always with a dead serious look, "I hear the flower's voice."

V

Uh, I know it sounds crazy, but at the time I didn't think so.

He'd be talking away perfectly normally about functions and equations and stuff, then suddenly go "ah" – and look off in another direction.

I got used to it. *There he goes again*, I'd think.

Flower voices. I don't know what kind of flowers. I asked him that too. "What flowers do you hear? Cherry blossom? Tulips? Any kind of flower?"

He didn't seem really sure himself. Just shook his head.

"White," he said once. "Beautiful, white flowers. In full bloom. Lots and lots of them."

That's all he ever said.

But, you know, there are all sorts of white flowers. Lilies, chrysanthemums, magnolias… If I mentioned any one specifically he just shook his head.

"Such a beautiful voice," he'd say.

He always looked kind of blissed out when he talked about that voice.

Yeah, he was good-looking, very clean-cut features. Used to look down at the ground a lot and had a kind of hangdog air, but when he smiled he was handsome. He always brightened up when he mentioned the flowers, so I was kind of glad when he talked about them.

Course, I didn't know if he really heard anything. I think he genuinely believed he could. But I didn't care one way or the other. Even though I was a kid, I knew he was a bit fragile mentally. So if he was happy, I was happy.

The gossip magazines and papers went to town about that voice. Put their own spin on it to pull in the readers. But, jeez, some of the stuff they wrote… like a voice from heaven came to him every day telling him to kill that family. They made out that's what he'd written in his will, but I don't believe it.

I read a few articles, but every one made him out to be some kind of weirdo.

Uh, the question is – was that voice real or not?

Huh? Yeah, I told the cops. But in the end they didn't seem to believe me. Nobody else saw that piece of paper except me.

Uh, two days before the murders. I saw him carrying around a small piece of notepaper.

I was on my way to a friend's house after school when I ran into him.

He had something in his hands, and was holding it real careful. And he had this goofy happy look on his face. I was curious, of course, so I asked, "Hey, what's that?"

"I got it from the voice," he said.

That was a shock to hear. Of course, I knew he meant the voice he was always talking about, but I never thought it was real.

So I asked, "What did you get?" and snuck a look at his hands. He had this piece of coarse straw paper. It had fold marks, and I saw two addresses written on it. In neat handwriting. I only had a quick look, but I'd say it was girl's writing.

I couldn't read all the addresses properly, but I could see one was in Yamagata Prefecture.

Big Brother didn't say a thing. He just giggled like a girl and kept walking towards home.

I didn't take much notice then. But somewhere in my head it registered that maybe Big Brother's voice wasn't just in his imagination.

I only started to think about that piece of paper again after he died. When the cops and media were swarming all over the place asking questions. To tell the truth, I forgot all about it up to then.

But I didn't mention it till the first wave of excitement had blown over and another detective came. The first detective who showed up was really intimidating. Mum didn't want me speaking to him, so basically it was the first time I talked about it.

That detective was like a teacher. Calm and serious. He

always came with a plump woman policeman, and she was a good listener too – easy to talk to.

Uh, when I told the detective about the paper I saw Big Brother with, he was very excited.

I didn't understand why till years later.

It was the Yamagata address. The person who'd supposedly ordered all that poisoned sake and soft drinks was in Yamagata. And the delivery address was the clinic where all those people died.

VI

Uh, that meant somebody gave Big Brother those addresses and asked him to write delivery slips. Doesn't take much thought to see the significance.

That's right. Someone else was involved.

I'd been racking my brains over the possibility someone else was behind the murders, ever since Big Brother got blamed for them. You know, the cops had no idea what his motive might be. They knew he wasn't in good shape mentally.

But they checked all his contacts thoroughly. Anyone who had ever laid eyes on him was investigated. The monk at the temple where he sometimes went to look at Buddha statues was grilled too. For days apparently. He was all riled up about being treated like a suspect.

The weakest part of their theory was the link between him and the supposed sender – the clinic in Yamagata Prefecture. And the Aosawa Clinic. Basically they couldn't find one. If the sender was someone from this city, it might be understandable. But how did the person know the address of the doctor's friend in Yamagata? That was the biggest mystery.

So if the memo paper I saw was in fact from the real culprit, then it's major evidence.

The cops searched Big Brother's apartment and the neighbourhood from top to bottom. Even the drainpipes. But they never found that memo. It was only small and would have been hard to find. So then they started to doubt me. Uh, it didn't suit them to believe me then. Said I was just a kid, that I'd made a mistake, that there wasn't really any memo at all.

I wasn't impressed by that. But I couldn't do anything, seeing as they didn't find it.

So after all that, it was left up in the air. The possibility of someone else being involved.

That pair of detectives – the man and woman – they kept coming back. Had me tell them about the memo over and over. But as time went on, and the memo never turned up, the male detective started looking grim. I could tell they believed me, but without evidence they had no choice but to take the official view that Big Brother had done it all on his own.

But it's true. I did see that memo. And I'm sure it wasn't Big Brother's writing. I'd know his writing because he'd been my tutor all that time.

His handwriting was distinctive. Tiny, but written with a heavy hand. What I saw looked nothing like his style. This was neat and flowing.

Yeah, I was frustrated by the way things turned out. But I couldn't do anything more. Back then I was more annoyed about not being believed than interested in knowing the truth. Didn't even dawn on me that the memo could prove Big Brother's innocence.

But when I look back now, there's one thing I'm sure of.

He was set up. I know it.

Uh, the real culprit? No doubt about it. A woman.

VII

Nah, I'm pretty sure Big Brother didn't have a girlfriend.

Uh, he hardly saw anyone. He was normal enough around children, but didn't seem to get on with adults too well.

I'm not surprised, though. All the adults in the neighbourhood treated him like he was somehow suspect.

But he had a double handicap. No job for one thing, and on top of that his landlords – who owned the hardware store – weren't exactly a poster couple for good neighbourly relations.

The husband and the wife were stubborn and crazy, the pair of them. Always stirring up trouble over everything, from putting out garbage to how to run the neighbourhood association. They built those apartments without a word of warning to neighbours. Then when tenants moved in and needed to use the private access road, the level of friction shot up.

The tenants were mostly bar managers and tradespeople. Hardly had anything to do with the rest of the neighbourhood. Big Brother stood out because he was there all day. A sitting duck for all the hostility directed at the hardware store and prejudice about tenants. It was his bad luck. Though he was the type to get picked on anyway. He had a habit of looking down – like he was saying sorry – that only made it worse.

But women are sharp-eyed.

Yeah, and Big Brother was a good-looking guy. Skinny but dignified, you know. I think he had a pathetic air that appealed to the ladies.

Women with their heads screwed on right weren't interested, but I noticed the younger girls looked at him. Hookers too. Uh, they often came on to him out loud.

He couldn't handle that at all. Made him go red and run away. I felt sorry for him.

They were really explicit, you know. "You're a man, don't pretend you don't get it," they used to say to him. I didn't get what they were saying either, and when I asked Mum I got in trouble.

I remember there was one girl who used to follow him about all the time. Her parents had a pork cutlet restaurant, or a coffee shop – something like that. I heard her begging him to let her take care of him. Said he needed someone like her to *soothe* his heart because he was sick. Stuff like that. She was a solid girl. And all thumbs as well. Big Brother nearly died of embarrassment. He nearly fell over himself trying to get away from her, but that only made her chase him even more.

Everybody killed themselves laughing. The hookers made fun of her something bad. You know, women can be really cruel to other, less good-looking women.

"Ooh, he's no match for a shameless girl," they'd say. "The cheek of her thinking she could soothe anyone's heart with that face... Though they say you get used to anything after three days."

Yeah, the hookers were merciless. But even their hassling didn't budge the girl. I don't know... they were all as bad as each other.

Then she suddenly disappeared. Once and for all. Rumour was her parents folded up the shop and moved to the mother's hometown. Don't know the real story, though. In any case, Big Brother was off the hook. I still remember how relieved he looked when he heard.

So that was the only sign of any woman.

But I'd bet my bottom dollar the flower voice was a woman. White flowers, beautiful voice. Yeah, had to be a woman.

Like I said, talking about the voice always put Big Brother in a good mood. But when that business first started, he was different somehow.

He started reading sutras about the same time and – uh, I don't how to put it – it was like he'd found a purpose. Something like that. I know it sounds cliched to say he found something to believe in, but I think that's what happened.

But I can't say one way or the other if that something was the voice.

Uh, before then he seemed kinda insecure. Like a leaf in a puddle, spinning in circles, with nothing to focus his life on – if you wanna get poetic. Battered by the elements, even. Hah, that's a good one too. But you know, in that time before the murders he seemed different, like he'd found a purpose in life.

Don't get me wrong, he was still always down at the mouth. It was more like he accepted his fate.

What did he find?

What did he see when he opened the lids on those bottles of drink and mixed in the poison?

He was methodical, good with his hands, you know. I can imagine him carefully putting the lids back on the bottles, one by one. Straightening the dents, making sure the beer didn't go flat, so nobody would notice they had been opened.

Then setting off with his death load.

Big Brother always ate like a bird. Barely touched food, so he can't have had much fuel in him that day. But according to reports, when he delivered the beer and juice he was brisk and snappy – nothing unusual about him. So what was driving him? He must have been running on something.

Yeah, what the hell was he thinking when he rode through that weather to deliver a load of poison drink?

VIII

The uproar in the city over the murders was huge.

Big Brother was laid up all through it, but nobody noticed. He was completely forgotten.

I was caught up in all the fuss too. It was a weird time. Cops everywhere.

Uh, the investigation was still going when summer ended. And all that time Big Brother quietly wasted away.

I didn't drop by to see him any more.

He wasn't up to hanging out with me, so I drifted away and got interested in baseball instead.

School started again at the end of summer, but it took a while before I thought of going to see how he was doing.

Yeah, I remember the strange feeling when I stood outside his door.

You know, I'd been inside heaps of times before, but at that moment I really didn't feel like it.

It was like I wanted to go in but thought I shouldn't, so I just stood there because I couldn't make up my mind.

Then this guy with a buzz cut came stomping up the corridor and I nearly jumped out of my skin.

Asked if I needed to see the person in this apartment. He sounded kind of rough.

When I said yes, he told me I should leave. Said the man inside was really sick and I'd be better off avoiding him because it might be bad enough to call a monk. Apparently he hadn't gotten out of bed in a long time. He was a scary guy, but I see now he was only trying to help me. It would have been bad for me if Big Brother had TB.

So I turned tail and ran. But you know, the strange feeling I had when I stood outside that door stayed with me. It was like the Big Brother I knew wasn't in there any more.

IX

Last time I saw Big Brother it was autumn.

It was fine weather that morning and I was heading for the park where I met up with the other kids to walk to school. Suddenly this white shadow-like thing brushed past me. Gave me a real start. I turned and saw Big Brother.

He was skin and bones. No wonder I took him for a shadow. He'd aged, and his hair was like straw. His clothes were so baggy I could tell his bones were sticking out.

"Hey," I called out to him. After a beat he turned and looked at me.

He was smiling, and I knew it was him all right, but he hadn't half wasted away. His skin was rough, like bark, and he had black rings under his eyes.

I was lost for words. He'd changed so much.

"I'm on my way to listen to the voice," he said.

Yeah, that's what he said, though I didn't ask. Then he turned round and went off. His legs were shaky, like it was hard to walk. And he looked like he might collapse any moment.

I watched for a bit then ran to catch up with the others.

The landlord found him less than a week later, I think.

It was fine weather the whole time, so I guess temperatures were high.

Apparently people in the apartments either side of Big Brother complained about the smell.

The neighbourhood had a field day gossiping. People said the landlord wouldn't have done anything if it had been winter. They said he only called the cops because tenants in the other apartments knew about it. If not he could have gotten rid of the body and advertised for a new tenant as if nothing had happened. At least that's what they said. Big

Brother paid rent six months in advance, so the landlord wouldn't have lost anything.

Uh, and they said it was a miracle he didn't get rid of the suicide note too. It was only because other tenants were with him that he couldn't dispose of it.

You know, Big Brother didn't have any close relations. So if his death had been put down to suicide because of illness, and the note and everything else in the room were disposed of, then the case might never have been solved.

But they found the note. And the cops realized its significance.

That was the start of the next stage in the whole sickening business.

X

The impact of the murders?

Hmm, I don't know. Big Brother had an impact on me. I became an engineer, didn't I?

Uh, and I still don't think he did it.

It was a set-up. Somebody took advantage of him being so vulnerable, and that person got away scot free. They planned it nicely, you know. Big Brother cops all the blame, while they make their escape.

A book? Nah, don't know anything about it. A book about the murders?

I didn't know.

It sold well? You must be joking.

The woman who wrote it must be one hell of a busybody.

So who did it? According to the book, I mean.

Not spelled out? Well, of course it wasn't Big Brother who did it.

But you know, all this talking has made me hungry. Okay if I order some cod roe spaghetti?

Uh, I never make it myself because it's a nightmare peeling off the skin.

My ex-wife hated anything with fish eggs. She was afraid of getting gout. It's almost always men who get gout, but she had some weird fears.

She was afraid of manholes too. Never, ever stepped on one. Cause when she was young she knew a kid who fell down one and drowned. Apparently the lid had lifted off in floods.

"*You* never fall down manholes, even though you always step on them."

She actually said that to me once.

Said it always scared her to bits to watch me and worry about when I'd fall in. Today? Tomorrow? She was on edge all the time just thinking about it. But she accused me of not noticing. Not having any feelings.

Can you beat that?

Ha ha... maybe it's why everyone around me dies. They get stuck with my share of stress as well as their own.

Uh, but you know, people like Big Brother who carry everyone else's stress for them end up dying.

He was a victim.

The temple where he used to go and look at Buddha statues took in his bones. The monk there is an interesting guy. Bit of an oddball. Of course, there wasn't a proper funeral. I wanted to say goodbye properly, but never had the chance. Rumour was the two detectives went to his funeral in secret. I don't think they believed he did it either.

XI

When I was in high school I had a flashback to a memory of Big Brother once.

Right in the middle of summer.

I was going home from a baseball match. Walking by myself on a road I never usually went on.

There was no wind. The heat was real bad and everyone was sick of it.

Uh, I was in a foul mood. It was hot, we'd lost the baseball, and I was tired. In those days coaches believed having the right spirit was everything. Didn't think about the importance of rehydrating in the heat. I was so tired I didn't even have the energy to drink.

I suppose I might have been a bit delirious.

Anyway, I remember feeling like death. Like I might collapse any time.

Then out of the blue I heard a voice say, "In that case, go and die."

Clear as a bell. Gave me a real shock.

So I stopped and looked around.

Everything was blurry in the heat because of the haze coming off the asphalt. But I couldn't see anyone.

Thought I must be crazy. The voice was far too clear to be just my imagination. But no one else was in sight.

Suddenly the words *bell-like voice* flashed through my brain. Because it was a bright, clear voice. Very soothing. A young woman's voice.

Then I looked up and saw a whole bunch of white flowers.

On a crepe myrtle tree.

The tree was so loaded with flowers I wondered how one tree could produce so many. They were pure, brilliant white. A glaring whiteness.

Gave me the creeps, actually. My head went light. Uh, I think my body temperature must have actually dropped because I still remember the chill I felt.

But I remember thinking, *Aha, so this is the voice Big Brother heard.*

Weird, isn't it? I'd forgotten all about him up to then. You know, the murders and the fact he'd died never entered my head from one day to the next. Uh, but in that moment I thought of him.

Anyway, I stood there half-dazed and realized at last I wasn't hearing things. The voice was real.

I remember my mind going in all directions. I was scared on the one hand and wondered what to do. But on the other, I realized that now I knew what had happened.

There must have been a window open in the house on the other side of the tree. And through it I heard several women's voices laughing and talking.

Yeah, the voices coming from a window on the other side of the tree made it sound like the flowers were talking. I felt better once I'd worked that out. Nothing strange about it at all.

The house was old, and posh-looking. But it looked run-down and neglected. It was Western-style, with three round windows.

Seems it used to be a clinic originally. There was a sign that had been painted over.

I felt more myself, so I went on. Told myself it was only coincidence I overheard somebody say "In that case, go and die" in conversation, just when I was feeling so bad in the heat. Telling myself that made me feel normal again.

But you know, that's what made me think Big Brother must have heard a similar voice.

Go and die.

That's what he was told that morning.

Bright and clear. Just like that.

Anyone might feel they had to follow instructions given by that voice.

That's why he said yes, went back to his room and put a rope round his neck.

9

SCENES FROM A LIFE

I

"Gosh, everything's gone quiet, hasn't it? The world's simply disappeared."

"Yes. Strange how that happens. All of a sudden the sound of the sea just vanishes."

"Oh, it's so lovely and quiet here. It really does seem like the world has disappeared. Ah, there it goes again."

"Yes."

"It's as if we're the only two people left in the world."

"It certainly is."

"Look, everything's gone all hushed again. It's unusual to last this long."

"In Spain they say 'an angel passed by'."

"Really? What a lovely expression. Does it mean a quiet moment like this?"

"Yes. It's what they say when people are talking and the conversation suddenly stops because everyone goes quiet at the same time. The Spanish are much more talkative than the Japanese so moments like that would be rare, I guess."

"I guess so."

"It's the kind of saying you might expect from a Christian country."

"My home is so noisy, though."

"I suppose it is. You're from a big family."

"It really is loud. Somebody is always there, and the TV or radio are left on at all hours. There's never a moment when an angel could pass by."

"But isn't it nice to always be surrounded by family?"

"No, it isn't. No angels could pass by in our house. That's why it's so —"

"So what?"

"Nothing. Just that at home there's never a moment when angels could pass by."

"It's better than being alone. Being with other people is much better."

"I wish I could be alone."

"You do?"

"Yes. I want to be alone."

"Why?"

"Or if I can't be alone, I want to be with people I choose. Not someone who might get in trouble if they're not with me, or a person who thinks I need company."

"Everybody cares about you a lot, you know."

"Am I asking too much? Wanting to be alone. I wish I could go to a country all of my own. Where there's only me. Or two people at most."

"Oh – it happened again."

"Lots of angels have passed by, haven't they? I'm sure they're all listening to us – just like Mama does."

II

Human beings are deeply sinful, my dear. We are born steeped in sin from the moment we enter this world. So we must spend all our life in repentance. Do you understand? Listen to your Mama.

Look at all the suffering, violence and bloodshed in the

world. If that is not proof of being born into sin, then what is? Happiness is fleeting. Nothing more than a faint ray of light in a sea of suffering.

That's why you must repent. Because from the moment we are born alone into the world we are in a state of sin. And it's very important to always be conscious of your sins. You must say your prayers, because somebody is always watching you, so someone will always see the sins you commit. Make no mistake about it.

Somebody always sees your wicked thoughts. Somebody always sees when you go astray.

III

"Have you ever heard of utopia?"

"Yes."

"I heard it's an ideal country, like Shangri-La in China. A place everybody wants to go to, a kind of paradise."

"Ah, like the Utopia of Thomas More's novel."

"Thomas More? Who's that?"

"An English philosopher and politician in the sixteenth century, who was executed for treason after opposing Henry the Eighth's divorce. The Renaissance had a big impact on his ideas, and he was the one who gave the name Utopia to an ideal society. He imagined it as one where religious or royal power had no sway over equality."

"Gosh."

"People thought it was a fantasy at the time, like science fiction now."

"It's different to what I imagined. I thought it meant something more beautiful, like heaven."

"I'm not surprised. But religious issues are big in Western culture."

"I had this idea it was a place I'd like to go, but I've changed my mind. I'll choose another country."

"Another country?"

"Yes, and I've already thought of a name for it. Our country. Just for us. Oh – someone's coming."

"It's just kids."

"Hisako-*chan*, Hisako-*chan*."

"Hisako-*chan*, who's this?"

"Yeah, who is it?"

"He's my *yuu jin*."

"*Yuu jin*?"

"Is *yuu-jin* his name, Hisako-*chan*?"

"Yeah, Hisako-*chan*, what's a *yuu-jin*?"

"*Yuu-jin* is another word for friend."

"*Yuu-jin*, *yuu-jin*, let's play together, *yuu-jin*."

"Come on, *yuu-jin*, let's play."

"Okay, we'll go and play in the church garden."

IV

There once was a lonely young man.

For a very long time he lived all alone and he wasn't very strong, so he was always nodding off. And when he did his sleep was filled with dreams of when he was a child.

After living alone for many years he used to say how strange it was that he could remember his childhood as if it were yesterday. For example... well, let's see... do you remember how Mama gave everybody biscuits last year? Didn't they smell wonderful? They were the shape of a bear and had tea leaves mixed into them. See how easy it is to remember when I remind you of the wonderful smell? And the feeling of excitement you get at Christmas. Those memories seem just like yesterday, don't they?

That's how the man was able to remember his childhood so clearly. In his mind he could picture himself wearing a straw hat and catching fish in the river, or letting off fireworks on the beach. These lovely memories meant far more to him than all the time he was suffering from illness.

This man adored fireworks. In the summer holidays he had great fun setting them off with his uncle and friends from the neighbourhood. He liked going to see firework displays and used to race off to see any firework festivals he heard of, even if they were quite far away. He was always happy to stare up at colourful fireworks exploding in the night sky like flowers. The vibrations from the boom when they exploded gave him a funny tickle in his tummy, and he could feel the rays of light from the flowers scattered way up high in the sky, shining down on his cheeks. You all know what I mean, don't you? Remember the faces of your friends when they're looking up at fireworks in the sky? How their faces turn black-and-white?

But this man was very, very lonely because he didn't have anyone to play with whenever he wanted, like you all do. All he did every day was doze and dream of the fireworks he'd seen when he was a child. Isn't that sad? You can play with your friends any time, but he had no one.

Listen, let's keep this a secret, shall we? Gosh, I know, why don't we go and play with him? We can take fireworks and have fun together. What do you think? Isn't that a lovely idea? Don't tell the others, though. We'll sneak over and surprise him. Imagine how happy he'll be. I can just imagine he'll be overjoyed.

10

AN AFTERNOON IN THE OLD BOOKSHOP DISTRICT

The editor

I THE DIARY

Sat, 2 Aug

Rain. Sudden humid weather getting to me. Must get a hat. Dropped in on 2, 3 and 5. K caught on fast and things went smoothly. Thank goodness. Spent 1.5 hrs on average with each. Mostly reminiscing. Nothing for further investigation. Everybody remembers the period well. Interesting all were nostalgic about it. No air conditioning in guest house. Too hot. Hope the tapes don't stretch. Transcribing is sweaty work. Went to M in evening but was shut. Notice on door said Closed for emergency reasons.

Sun, 3 Aug

Weather changeable. Humid, can't sleep. Went to see 1, 7 and 8. 1 passed away and 7 in hospital. Got permission to visit. Will get someone to say I'm coming. 8 finished in under 20 mins. Transcribing time-consuming, will concentrate on that today. Evening storm. Slightly cooler afterwards.

Mon, 4 Aug

Weather suddenly fine. Summer full-on now. Walking hard work. Drinking too much Coke. Not good. Saw 7 in K— Citizens General Hospital. Brought back memories. Remembered me. Got introduction to 21, luckily. Offered to make contact for me so I accepted. Dropped by M but still closed. Heard from neighbour that a relative died. Looked in S and T. Discovered several back issues of G. *Did transcriptions in evening. Slow progress. 5 mins' talk takes ages to write down. Wish I knew shorthand.*

Tues, 5 Aug

Fine. Awful heat. Went sightseeing today as K seems worn out too. Saw the gardens and ate cold Chinese noodles. K very impressed by blue room. Sent K back to guest house and visited 4 alone. Rather hostile. Questioned my motives. Occasional silences. Feeling tired. Looked in Y, A and H. Cramped, hard to find things. Didn't look likely to have back issues of G. *Went back to guest house and had drink with K. Couldn't get a word in edgeways. He seems tired. I feel bad. Might increase his pay.*

Wed, 6 Aug

Fine, occasional cloud. 9 and 12 still away. 10, 11,15 and 16 refusing interviews. 11 claims to be away for early summer holiday but it's an excuse. K seems down, hung-over maybe. Told him to rest and concentrate on transcribing while I visited 13 and 14. Didn't expect much but results surprising. Though can't work out how to connect them from outsider's perspective alone. Dropped by M and it was open. Tired so only had quick look to check location of shelves.

Thurs, 7 Aug

Fine. K down with summer cold. Said he's okay if he can stay out of heat so told him to transcribe. But the rooms are hot as hell too. Ended up drinking gallons of soft drinks. Spending a lot on fluids. Using up lots of tape too so bought a stack, but it's expensive. 9 passed away. 12 still away. 17 and 18 will only speak on the phone.

Fri, 8 Aug

Cloudy, occasional sun. K recovered. Will concentrate on transcriptions. Went to see 21. Took all morning. Very useful. Tried my luck with 20. Rambling. Waste of time. Went to M. Listened to owner.

Sat, 9 Aug

K returned to Tokyo. Took tapes to do at home. Hugely grateful. Saw 19 in morning. Went to M and spoke to owner. Will get a bunch of G back issues together for me. Did nothing much in evening. First time in long while. 21 called. Just remembered something. Will visit again tomorrow.

Sun, 10 Aug

Visited 21 again. Quite shocking. Predicted it, but still unexpected. Went back to room and sorted out information. Don't know when I can come back. Many people away next week for Obon break. Went to M and spoke to owner. Looked for books together. Bought a few. Did transcriptions by myself at night. Then homework. Wish I had more help, but can't ask anyone else. Will have to do it myself.

II

Yes, that is indeed her handwriting.

Ah, seeing it again like this brings it all back.

A solid, steady hand with a uniform touch, yet one that reveals no emotion.

My memories of working on this book have faded over time. Especially as it has been many years since I worked in that particular department.

I wish that I could have stayed in book production, but with the pressure of younger editors coming up I had to go into management, which is far less interesting.

However, if you ask me about a particular title it all comes back immediately. I can recall every book I had a hand in and hold each one in great affection, regardless of whether they sold well or not.

Your call took me by surprise. I was not expecting to hear that title mentioned again after so many years. But the mind is a mysterious instrument. The moment I heard it I experienced a veritable physical sensation of memories flooding back.

Yes, that title did extremely well.

Yes, that is true. And it was also quite the talk of the town. Readers were familiar with the case from the news, yet many had not realized the scale and seriousness of it.

However, we did also receive many calls of complaint.

In the main these expressed dissatisfaction with the title. We were reprimanded for using the word *festival* in connection with such a tragic incident. However it was an apt title, in my opinion, and quite in keeping with the content. For one thing, the word *festival* is also used in religious contexts, and I believed that the book did convey convincingly the gravity of that period for the author. Therefore I stuck to my guns, as it were, on that issue.

Yet it never made it to paperback. The author's refusal to grant permission was one reason, but generally speaking, topical publications such as this are difficult to sell in a paperback format.

The author?

Well, I have to say that she was an enigma. For a university student she was very composed and self-assured.

When it comes to publishing a book, most authors show some degree of excitement about it, but she never did. No, although she seemed surprised by all the attention, she did not appear to be pleased by it.

If anything she implied it was all rather a bother. You do know that she turned me down initially?

Yes, when I first approached her. But in the end she was persuaded. She gave the impression that it could not be avoided, and told me that this was the first and last time she would do *anything like this*. By *anything like this* I rather think she meant getting involved with strangers to research a project and write about it.

I heard her say more than once that this was not part of the plan.

She had meant to use her research as material, and had never intended for other people to see it.

Yes, I believed her implicitly. I do not think it was simple modesty.

Of course, I understood her feelings to some extent. After writing a book there comes a point when the author must make a decision whether to continue to write and become a writer, as it were, or accept that the first book has been a one-off. In the course of my discussions with this particular author I had the distinct impression that it would be the first and last time for her. It was clear to me that she was resolved on this.

To be honest, I hardly saw her again once the book came out. I could count on one hand the number of times I met her after handing over the advance copies. We had a flood of requests for interviews after it was released, but she would never consent to any. She instructed me to refuse them all, as she was simply not interested. Naturally the publicity department were tearing their hair out, as it were. Well, of course they would be. The media were banging on our door, so to speak, and we only had a bare minimum of information about the author to give them. I resorted to the excuse that she preferred to stay out of the spotlight due to her connection with the case.

In the eyes of the public, however, it appeared as if we were the ones stonewalling and putting up barriers to hide her. That was a major misperception.

She did not show any interest whatsoever in sales or reviews. It was almost as if once the book was published, it meant nothing to her any more.

III

Yes, my word, I was tremendously excited the first time I read it.

Why was that? Because I could not believe it had been written by a slip of a girl barely past twenty. The writing was dispassionate and meticulous, and her style was poised. Had I not known the author was a university student I could not have pinpointed her age.

It also had a certain… er, this may not be the right expression, but let me venture to say that it had a certain ominous… or perhaps, shall we say… *sinister* undertone.

Hmm, that probably does not clarify things much. Allow me to rephrase. One could say that from it there emanated a cool gaze and mysterious ambience that was not entirely of her creation, and which existed only between the covers.

I am sure you know there is such a thing as a fluke.

It could be called *chance*, or *beginners' luck* or some such term, but it is indeed real.

Well occasionally it happens that a work comes to be possessed by a quality the author never intended. This was one such book, though we will never know if it was a fluke or not as she never wrote another.

The subject matter was deeply fascinating and surrounded in much mystery. It is still often referred to in conjunction with the Teigin Incident. Given all that, I did anticipate that the book would cause a stir.

I am not in a position to judge if what she wrote was the truth. However, I do believe that in the case of this book that is not the issue. In fact, I would venture to say that in terms of genre it is closer to Capote's *In Cold Blood*. It is a work that cannot be classified neatly into any particular genre. Neither fiction nor non-fiction. I would also be hard-pressed to call it *literary*, because of ambivalence about the style. However, one could say that is another of its attractions.

Of all the titles I had the privilege to work on, this one was an original. Quite singular. It resembles no other work I know. Yes, this book was special. Almost as if it came from another world, so to speak.

IV

That is correct. Undertaking to accept this cardboard box was her first condition.

Yes, it is the complete set of materials that she used to write the book.

Everything is in here. I do not believe she has anything in her possession any more.

There is also a stack of tapes in the box. Although, by now they might have stretched and become unusable. You may find that they are no longer audible. I kept the box on a shelf at work amongst my personal belongings, and that was the extent of my caretaking. However, in my defence let me say that she did make it plain she did not want to keep the materials and told me unreservedly to burn them, throw them away, or to do whatever I liked with them. She sent them to me once the proofreading was finished, apparently with no regrets.

No, apart from a quick look through, I have never examined them thoroughly. Knowing that these were her research notes was enough for me. I felt no need to go through everything.

However, had I been instructed to dispose of them, well, I think I would have hesitated.

That notebook is a diary of her interviews.

You can see how matter-of-fact it is. As is she a very matter-of-fact sort of person.

She assigned numbers to each of her interviewees, and there is a separate list of those at the end. There were close to forty people on it, although she did not have contact with everybody. Some were unable to be located and others refused to talk with her.

K was apparently another student, a boy younger than her, who helped with the interviews. He seemed to have difficulty coping with the heat in the Hokuriku region.

I beg your pardon?

The alphabet letters, you say? Ah, I believe they indicate second-hand bookshops.

V

Apparently she referred to each second-hand bookshop in the city centre by the first letter in its name.

You are correct. *The Forgotten Festival* makes no mention of her visiting bookshops.

This book is a seamless blend of reportage and fiction, past and present, yet although it reveals where she did her research and interviews, the old bookshops are completely omitted.

I do not know. I had no cause to think there was any significant reason. Perhaps she had the overall effect of the book in mind and wanted to keep things simple. I personally believe that she chose the best way.

Ah, *G* in the diary is that one – the thin magazine.

You will find a bundle of back issues in the box.

It looks to be a magazine with a small circulation. A local tattle magazine. It contains local news, gossip and scoops, et cetera, which would only be of interest to a very limited readership. She appears to have collected copies published around the time of the murders.

I believe she was looking for any rumours circulating at the time, articles with leaks on the police investigation or anything that the medical fraternity might be saying about the victims. When one is an outsider, it is extremely difficult to be privy to local rumours. Even more so when the victims are people of influence. Apparently she wanted to look into the past and reputation of the murdered family. In the end, however, she never found anything to back up any suspicions she may have had.

Despite its sorry-looking appearance, this magazine does have a certain *je ne sais quoi*.

One does not expect much of the content.

Well, because it consists almost entirely of juvenile insults, it reeks of amateurishness, and the advertisements are almost all related to the sex trade.

Nevertheless, for someone such as myself accustomed to publishing commercially viable magazines, it does have a raw appeal that leaves a strong impression.

I see in it the origins of the mass media. Because the mass media is, after all, really only a fancy version of a local community noticeboard.

To flick through something like this can be rather enlightening, and even moving. One sees how people became able to communicate and spread information, which in turn lead to the formation of civil movements and newspapers.

My interest was piqued by that magazine and therefore I read it cover to cover, yet I came across nothing about the clinic. However, I cannot say with complete certainty that there never was anything to be discovered, as I do not have all the back issues.

That is indeed true. We can assume that she invested much effort in investigating second-hand bookshops.

The city is not only an old castle town but it is also an old university town, hence the proliferation of bookshops. As these are concentrated in specific areas, it would have been relatively easy enough for her to visit them all. Second-hand bookshops are perfectly suited to the ambience of an old city, do you not agree?

Yes, this district is one of the biggest specialized second-hand bookshop areas in the world, but much has changed over the last few years.

I do find it delightful that used bookshops are once again in fashion with young people.

There are two kinds of people in this world, I believe, those who frequent bookshops and those who do not.

I beg your pardon?

What about the notebook?

Number six is the only interviewee to not be mentioned?

My word, you *are* thorough.

How sharp of you to have noticed. Never fear, I am not putting you to a test or any such thing.

To tell the truth, it bothered me too when I first read that notebook. I found myself unconsciously ticking off each person as they appeared. Yet six never does. Was it someone in the same profession? Someone else?

I raised it with her too. Who is number six? There is no record of this person in the list at the back either.

She told me that it was a woman who survived.

This woman had apparently gone overseas, therefore she was ultimately unable to ask the questions she most wanted to. That was her only regret, she said.

VI

When it comes to one-book authors, Margaret Mitchell leaps to mind.

Her story is quite remarkable. She sent her manuscript in a trunk to an editor and then pestered him with numerous telegrams. He started reading the manuscript on the train, rather unwillingly I believe. However, that manuscript turned out to be *Gone with the Wind.*

I do envy that editor.

Imagine having the incredible fortune to be the very first person to read that book. What if he had lost the pages? Or worse, simply dismissed it as another tedious manuscript and passed it on for another editor to discover? I quail to think what might have happened.

Whichever way I think, it makes me shudder.

Margaret Mitchell poured everything she had into *Gone with the Wind*, and declared afterwards that she would never write another novel. And she never did, which I think is magnificent. She gave her all to what became her one and only great work.

Oh no, I do not mean to suggest in the least that this book compares with *Gone with the Wind*. I was merely discussing the work of an editor.

Novels such as *Gone with the Wind* are what make an editor's work such an adventure, one that is both fascinating and daunting.

I spend my days ploughing through a mountain of envelopes on my desk, searching for that as yet undiscovered masterpiece and am rarely – if ever – rewarded. Yet, when one least expects it, something surfaces from an unforeseen quarter. The production begins and it is sent out into the world, as if that were the plan all along.

I sensed from the beginning that she had no interest in pursuing the path of a writer, so I did ask her once what kind of career she was interested in.

She looked at me with a terribly serious expression and said, "Hmm, let me see." She was never one to smile much.

And she said, "I don't really know, but I can tell you that this is not it."

Then I asked if there were something she wanted to do. After thinking that over for a while she said that there was something she wanted to know. That was all. Then she told me, as if the thought had just occurred to her, that to be honest she had not thought that publishing the book was a good idea in the beginning, but that now she was grateful. Because she believed that publishing it would help her to discover something which she wished to know.

I persisted in asking what it was, but she would only repeat that it was a private matter. Ultimately, she never told me.

VII

Incidentally, I did receive an odd telephone call about a year after the book came out.

Crank calls are not uncommon in this business. Usually the caller says something along the lines of *I am the author of such and such a book so please send any royalties to this account*, or complains that a particular title was a disgraceful plagiarism of their life, and so on. You would be surprised.

However, this call was not odd in that sense, which is perhaps why it left an impression on me.

The caller was a middle-aged woman. She sounded refined and confident.

She told me that she had read the book and wondered if by any chance the author happened to be Makiko Saiga. She claimed to be an old acquaintance of Makiko's and said that she wanted to get in contact with her.

Nothing in her manner struck me as odd.

Since the book was written under a pen name and contained no photographs, I suspected that she was telling the truth about knowing the author.

However, Miss Saiga had already instructed me to never give out her details to anyone who asked for them, especially people who had known her as a child. She said that if anyone were to enquire, I was to ask for the person's address and say that the author would be in contact. Which is what I said in this case.

I said my piece and the woman went quiet for a few moments.

I could hear some kind of background noise, which I had noticed from the first but was unable to identify, although it crossed my mind that she may have been speaking outside.

In that brief period of silence, however, it suddenly struck me what the sound was.

The sound of waves.

The woman must be calling from somewhere very close to the sea. And for the life of me I cannot say why, but at that moment I had an image of the ocean on the Hokuriku coast.

When she spoke again it was to praise Miss Saiga for all the effort she had put into researching her book, and said that she must have visited K— city numerous times and spoken to many acquaintances to have recorded the events of the past with such care.

Her tone was different. She sounded wheedling and gave the impression that she wanted something from me, though I could not fathom what that might be. However, my guard was up.

I replied, with some caution, that yes, Miss Saiga had been very conscientious in her research. Then I asked for her name and contact details in a businesslike manner.

She gave no answer. Instead, she was simply silent, then all of a sudden she hung up.

Again, I cannot pinpoint the reason why, but this unnerved me.

However, in that gap before she hung up, I overhead a brief snatch of conversation. And I could tell that there was another woman next to the caller, who was much younger and spoke in a very sharp voice.

My instincts told me *she* was the one who had asked the middle-aged woman to make the call. Hence, the person who was really acquainted with the author must be the young woman. The actual caller did not know her at all.

I was rather uneasy about all of this.

Why did the young woman not make the call herself if she knew the author? And why would she not give her name?

I pondered this for some time after putting the receiver down.

It was most disquieting. What *was* it that she wanted to know?

VIII

Are you in the process of writing a book?

Is it by any chance another review of this case?

A non-fiction work about a work of non-fiction? Hmm, that is an interesting concept. Currently there is a boom in books about the Showa era. Perhaps because the last generation to have experienced war is growing old and feels a sense of crisis. Personally, I would like to see more younger people with international experience bring a fresh and objective perspective to bear on the period.

Have no fear, I am not asking you to answer that.

Keep your ambition close to your chest, is what I always say. If you speak of a project before completion the magic will disappear. You have to let it mature inside you, not bring it out for discussion with anybody.

Look out of this window. See how the street fills up with more and more people once afternoon comes.

Students, businessmen killing time, academics, foreigners.

No doubt there are editors, writers and researchers amongst them, each one engaged in their own mental and spiritual pursuits according to their own particular style. Patiently working on pet projects, nursing ambition, their sights set several years ahead. Researching. Thinking. Writing.

Some will founder along the way, of course. Some manuscripts will end up discarded, never to be seen by anybody. Others, however, will blossom and be sent out into the world to bear fruit, as it were, producing excellent results.

There are also people walking around down there with the seeds of ideas in their heads that have not yet germinated into words on the page.

I always feel heartened to look out of this office window onto a street lined with second-hand bookshops.

I feel reassured that the world is full of books that people are steadily reading their way through. No matter how much information may be available, or how easy it is to come by, when all is said and done books can only be read by working one's way through them, line by line, page by page.

There is an old saying to the effect that when an elderly person dies a library disappears.

That undoubtedly holds true for each and every one of the shops on this street.

I have haunted this area since my student days. I was nervous at first about going into the bookshops because I felt as if anything I did would be scrutinized by the owner and my intelligence judged. I would think long and hard before pulling any book from a shelf.

Yet once I overcame my nervousness I discovered that the bookshop owners have an astonishing trove of knowledge.

On one occasion I was looking for reference materials, searching for a certain novel in translation, and when I mentioned the title to the shop owner he told me – off the top of his head – that three translations had been put out by different publishers before the war, but all were out of print now, though the most recent, which was the 1944 version, had been on that shelf over there until very recently. I was flabbergasted, as you might imagine.

I had many similar experiences at other bookshops and have learned a tremendous amount from the owners over the years. I continue to benefit from their erudition to this day and have the greatest respect for them and the storehouse of knowledge that they acquire in the course of their daily business.

Which is why I hope they will always be there. May that precious storehouse of knowledge always be safe from unforeseen events too, such as earthquake or fire. I sincerely hope that from the bottom of my heart.

What? Yes, I suppose I am slightly emotional.

Perhaps you are not aware. The M bookshop referred to in that notebook no longer exists.

It burned down.

IX

I discovered this only recently myself.

Last week I went on a business trip to K— city. Since you had just contacted me and I was feeling slightly nostalgic, I put the book into my briefcase to renew my acquaintance with it on the train. It was an emotional journey in more senses than one, so to speak, to flick through it again and read the occasional section. Of course, it made me think of her research notes again as well.

As I had a bit of time on my hands when I arrived, I took a walk through the second-hand bookshop district.

In particular I wanted to look in the M shop.

But although I searched all over I could not find it anywhere.

Eventually I asked a local and was told that it had burned down quite some time ago. Apparently the fire had begun in the residence of an elderly person who lived alone behind the bookshop, and had spread from there. This neighbour had also died in the fire.

The couple that owned the bookshop lived off the property and were unharmed. Their rare books were kept in a safe at home, fortunately. However, everything in the shop was lost. You can imagine how all that paper must have fuelled the blaze. I expect it went up in a very short time.

The owners were insured, but it is not as though their stock of books was replaceable. Apparently they have decided against reopening the shop.

I was rather upset about the whole incident. Whenever I go on a business trip or holiday I always like to visit the second-hand bookshops. And in this case the M shop's connection to a book that I had worked on made it doubly interesting to me.

What year was the fire, did you say?

Well now, I think it was a year after the book came out...

Yes, that is correct, now I think about it. It would have been just around the time we received that strange phone call. But I could not say now which came first.

x

I never met Miss Saiga again, but we do exchange New Year greetings cards. She almost never writes any news of herself, though she did write that she had found a job at a pharmaceutical company and had married. It was my impression that she was well and truly set on her path in life, and so I refrained from further contact with her.

However, I did receive one postcard out of the blue.

I think that would have been about six years after publication.

The message was very simple.

She had had reason to go back to K— for the first time in a long while, and the crepe myrtle was in full bloom again. Something like that… it was a very dry letter.

You will not find that postcard in the cardboard box, however. If you want to see it, I can bring it with me next time. But truly, that was all it said.

A poem?

Ah, you mean the poem that was left at the scene of the crime.

She did not put the poem in her book, but she did know the wording. She showed it to me, in confidence.

So you know about it too?

All that was said about it in the newspapers at the time was that it contained a foreign name. Even now nobody knows the significance of that name, and although it was believed the perpetrator wrote the poem, that too was never confirmed.

It is a curious poem, though, if it can be called that. Is it really a poem, I wonder, or a letter?

Apparently the police researched thoroughly the possibility of it being a quotation of some kind, but came to the conclusion it was most likely invented by the person who wrote the letter. The name Eugenia is not common by any means. People connected with the case were questioned repeatedly about it. Was it significant to them? Was it a pet name for anyone they knew – that kind of thing – but in the end the police dug up no clues whatsoever.

If you take it as written, it can be read to mean that Eugenia refers to that family whom the sender knows and has come to take revenge on. But in the end police were never able to find any connection between the perpetrator and the family.

The handwriting was also very bad. Whether that was intentional we do not know, but it did make it difficult for experts to identify the sex or age of the writer.

It was found on a table under a single flower vase. That fact alone suggests that it was put there in order to be discovered and read.

Miss Saiga and I once looked that letter over together and discussed it. What kind of letter it was, who had written it and for what purpose, et cetera.

She asked me my opinion.

In my profession I am used to dealing with handwritten manuscripts and various types of handwriting, but I could not be sure of anything with that example. I gave her my honest opinion nonetheless.

It was my feeling that a woman wrote the letter. There was something about the writing and choice of words that did not seem quite masculine to me. I think that is what I said to her. That was my impression, anyway.

Then she asked if I thought it could also be taken as a love letter.

I told her that I did think it could be read that way.

Though as a love letter, I did feel that it was somewhat threatening. I am sure the intended recipient would feel alarmed by it.

That is basically what I told her. These days a woman who sent that might be said to have paranoid, stalker-like tendencies. But the word *stalker* was not in use back then.

I asked her for whom she thought the letter was intended.

And she replied, quite matter-of-factly, "That whole family, don't you think?"

In which case it would mean that the person who wrote the letter had some kind of grudge against the family.

But when I put it to her like that, she shook her head.

"I wouldn't know anything about that," she told me. "I don't know if the person had a grudge against them, but I do think that this letter was addressed to the family."

Her answer was so cool and matter-of-fact that somehow I could not dispute it.

But in that moment, I did think it conceivable that she had an idea of the perpetrator's identity.

She appeared to think it over for a while and then spoke again, in a manner that suggested the thought had only just occurred to her:

"The person who wrote this letter is in darkness."

"In darkness?" I replied.

"That's right. I have the feeling that this person is in a dark place," she repeated.

"A dark place? What do you mean?" I asked her. "That person's surroundings? Or their mental state?"

Again, she shook her head in answer.

"I don't know. I just have a feeling it might be both."

Then she pointed at the letter.

"Look at the second half. 'The song that rises to my lips / The insects of the woods crushed beneath my shoes in the morning.' See how it continues, 'And this tiny heart of mine ceaselessly pumping blood.' I think these are sounds the writer hears."

"Sounds?" I asked her, then reread the poem.

"Don't you think the writer is describing what he or she is hearing, not seeing?" she said. "The writer hears a song, the sound of insects being crushed underfoot, and the sound of a heart beating. *Hears,* not sees. That's why I sense darkness in this poem."

"Point taken," I told her. Then I put it to her that the *long ago dawn* in the first half suggested a visual sensation.

Once again she shook her head in answer.

"Before that comes the word *shivering*. Which suggests that this writer senses changes in time and the nearing of dawn, through changes in the temperature. A person in darkness perceives the passage of time through their skin."

Once she had said that much, even I could see who she suspected.

The girl who survived, the one who had lost the light.

Therefore I asked Miss Saiga – circumspectly, mind you – if she believed her to be the author of the letter.

She hesitated a while, then mumbled, "I don't know."

She spoke flatly and without expression. It did not sound as if she were speaking reluctantly; she truly did not seem to know.

That was very like her. Though she was articulate and direct, one never knew what she was thinking. She had a certain aura, as if there were a grey mist hanging over her that warded off anything more than superficial interaction. I always felt slightly uneasy when speaking with her.

However, I *was* greatly impressed by her interpretation of that poem. It gave me a new appreciation of her ability to investigate and analyse complicated issues. In fact, I believe that for her, writing the book was an exercise in her utilizing her talent to the maximum.

XI

What is the truth, *really*?

How *do* you go about proving what happened on a certain day in a certain place?

Say a murder takes place at an isolated house in the mountains.

Four people, with complicated interrelationships, kill each other.

Everybody involved dies, and several months go by. The house was cut off from society to begin with. Nobody knew there were four people there, nobody knew they even existed. Eventually a storm comes and the house is flattened by a landslide, then finally the land becomes a wild field. The house and bodies are never discovered.

In such a case, did something happen? Naturally it was a tragedy for those involved. But what is it to us? And to the world? There was violence, but if that is never made known to us, is it not the same as if nothing ever happened?

In one sense, something can only be recognized as having happened if there is a record of it.

Miss Saiga said that she wrote the book as material.

At the time of the murders she was still in primary school. It is my guess that writing about them was a way for her to confirm to herself that it happened. And through that process she was finally able to recognize her connection. I feel sure that book was written for herself. Through writing about the crime, she *discovered* it.

In the process, she also discovered the culprit. The person she believed to be responsible.

I remember that she did do some research on the law regarding the statute of limitations.

She was particularly interested in the suspension of the statute of limitations and looked into cases of suspects going overseas. Apparently time spent abroad can extend the deadline on the statute of limitations.

I am sure you can see where I am heading with this. Who it was that she suspected.

There is the matter of the letter, but it is likely that she had suspected this person for quite some time. At least, that is what my instincts tell me.

And they also tell me that she is in pursuit of this person even now. But, strangely enough, I do not think that her aim is to apprehend the person in question or extract a confession. It is my belief that her object is something different. That the pursuit of this person has become her mission in life and, as with the book, she does it only for herself.

But let us say that she did manage to get hold of the truth. If she did, well, I for one do not believe she would write a book about it. If she herself is satisfied, that would be sufficient for her. A shame, is it not? It is a strange trait, if I do say so myself. Another fact gets buried. And with no record then, regrettably, it will be as if it never happened.

So, if you do happen to write about her or about this case, I beg of you, please do keep me informed. Make sure to keep backup copies of your material. And, just to be on the safe side, please do telephone me often.

Promise me that much, all right?

11

THE DREAM PATH: PART TWO

The detective

I

Sorry about the racket before. The grandchildren are here – my youngest son's boys.

We're a very male family. The eldest son's got two boys too.

Course I'm fond of them, but they do get excited. I can last hours if I'm interrogating during an investigation – even now – but when it comes to playing with the grandchildren, just half an hour does me in. And they get heavier every time I see them.

Ah, but I never imagined the day would come I'd hold grandchildren in my arms. Happens before you know it. One day suddenly there were these little kids calling me Grandpa... it was a real shock, I tell you.

Not at all, I feel more relaxed outside. And it's easier to talk while walking.

Facing someone over a table reminds me too much of the job. Makes it hard to settle down for a proper chat.

No, I don't do much now. Teach kendo to children once a week, that's about all. I'm just your average retired senior citizen.

Isn't this evening breeze pleasant? I say, how about we go to a small bar I know? My regular. No obligation of course, we can split the bill. It's quiet, cheap, and the food is good. The kind of place I like, but they're not easy to find. The bars I used to go to when I was still on the job have almost all gone now. It's hard to find a new place, so I pray this one won't close on me.

Come here a lot, do you?

I see, quite a bit. So you'd have a general grasp of the geography of the city then. Have you walked the streets much?

Oh, I see.

Well, I'm not one for crowds, so let me show one of my favourite routes along the backstreets.

Origami?

Never do it any more. It's a funny thing, but the minute I retired and finally had the time for it, I lost interest completely. I used to have the concentration for it in my spare moments at work. It was an escape from the busy, brutal atmosphere, I expect.

II

Recently I've been doing a lot of thinking.

What I think is that everybody has a particular time in their life that they find themselves going back to in unguarded moments. Could be a period of success, or a time they can never forget, something like that. Not necessarily always a good time, though. For some it might be a period of depression or withdrawal. Whatever the case, good or bad, there's one particular period in a person's life that's central to them.

For some it's childhood. Others their student days. Or after achieving fame and recognition. Could be any one of all kinds of life experiences, but for some reason when a switch goes on that person finds themselves going back to that same time in their mind, over and over. Always the same.

Don't you have a touchstone period like that?

For me, it was that case. Working that case in the 1970s was a defining point in my life. Sometimes I'll be doing something and suddenly don't know where I am. Whenever that happens, what I *always* see in the back of my mind is me, working on solving that case. Even after all these years.

In fact, if I'm really precise it was the first time I came face to face with *her* in the hospital. That's the moment.

My zero hour.

Am I being clear?

If my life were a book, the thickest section, the one with the most dog-eared pages, would be the one about that case. The spine would be bent from being opened to those pages so often. And the book would always fall open to that place. That's how I see it.

III

I still don't understand why I felt so convinced.

Call it a personal prejudice if you like – I admit it.

But I'll be honest with you.

I wasn't searching for who did it. I was trying to prove *she* did it. Every day, rushing around, doing everything I could possibly think of. All I was doing was trying to prove her guilt. That much I can tell you.

Yes, let's say it *is* unbecoming of a detective to be swayed by a preconceived idea. With no supporting evidence to boot. All I had to go on was my instinct. The person under suspicion might well take exception to that. And rightly so.

Ordinarily I'd think as much, too.

But that case, and that case alone, was different.

It was the only time I felt one hundred per cent sure that I knew who did it.

My conviction never wavered. If anything, it's only grown stronger the older I get. Most of the time I forget about it, but then something reminds me for some reason or other, and there are times I can't sleep at night for frustration and regret.

We were defeated.

She beat me.

I put so much into investigating that case, my colleagues said I worked like a maniac. I could see they sort of admired me and assumed I was motivated by gut hatred for a mass murderer. But my real motive was different. Because from the start I *knew* who did it. The problem of identifying the culprit was never in my head. I didn't want to be beaten by her, pure and simple. That was it. I didn't want her to win. Everything I did was driven by that motivation.

You're asking why I was so convinced?

I've thought about that a lot too.

Frankly speaking, even now I don't know. All I can say is I knew the moment I laid eyes on her. I could feel a kind of transparent malice, exactly the same as I found at the scene of the crime – that's all.

Ha ha… like falling in love at first sight?

Yes, I see what you mean. It's like two sides of the same coin. The only difference is whether you react to her charm and virtue, or what lies behind that. Another detective who went with me once to interview her was so taken in by her beauty he kept going on how we had to protect the poor girl, and for her sake we had to do everything to catch the murderer, that sort of thing. Seeing his reaction helped convince me too. There's a fine line between good and evil.

We both saw the same person, but our reactions were poles apart.

I can't deny it might have been a warped kind of attraction. She got under my skin. I was bewitched by her then, and haven't stopped thinking about her since.

IV

On the face of it the search for the man in the yellow raincoat was our main priority, but she became uppermost in my mind very early on, and I began looking into her friendships, standing in the family, et cetera.

The Aosawas were such an old, prominent local family that I expected a lot of resistance to our inquiries. I thought the local medical association wouldn't be too happy about being scrutinized either.

But surprisingly, most people in the community were more than willing to cooperate. There was a tremendous amount of sympathy for her, being the only survivor and losing all her family, so people were happy to do anything that might lead to finding the culprit.

We interviewed more than six hundred people, ranging from those who had had long-standing connections with the family to people who had only ever exchanged a few words.

But nothing came up.

There was no trace of scandal. You often find with old families that there's some kind of skeleton in the closet. But we didn't find anybody with a grudge – medical negligence, for example – or children with the wrong sort of friends, or good-for-nothing relatives. They were so clean it was almost unnatural. No matter how deep we dug, we couldn't find any dirt.

So then I thought, well, what if there was some kind of issue in the immediate family? Something that wouldn't leak out. It was my belief that for her to be the culprit, there had to be something that would smoulder away – a family dispute, or some kind of grievance with the household environment.

I put together a list of schools the children attended, workplaces and private friends, and methodically went through the whole list interviewing people.

But I couldn't dig up anything from there either.

The parents were of good character. The children got along fine. They all did well at school, were cheerful, bright, admired by everybody. *That can't be right*, I thought. I started to worry I might be way off the mark.

What *was* the motive? I couldn't find *any* reason to believe her to be the culprit. Was it a murder without motive, perhaps? Or an impulse crime?

Those thoughts just didn't correspond with my impression of the girl I saw in hospital.

I couldn't believe I was wrong about her.

I just couldn't be.

I racked my brains over it, day after day.

One theory I considered was that she'd intended to kill herself and take the whole family with her. Once she had made sure everyone else was dead, she would follow.

That seemed more like her than anything else.

But in that case, what would be the motive for killing herself?

Was she depressed about her future?

As far as motive went, that line of thought was a dead end.

She'd been blind since she was little and was used to it, not to mention that the Aosawa family were so well off there was no need for her to work. In fact, she could live a life of luxury without ever having to work.

In which case, maybe getting exclusive control of the family money was the simplest explanation. But I wasn't convinced of that either. It would have been much easier and more convenient to have a family member as a guardian.

Gradually, the investigation began to stall.

Everyone was starting to get in a panic.

That was when a random killer theory was floated. A killer who wasn't particular about location. Any house with a large number of people in it would have served the purpose.

But that theory didn't fly either. Namely because of the delivery slip. The slip with the sender's and recipient's names and addresses on it. It was because of the delivery slip that nobody thought twice about serving the drinks. The existence of that slip put paid to any random killer theory.

So we were clutching at straws by then, and the scope of the investigation was widened to include victims' past friendships and medical associations from other prefectures.

By golly, that inquiry dragged out painfully, with no end in sight. Hopeless, it was – we didn't even know what to look for any more. It felt like the summer was never going to end.

When I look back now on that case, I think of the moment I met her in hospital as my zero hour, and the rest was simply footwork, plodding the streets in the heat. Fed up, knowing it was useless, but not knowing what else to do. That summer I nearly lost heart.

I have this abiding image of my colleague and me, sheltering from the sun under a canopy outside a small grocery, where I bought us adzuki bean ice creams to eat. We were exhausted from the heat and too tired even to talk after trudging the streets since early morning with nothing to show for it.

I suspect a part of me still walks those summer city streets. Sometimes that's what it feels like.

V

That's why when that young fellow suddenly turned up as a corpse I was furious more than anything.

What – the culprit turns up from somewhere off the radar, complete with suicide note…

It was like he came from another planet. We hadn't been even remotely close to finding him. That's what it felt like.

But now we had the baseball cap and all the other physical evidence, so it was no wonder the top brass brightened up all of a sudden.

After I checked it all out, there was no doubt in my mind he was the one who had delivered the poison drinks.

But what was his motive? And what about the delivery slip?

So then I started to probe his connection with the Aosawa family, and I was sure I'd find something this time.

But we drew a blank again.

We turned every stone, but there was no point of connection between him and the Aosawas that I could find.

So I was over the moon when I heard about the boy living nearby who had seen him take a memo into his flat. *This is it*, I thought.

I've never worked harder at dragging through mud, literally, than I did then. I even got thanked for making the town cleaner! It's fair to say I was like a man possessed by the thought of that memo. Nearly drove me mad not being able to pass by without checking any scrap of paper I happened to see dropped in the gutter. Wherever I went, I always had my eyes glued to the ground, looking for those scraps of paper. Didn't matter how far it was from where he lived, if I saw a bit of paper on the ground, I couldn't be satisfied till I'd turned it over to check. I was that obsessed.

But in the end we never found that memo.

I don't think the boy was lying. I believe what he saw was a copy of the information that was written on the delivery slip.

But ultimately we could never prove it because we didn't have the physical evidence.

The bosses were counting on that memo, but the mood changed once it became clear nothing would turn up, and everyone started saying the boy had made a mistake. Then opinion at the top began leaning towards the theory that the man had acted alone.

There was no mistake that he'd done it, and I think they just wanted to put an end to an investigation that had grown too big.

But I was against it.

The existence of that delivery slip was evidence of an accomplice. I maintained that considering the mental state of the man who had actually carried out the crime, the main culprit must be tied in with that somewhere.

A lot of colleagues working the case thought so too, but the top brass had a different opinion.

It was clear they wanted the investigation wrapped up. And in fact it did end, with the conclusion that the crime was the work of a single perpetrator.

VI

I had a lot of sympathy for the other survivor, the woman who helped at the Aosawa house. She copped a double blow.

She suffered the after-effects of the poison for a long time, and on top of that was the butt of vicious rumours that she was the one who had done it.

After regaining consciousness she was so overcome with guilt at having survived that she often said she wished she had met her end too. It was tough for the family, as you can imagine, being looked at suspiciously by everybody, but they all pulled together and did a fine job of getting her through it all.

The only time I felt any kind of rage, I suppose what you'd call ordinary human anger, was when I was with that woman and her family. When I was with them they made me feel like I was carrying out my job like any responsible person.

She was tormented by guilt something terrible after leaving hospital.

When the investigation closed I went to pay a final visit, and she broke down in tears, howling, saying she shouldn't have survived. It really made me see red again, I tell you.

That same day I went to see the other survivor as well.

I wanted to see her before my anger cooled off.

She was already back at home by then, without her family of course.

I still think about it sometimes.

I wonder if in truth she really *could* see. I couldn't help thinking that, and I know a few other people who thought the same.

That day was no exception.

When I opened the door, there she was, standing there, waiting in the entrance hall as if she'd seen me coming.

And she called me by name before I could give it myself.

She wore a navy-blue dress. It looked like a mourning outfit but was very becoming. Made her look quite the stunning beauty.

She knew I suspected her.

Probably from the first time we met.

She had sharp instincts, that girl. From the moment I laid eyes on her I thought she did it, and likewise, she knew from the moment we first spoke that she was under suspicion.

We spoke a number of times. I had her repeat her testimony and asked a lot about her family. Of course, on the surface of it I never mentioned my suspicions. But we both understood the game. We both knew this was a chase, and that one of us was hunting the other. That was our secret.

That day I informed her that the investigation was closed, much to my regret.

That's all I said.

But I know she understood.

I took her hand and put an origami crane in it. I gave one to the other survivor too. It was a piece called the Dream Path, two cranes joined at the stomach and facing each other, as though one has landed on a lake and sees its own reflection.

I explained this to her and she felt it to check the shape for herself.

Then she looked at me with a smile.

"Detective, we're like these cranes, aren't we," she said.

Calm as anything.

"Why's that?" I asked.

"Just a feeling," she said, and tipped her head at me.

Then there was silence. I had a feeling she had told me something very important, but for the life of me I didn't know what.

After a bit she asked if I thought people's dreams are connected.

I told her that the dreams of people who are thinking about each other are.

"Gosh, that's nice," she said.

And that was it.

I haven't seen her since.

VII

I wasn't in the country when that book came out.

I was in Malaysia at the time. Did a stint as an instructor for an information and training exchange with the Malaysian police. It was part of one of those vague workplace education schemes that large organizations tend to set up every now and then.

So I didn't know about it for a while until after I got back.

A former colleague told me. Someone who had also worked on the case. He told me that a young woman from the neighbourhood who'd been a child at the time had written a novel about it.

Even then I wasn't keen to read it. That case had been nothing but a bitter defeat for me, so I had no desire to see it rehashed and twisted into any kind of fiction. And I was also annoyed by the thought of reading something I didn't really want to.

But deep down, I was curious to know.

So finally I bought it one day when I went up to the National Police Agency in Tokyo and wanted something to read on the train. But I ended up having work discussions both ways on that trip and I didn't read it then.

It wasn't till a few months later I finally got round to it.

Then I kicked myself. To be frank, even now I'm still ticked off I went on that Malaysia trip.

Don't get me wrong, I have no problem with Malaysia itself. I was just shattered that when the book came out I wasn't in the country.

If only I'd read it as soon as it was released. Just a bit sooner – six months, even – I might have been spared all those sleepless nights, tossing and turning.

VIII

My first thoughts about the book were how well the author had captured the atmosphere of the time, despite having been so young when it happened.

It was obvious she'd done her work. She described the townscape and the social setting in great detail. As I was reading I could see clearly in my mind how things had looked back then.

You know how quickly cities change here. Buildings being knocked down and new ones going up before you know it. Commercial tenants coming and going, with new exteriors every time a new business moves in. You're always seeing places you know are new, but you can't quite remember what used to be there before.

At any rate, I'd never experienced anything like this before with fiction. While I was reading, I had a picture of the scene at the time in my mind, clear as anything.

The book was about the murders but wasn't written as a mystery and didn't have any kind of conclusion, so the actual content didn't leave much of an impression on me.

But – there were a number of places where I felt something was wrong, you know, not quite right.

I couldn't put my finger on the reason, though. It was just a vague feeling, and I didn't think too much about it at the time.

But then a few days later – I think I was just walking along the street – it suddenly hit me.

Immediately I rushed home and started reading the book again, very carefully.

This time I marked all the pages where I noticed something odd.

When I reached the end, I went back and checked all those pages.

And there was no mistaking it.

I was certain.

The author's descriptions of certain places differed from reality. Intentionally, it seemed. That's what I realized.

She'd written in such detail about the geography and physical appearance of the town – to an almost unnecessary degree – it was obvious when I looked that she'd deliberately falsified the descriptions in certain places.

Can you guess what those were?

The second-hand bookshops.

Yes, there are a lot of them in this city. As might be expected in a place with many universities and a long cultural history. A real scholars' town, it is.

But the book doesn't mention a single bookshop. Or rather, in places where they *should* be mentioned, she puts in another kind of shop. She goes into great detail describing the old established shops in the downtown area and records them with great accuracy in accordance with maps from the time, only the second-hand bookshops are not mentioned.

What was the significance?

I scratched my head over that one.

The fact of her being so hair-splittingly precise in other parts made it clear it was deliberate. But why? Why would she do that? Was it some kind of game?

It was very strange. Not many would notice it, either. Anyone who didn't know the city, or what it was like at the time, wouldn't have any idea. And if they did, then what of it?

I thought about this a lot but couldn't come up with any explanation. Maybe it was for her own personal reasons. I couldn't make any sense of it, and in the end became so busy with other things I forgot about it.

Several weeks went by.

My son was leaving home to get married and I helped him move. In the process, I noticed a stack of books in the passageway bundled up with twine.

When I asked what I should do with them he told me he'd called a second hand book dealer to come and collect them. He was a bookworm who could never get rid of anything he'd read, but with moving to a smaller place he couldn't very well take them all with him.

And that's how I got the idea.

It hit me as I was staring at that pile of books on the floor. I realized something crucial.

I realized that I'd overlooked something very important in the investigation.

IX

The young man who did it was very tidy.

There was almost nothing in his flat. It was always clean, apparently, and he didn't appear to have many clothes, but everybody testified that he always wore neat, clean shirts and his trousers were properly ironed.

Which is why I didn't pay much attention at the time, though his flat was empty and he had very few things lying around. We cleaned out the rubbish bins and drains looking for the memo.

But if you think about it, there *was* no reason for him to throw away that memo.

The boy who lived nearby testified that he was carrying

it about very carefully, treating it like a precious object. To me, that suggests blind worship of the person who drove him to carry out the murders. That's why he had held the memo in that manner.

I reread the boy's testimony.

And I discovered something I'd overlooked, despite reading it over and over at the time.

The boy said that the man was a good teacher. He also mentioned that sometimes the man got out his own science and maths textbooks to help explain theory and whatnot to the boy in terms he could easily understand.

He'd graduated from a good university with a science degree majoring in chemistry.

And he also worked at a place that made agricultural chemicals, so we should have found books on that subject in the flat too. Textbooks and academic books are expensive, not the kind of thing you throw away.

But we didn't find any books at all in his flat.

Before taking his life he'd put his things in order.

Yes, that's right. It stands to reason he would have taken his books to a used bookshop.

And – I'll bet my life on it – that memo is stuck between the pages of one of those books.

X

Imagine my shock when I realized this.

I bet you can't.

For a moment everything went black. I couldn't breathe. Even thought I might be having another heart attack. Then straight away I calculated the statute of limitations.

Why? Because I knew that Hisako Aosawa had married and gone overseas. She was legally an adult by then.

If she was overseas, the statute of limitations would be suspended. We still had plenty of time.

Of course, there was no guarantee those books were still in the bookshop.

They could have been sold by now, or even destroyed.

But second-hand bookshops operate on a different timescale to other businesses. Time stands still in those places. The same book can occupy the same corner of the same shelf for years on end.

The more I thought about it, the more on edge I became. The suspense nearly killed me.

I dug out an old map and set about searching for bookshops that had been open back then and were still open.

And what do you know, I discovered a shop not too far from where he lived that specialized in the natural sciences.

It had to be where he would go to dispose of his books. I had a gut feeling.

The name of the bookshop was somehow familiar, though. I had a feeling I'd heard it very recently.

I told myself it was only imagination, but the nagging feeling in the pit of my stomach wouldn't go away.

So next morning I set out for that bookshop first thing.

And when I got there, I realized immediately why the name seemed familiar.

Not two months earlier it had burned down. I'd heard the news on TV and radio, that's why I knew the name.

I shook when I saw sheeting over the burned-out remains.

It meant that someone else besides me had read that book and thought the same thing.

And whoever it was had no compunction about tying up loose ends. Resorting to destroying evidence without even knowing for sure if the books were in there or not.

The calculation and daring of it was chilling.

I looked into the incident. Apparently the fire had started in the house of an elderly person behind the shop and spread from there. This neighbour lived alone and had been in and out of hospital the last few years. He had died in the fire, so it wasn't possible to determine the cause.

That news also made my blood run cold.

It was an all too believable scenario for a house fire. And on the surface of it, it didn't look at all like the bookshop was the actual target.

It was nothing to her to burn down the house of an elderly person in order to destroy the bookshop.

This got me all riled up again, and I decided to find out where she had been at the time of the fire.

Turns out she was out of the country that day, but I learned she'd been here for six months not long before that.

I can guess why she came back.

She probably heard rumours about the book. Maybe she came back to get hold of it, or maybe she read it overseas and decided to come back. Either way, I have no doubt she came to the same conclusion I did.

It felt like a punch in the gut when I realized that. She'd beaten me again.

XI

So then I began wondering about the author's intentions. Why had she written the book?

It looked to me as though the author had reached the same conclusion I had, and was hinting at that by writing this book. I started to wonder if maybe she knew something, or maybe had further proof.

So I sent her a letter.

I started off with telling her that I'd been connected with the investigation and that reading her book had brought back memories, et cetera. Then I asked directly why she had altered the information about the bookshops.

When I got a reply sometime later, it wasn't what I expected.

She wrote that she'd gone to many second-hand bookshops as part of her background research on the period, and the owners had been kind to her, so she had felt awkward about writing about them directly in her novel. That's why she had made those alterations. It was for personal, sentimental reasons. There was no deeper meaning.

Well, there was nothing I could say to that. And anyway, if she had been in possession of some kind of proof, it would have been quicker to write about it. I didn't think she was lying, because there was no reason for her to cover for the perpetrator.

She was a bit of an enigma, though. Did she *really* change the details of the bookshop for sentimental reasons? And why had she written the book in the first place? I still didn't understand.

But in hindsight, I suspect she herself didn't really understand either, that's my bet. She was witness to a shocking incident as a young girl but couldn't take in its significance at the time. And because she couldn't process it, the shock stayed with her as she grew up. Then the only way she could find to express that was through this book. That's my take.

XII

That's how she beat me again.

The second time was a real kick in the teeth.

Only the two of us know about it. Just me and her. I don't know where she lives now, but in this big, wide world, she and I are the only two who know the truth. It gives me a strange feeling to think that.

But that defeat changed me.

Up until then it was in the past, over and done with. Something I wished I could forget about but couldn't. That was my position.

The second time she licked me I got wise.

I still didn't know.

It was still going on.

After all this time she'd read that book and taken steps to deal with it quick smart. That told me something. It told me that for her, too, it still wasn't over. It was a sign that she knew if any new facts came to light, the rope could tighten around her wrists.

Which meant there could be a third chance.

As long as the statute of limitations was suspended, it was still possible to apprehend her.

That gave me hope. Maybe I would see the day when she was caught.

Heaven's vengeance is slow but sure. Lately that saying often pops into my head. I don't doubt there will be a third time, and when it happens I won't see it coming. But there will be a moment when, quite by chance, her guilt will be exposed. I feel sure of it.

I'll stake my reputation on it.

I believe what she said the last time we met. That we're like those two origami cranes.

It's true, we are alike. The way we think and see things. Our actions mirror each other's, like the two cranes facing one another.

In a sense, we think of each other more than anyone else in the world.

There's a part of her that I understand better than anyone else in the world.

That's why we connect in our dreams. Maybe her dreams told me the truth about the second-hand bookshops.

That's why there will be a next time.

And when it comes, again her dreams will tell me.

One day I'll see her again. I know it. I can feel it in my bones.

XIII

Sometime later I received a phone call.

From the other survivor. The woman who helped out with housework.

I think it was just before I retired.

I knew from reading the book that she'd cooperated with the author. She told me on the phone that after the interviews were over, she had remembered several things.

So I went to meet her, near the house where she'd been brought up.

None of her family lived there any more, but it was near the sea, as was the school she'd gone to, and she'd grown up with the sound of the sea.

We took a walk along the seashore.

She'd aged, but she looked much calmer than the last time I'd seen her. I got the feeling that passing her last years in peace had been a saving grace for her.

She told me she'd been thinking about her childhood a lot recently. Looking at the sea through the classroom window and hearing its roar in the background. She remembered playing games with her friends on the beach. How they'd throw a ball into the sea and compete to see who could be the first to grab it as the waves washed it back.

She got quite misty-eyed talking about it. Told me with a laugh that she'd asked her daughter to scatter her ashes in the sea there.

Then she started talking about a phone call that came on the day of the murders. Said it was from a young girl who seemed to be confirming if the murders had taken place.

Well, you could have knocked me over with a feather.

Vital testimony like that surfacing so late in the game. Who'd have imagined?

Who in blazes had made that call? Was there another accomplice?

You can imagine how my mind was in a whirl, but I kept calm and noted down what she remembered of the telephone call.

It wasn't much to go on.

She was apologetic. Said she'd not realized at the time, but she had a feeling she knew the voice, though she couldn't put a name to it. Looking through photo albums and lists of names from the period didn't jog her memory.

I gave her my home phone number and told her to ring me if she remembered anything else. If she did, I was likely to be retired by then.

She pointed out a small church nearby, on the other side of a pine grove, where apparently Mrs Aosawa used to go and lend a hand several times a year. She used to go there with Mrs Aosawa at Christmas and New Year to deliver sweets and toys for orphan children that the church cared for. Mrs Aosawa also took small gifts to the residents of a nearby nursing home who attended the church, and helped with making cards and cleaning.

She had quite a spark in her eye as she told me all this.

It was heartbreaking to hear her reminisce about the past like that, but I was glad she could manage to talk about it.

She said that she'd been to that place with Hisako.

Hisako liked listening to the sound of the sea, apparently. Sometimes she begged to be taken to hear "Kimi's sea". When told the sea didn't belong to anybody, Hisako would only laugh and repeat, "It's Kimi's sea."

There was a small park surrounded by pine trees next to that walkway, where it seems Hisako had a favourite bench. She used to sit there and listen to the sea for long stretches.

We went and saw it. A very interesting bench it was, what you call a love seat. Made of stone, but in an S-shape so two people can sit and face each other. The only difference from an ordinary love seat was the backrest was so high you couldn't actually see the other person.

The upper part of the backrest had a thick coloured glass inset – a bit like a stained-glass window. I remember it had a red flower pattern. When somebody was sitting on the other side, you could see the blur of their head through the glass.

Sounds interesting, doesn't it?

Hisako was proud as punch of it, apparently. As if she owned it.

Kimi told me she used to sit there with Hisako and chat. It seems Hisako used to get very irritated because she could never be on her own. Somebody always had to be with her whenever she went somewhere, because of her blindness. But sitting on that bench she could feel as if she were by herself. Kimi used to let her be as much as possible. She told me she'd do her knitting or read a book, to try and give Hisako some space.

I had no wish to sit in the spot she used to.

I was afraid I'd lose myself somehow, became part of her.

Kimi didn't sit on the bench either.

The two of us just stood there for a while, listening to the sound of the waves.

Waves that she used to listen to. The same ocean that she might be listening to even now, way across the other side of the world.

When you think about it, the world is connected by the sea. It literally connects me to the place she is now.

I think Kimi had much the same thought. "I wonder what Hisako's doing now?" she said. "I didn't like her going overseas after marrying, but looking back now, it might have been for the best."

I didn't say anything, just agreed with her.

Deep down, though, I was thinking I didn't know if it really was for the best or not.

I thought it would be a long way off in the future before either of us knew the answer to that.

"I still have the origami cranes you gave me," she told me when we parted.

Which set me wondering if Hisako Aosawa still had the cranes I'd given her.

In the end I never heard from Kimi again.

The next phone call I received was from her daughter. To inform me her mother had died and to tell me the date and time of the funeral.

12

EXTRACTS FROM THE FRIEND'S FILE

I

SUSPECTED HEATSTROKE FATALITY

On the evening of the 26th a woman was found collapsed on a bench by staff at K– Park. She was taken to hospital with cardiac arrest and confirmed dead.

The woman was identified as Makiko Yoshimizu, 42, a housewife from Hino in Tokyo. She was on her way back to Tokyo after visiting her husband in his current posting in Fukui. The weather on the 26th was particularly hot, with the temperature in the city reaching a record 100 degrees Fahrenheit. The cause of death is believed to be heatstroke brought on while she was sightseeing in the city.

RESIDENTS FILE PETITION

City residents have begun a petition calling for the preservation of the former Aosawa mansion in the Nakaogaki district, after learning of a decision to demolish the building.

The residence was built in 1957 and designed by leading modern architect Kenzo Murano, who in his later years rarely undertook commissions for private homes.

Unusually for a residential building of the time, reinforced concrete was used in the construction. The structure was a combined clinic and residence that incorporated Japanese and Western styles into the overall design rather than simply separating them into Western architectural style for the clinic and Japanese style for the residence. Its distinctive appearance is a familiar sight to city residents.

However, it has been virtually uninhabited since a major crime took place there in 1973. This, along with soaring land prices, has contributed to difficulties in maintaining it, and the Aosawa family is therefore preparing to sell it. Upon learning of plans to demolish the building, local residents, fearing the loss of such a valuable architectural artefact, launched a petition calling on the prefectural government to recognize and preserve it as a cultural heritage site.

Kiyoshiro Kawataki, 73, who represents the Round Windows House Association, had been a patient of three generations of doctors in the Aosawa family clinic and told us, "The building is a familiar symbol of the district and a valuable part of our architectural cultural heritage as well. Experts have confirmed to us that it is still structurally sound, and we plead for it to be left as it is."

II

A RESPONSE REGARDING THE RECENT INCIDENT IN THE PARK

I recall that on the afternoon of the twenty-sixth there were fewer visitors than normal, in all likelihood due to the severe heat and approaching end of the summer holidays.

It is my custom to make a tour of inspection of the whole park every three hours when there is no other pressing business, and at one o'clock in the afternoon of that day, I did not see anybody fitting the description of Makiko Yoshimizu. Other staff members also confirm this.

As it was late in the day, the strong reflected glare on the asphalt and dry pathways would have raised the temperature to close to 120 degrees Fahrenheit. Staff had sprinkled a certain amount of water on the paths for cooling purposes, but at such a temperature this would not have had any significant effect.

Apparently the first sighting of a person matching the description of Mrs Yoshimizu was reported at 3.30. One of the cleaning staff witnessed a woman with a child talking to another woman sitting on a bench. The cleaner's impression was that the woman and child were not acquainted with the woman on the bench, and instead were passers-by who happened to exchange a few words. This staff member cannot be certain her memory is accurate, as the park is a large one with many visitors. I ask for your understanding of this.

Next, at around four o'clock, two gardeners observed the woman sitting on the bench with a bottle of lemonade in her hand. She was alone, and there was no sign of the aforementioned woman and child at that time. She appeared to be resting, and the gardeners did not sense anything unusual. Then, at 4.30, I discovered Mrs Yoshimizu collapsed on the bench. It was near closing time and park staff were about to carry out their final inspections for the day. Initially I thought she was asleep. She appeared to be leaning against the bench and dozing. When I approached and called "hello", she gave no response. Her silence seemed unusual, so I touched her on the shoulder and called to her once more, and as I did so she slid over and collapsed on the bench.

I was shocked by this and quickly called other staff, who rang for an ambulance. At this time she did not appear to be conscious. I later heard that she never regained consciousness.

It pains me greatly that we did not find her earlier, as I learned that she has a young child. The staff and I will wholeheartedly do our utmost to ensure that such an incident never happens again. I regret that this is all the information I can provide on the last hours of Mrs Yoshimizu.

III

BOARD OF EDUCATION INSPECTS AOSAWA RESIDENCE

The Prefectural Board of Education invited experts to inspect the Aosawa residence in Nakaogaki after receiving a petition with close to ten thousand signatures calling for the building to be preserved. In discussions with the citizens' group leading the campaign, group members, local historians and architects all stressed the rarity and value of the mansion. Heated discussion continued for two hours, ending with the Board of Education undertaking to review the case and report on the result of their review.

DECISION TO DEMOLISH AOSAWA RESIDENCE

The Board of Education announced its decision not to recognize and preserve the Aosawa residence in Nakaogaki as a cultural heritage site.

The Board explained that their decision was based on a number of considerations: one, that other cultural properties in more urgent need of preservation should be given priority; two, that the Aosawa residence is located on prime development land, hence the cost of maintaining it would exceed prefectural budget resources; and three, that the Board has taken into consideration the wishes of the current owner to dispose of the building.

The citizens' group responded angrily to the decision, saying that the cultural heritage registration system was meaningless if it did not preserve those buildings with strong roots to the daily lives and memories of ordinary people. It stressed that the landscape was changing rapidly and with each passing day important historical buildings were being lost due to the scrap-and-build mentality of the Japanese construction industry. The group also accused administrative officials who handed down the decision of being in collusion with the construction industry, which it said is more concerned with securing contracts to construct new buildings than taking the time and trouble to build superior quality structures to leave for posterity.

Demolition work is scheduled to start as early as the middle of next month; however, the citizens' group is taking a hard-line attitude and saying that resorting to force is not out of the question.

IV

MORE INFORMATION ABOUT THE INCIDENT IN THE PARK

When I spoke to Mrs Yoshimizu I saw no lemonade bottle. She had collapsed in such a way as to be lying prone on the bench: therefore, if there were any bottle I feel sure that I would have noticed it. I also did not see any objects lying on the ground at her feet. The cleaning staff I spoke with confirmed that very little rubbish had been thrown away that day, and no bottle was found in any of the bins in the vicinity. The park has clear views and cleaning staff do a thorough job, therefore it is my belief that if a lemonade bottle had been left lying anywhere it would have been conspicuous. It is possible that Mrs Yoshimizu returned the empty lemonade bottle to the teahouse where she bought it. With this in mind I also made enquiries at the teahouse; however, I was told that the wooden bottle return box is kept outside, and if anyone had returned the bottle the staff inside would not necessarily be aware of that.

The identity of the mother and child who exchanged a few words with Mrs Yoshimizu is not known. All I can say is that they appear to have been in the area by chance.

According to the description of the staff member who saw them, the woman was plump and middle-aged, and the child was a small girl around two years old. She did not see their faces, apparently. However, she did say that from their dress they appeared to be local visitors, not tourists.

I hope this answers your questions.

V

DATELINE: CITY OF K—,

THIRTY-ONE YEARS SINCE THE AOSAWA MURDERS

Even *The Forgotten Festival* Came to Be Forgotten

There are things that happen on this earth which can only be described as a strange twist of fate. Like many people, there was a time when I too would have scoffed at such an idea and regarded it as not worthy of serious consideration. However, in the course of my life I have encountered things for which there can be no other explanation. In fact, I recently became aware of one such incident which forces me to the conclusion that there can be no other explanation.

The other day I came across a brief article tucked away in a small newspaper. It was about a housewife who had died of heatstroke in K— Park while on her way back to Tokyo after visiting her husband at his regional posting. At the time I read this article I did not pay it any particular attention. However, my interest was immediately aroused when I discovered from an old acquaintance who I happened to see a few days later that this woman was the author of *The Forgotten Festival.*

My acquaintance was a former police officer. He had been in charge of the investigation into what came to be known as the Aosawa Case, and as a young reporter at the time I had followed him around for over six months, hounding him at all hours of the day and night for updates on the case.

A mass poisoning with an unprecedented number of deaths had inevitably led to parallels being drawn with the Teigin Incident. The investigation into the crime was closed after the suicide of the suspect, yet doubts about his guilt have continued to be expressed in various quarters ever since, together with claims that he was falsely accused. A quarter of a century later the truth still remains shrouded in darkness, while the incident slowly fades from the city's memory.

In recent weeks, however, the Aosawa Case has once again come to public attention due to the publicity surrounding the campaign to preserve the Aosawa residence, the scene of the murders. I myself sought out that old acquaintance again after my memory was refreshed by this campaign.

The Forgotten Festival: how many would recall that title now? The book became a bestseller after a young woman who had been at the scene as a girl wrote about the incident in a novel more than ten years later. I remember vividly how its publication once again brought the Aosawa Case into the spotlight. The author was roundly criticized for using the word *Festival* in the title, but she maintained silence on the subject and after that one volume never published another book.

I cannot help but see it as a peculiar twist of fate that the author should have died here, in this city, just as it is in the process of attempting to eliminate all trace of the house where the murders occurred. It is as if time has been turned back.

She had been at the scene of the crime with her two elder brothers. I contacted one of them after her death and he agreed to a telephone interview on condition that I did not give his name. When I asked what his thoughts were on his sister dying in the very city where the crime had occurred, he told me bluntly, "When all is said and done, she wasn't ever able to get away from it. She didn't tell us she was going to write that book, and never once mentioned the murders again after it was published, but it seems she could never put it behind her."

The family moved away from the city when the father was transferred shortly after the incident; however, soon after that the parents divorced. The younger of the two brothers apparently committed suicide in his twenties.

"We weren't especially conscious of it, but I do think now that all of us being at the scene of the crime as children did have something to do with it," he told me. "My sister's book was called *The Forgotten Festival*, but for us it was *The Unforgettable Festival.*"

Though I said nothing in reply, the thought I had was that even a book can be forgotten. The cruellest thing in this world is to be forgotten; yet time will bury the furore of the past and silence the chatter that was once on people's lips.

Almost everybody directly associated with the crime is deceased, and those who know anything about it are departing this world in quick succession. There is an old saying that truth is time's daughter, but I have to wonder whether time will ever tell us the truth of this affair.

VI

STAND-OFF WITH CITIZENS' GROUP CONTINUES

A citizens' group disputing the decision to demolish the Aosawa residence is continuing its daily protests outside the house in a stand-off with construction workers attempting to begin demolition work.

Police were called in on the morning of the 18th after a confrontation when workers attempted to enter the premises. The contractor in charge of the demolition has postponed work on the grounds that it is dangerous to both parties, and has appealed to authorities to persuade the citizens' group to desist. However, the prefecture is unwilling to intervene as the Aosawa family has requested the demolition and therefore it is no longer a prefectural concern. The deadlock appears set to continue for some time.

VII

A LETTER FROM JUNJI

I tried to start this letter with "Dear" but couldn't do it. It's my first letter to you, isn't it? I'm not good at letters or writing, so it felt strange to even have to think about how to start a letter.

You must wonder why I'm writing. I don't really understand it myself. We could just as easily meet and talk, but there are things I can never actually say, so for some reason I'm writing this instead.

I think I told you once I've never felt comfortable in my skin. It's like there's an outer me that's the container, and another me on the inside, and the two don't fit together at all.

Of course, I know how people see me. Even as a kid I was always restless and fidgety, an insignificant little nobody who couldn't say anything clever. That was me. Always a hanger-on. A busy live wire with no real friends. Nobody really cared if I was around or not. That's who I was back then, and I doubt if things will change.

I think it was reading my sister's book that brought this masochistic mood on. (I told you about that book, didn't I?) Maybe being caught up in all that as a kid has something to do with it too.

Being a thoughtless show-off, naturally I enjoyed the fame that came from my sister writing a book and me being connected to it all. I admit it. In the beginning, that is. But later I felt overwhelmed by enormous anxiety one night all of a sudden. It's terrible. Every single night I have the same dream. I dream about the murders. In my dream, I'm laughing. I see people writhing on the floor in agony and I laugh at them.

In my dream, I did it. I see a son of the family, the one who always looked down on me. I see the housekeeper who put on airs because she was in charge of the kitchen for an old establishment family. I see all the people in that house who gave us the cold shoulder because we were outsiders who didn't understand how great that family supposedly was. I see them all on the floor writhing in pain, and I mock them with my laughter. I was infatuated with the children in that house, always over there following them about, but I knew they never accepted or even liked me. I hated myself for being looked down on and hated them for doing it to me. That's why I went over to the house that day.

I don't know what to do. I don't know if I should keep writing this.

I bet you're wondering now. You can't imagine what's bothering me. Why I'm writing this letter.

The house we lived in then was old, with a very small garden out the back. A damp, dark garden with shrubs, paper plants and camellias. A breeze-block fence separated our house from next door, and neighbourhood cats used to walk along the top of it, like a pathway.

Sometimes I'd be doing homework or something in my room and look up straight into the eyes of a cat walking along the top of the fence. The cats used to sit on the paving stones underneath the paper plant sometimes and groom themselves.

The first time I went over to that house that day, the drinks had just been delivered. It must have shown on my face that I wanted some, because the housekeeper gave me a bottle of cola. She opened the lid for me.

If I'd drunk it then things might have been different. I might have been the only one who died and everybody else would have been saved. I might have been remembered as the unlucky hero who saved the day. But that didn't happen.

I might give the impression of being careless and slapdash, but deep down I'm actually deeply suspicious and spineless. Always quick to run away if I sense trouble. When the housekeeper opened the bottle I was surprised the lid came off so easily, because exactly a week before I'd copped it from Mother for breaking a promise to only drink one bottle of cola at a time. She'd caught me just as I was about to drink a third bottle, so I'd done my best to put the lid back on. It looked all right, but a few days later when I took it from the fridge again to drink, the lid came off just like that, and the cola was completely flat.

So I knew. I knew somebody had already opened that soft drink and put the lid back on. I was instantly suspicious and took the bottle back home. It had a strange kind of sour, bitter smell. As I was going inside I saw a white cat walking along the top of the fence and thought maybe I could use it as a taste tester. So I squeezed down the side of the house to the back garden and found the cat just where I thought it would be, licking itself.

I poured some of the drink in front of it and the cat only licked a tiny bit, but the effect was instant. Straight away it stumbled and had a sort of fit. It must have sensed danger because it made a kind of warning cry and got away from there as fast as it could.

I thought about what this meant. Or at least I think I did. I don't know if I really did think about it. Looking back, I still don't know what I was thinking at the time.

Anyway, I decided not to drink the cola. I poured it down an outside drain, took the bottle back to that house, wiped it with my shirt and put it in the case at the back door.

I never told anybody. I think I understood that people in the house would drink that cola, and though the result was what I expected, it was also not what I expected.

I went home again and called my sister. I still think about what was in my head then, over and over, even now. What was I thinking? Why didn't I tell anybody about the cat? Why didn't I tell anybody about the lid, and the strange smell?

I don't know. I truly don't know.

In my dream, I'm laughing. I watch everybody and laugh. The white cat lies on the ground between all the people rolling around. It trembles and its legs stick out at weird angles.

Sorry about this letter. I'm really sorry to leave you a letter like this.

I'm too scared to sleep. The thought of seeing those people and the white cat in my dreams terrifies me.

VIII

CITIZENS' GROUP PROPOSES DISCUSSIONS

A citizens' group has put forward a new proposal regarding the long-standing impasse over the Aosawa residence. Their proposal is to include Hisako Schmidt (now resident in the United States) in discussions to confirm the final decision on the fate of the building.

According to the Aosawa family lawyer, Mrs Schmidt has already received the proposal and approved it. She is expected to return to Japan by the 16th at the earliest to participate in talks with the group.

13

IN A TOWN BY THE SEA

The friend

I

And now here we are. In an unfashionable town by the sea, late in the day on an early-autumn afternoon, the two of us standing side by side as we look down on the ocean. A sea breeze blowing over us. The sun's rays, though dazzling, hold only the illusion of heat, and the freshness of sunlight at the beginning of summer has long since faded.

This feels at once like the end of a very long journey, but also as if no time has passed. I struggled to reach this point, and now I'm here it feels dreamlike. All the people I met along the way are mere figures in the distance, while this woman with me now is like the first person I've ever met in my life. Yet she seems to be in the most distant place of all.

The sound of the ocean washing over us on this hill takes the uncomfortable edge off the silence between us. We start walking.

She watches the windbreak forest sway in the wind as she paces slowly along the walkway. All I can do now is wait. Wait for her to break the silence and speak. This is all there is left for me to do.

It puzzles me that I still cannot form a fixed visual impression of her. Perhaps it's interference from the light reflecting off the sea. Or was the image of her that I created in my mind somehow biased? I follow her with my eyes to gauge the truth of this, but I still cannot see her distinctly.

She is much smaller and more delicate than I expected. Thinner and more modest than in my imagination. Her complexion is fair and her face still beautiful, but her skin is thin and the lack of flesh on her neck and shoulders gives her a forlorn, pathetic air.

This is not how she's supposed to be; I can't quite believe it. The woman I know, the woman that everybody spoke of, was not like this. Her appearance is unsettling, and I can't understand why.

Suddenly, she whips around to face me and says, "So you're a friend of Jun's from university. That funny little boy. The middle child in that family who used to live nearby. That does take me back. He could never keep still, and was always making people laugh."

She looks at me with faraway eyes, as if searching through her memory.

I return her gaze. Though I cannot see her pupils because of the sun at her back, I know I must be reflected in those eyes.

Eyes through which Hisako Aosawa now sees.

II

"I had no idea Junji had died. How old was he?"

We proceed slowly along the walkway, side by side.

"He was twenty-seven. It was very sudden," I answer. My own voice sounds like a stranger's. It seems unreal to be talking with her now, like this.

"Gosh, that long ago? He was so young." Her voice goes up in surprise.

I think about the long journey to this point, the sea a pounding accompaniment to my thoughts. I think about the letter from him that started it all. It still sits in my drawer, growing old along with me, though its writer never does. How many times have I reread it? How many times have I wished I could ask him what it means? Though of course I know there will never be an opportunity for that.

"Dear me, how tragic," Hisako Aosawa says, oh-so-tactfully, in consideration of my feelings, I suppose. From her tone I can tell she thinks Jun and I were romantically involved. I deliberately don't inform her otherwise.

The roar of the ocean smothers the silence between us.

Jun and I weren't particularly close. In fact, we were cool if anything towards each other in university tutorials. But we both recognized that we were kindred spirits. We both knew how uncomfortable the world could be for people like us, those who make compromises without any resistance to speak of yet still feel out of place. Who have no faith in their own kindness or goodness. Who are conscious of another, different world below the surface of this one.

We both knew we were that kind of person. Which is exactly why we avoided each other. For fear of being called out.

He was a lively, skilled conversationalist who was popular in our tutorial group, but I kept a distance from him because I saw what he was really like, and he knew it. In my memory he is always alone, returning my gaze with troubled eyes.

Hey, you get it, don't you? I bet you feel the same, he's saying to me. Wanting my approval.

When I read that letter, I was perplexed. It made me feel he wanted my permission for something truly awful. And I turned out to be right.

The heavy salt-laden breeze lifts my hair.

It's strange. These last few years all I've thought about is Hisako Aosawa. I forgot about Jun, the one who originally set me on this path. He was shunted to a corner of my mind while I became fixated on the crime and finding out what happened afterwards. Yet now that I have finally found her, for some reason all that passes through my mind is memories of him.

"When did you regain your sight?" I ask.

"Two years ago," she replies. "I took part in clinical trials for a long time. To cultivate and regenerate the nerve cells, and then I had a transplant operation. I was told the chances of success were very low because it fails for many people, but it worked for me. It was a miracle."

She speaks softly, but her bleak tone suggests that she considers her recovery to be anything but a miracle.

"What was it like to see again after decades?" I ask, pretending not to notice the unhappiness in her voice. I suspect some kind of trap and am wary.

"I was disillusioned by so much beauty, I suppose."

Did I hear right?

"Disillusioned? Did you say disillusioned?" I ask.

She smiles faintly. "Yes. Disillusioned. It was a long time before I became used to being sighted again, because my world before that was so much more interesting."

In her voice there is a note of quiet despair.

"Your world before that? You mean the world in which you could not see?" I ask tentatively.

"Yes."

She turns to face the sea. Already she appears to have lost interest in my question. Beads of light blur the outline of her figure.

In the end it was decided to demolish the Aosawa

residence. Because that is what Hisako Aosawa wished. I heard it announced on the news.

"I want to forget the whole thing," she said. "I don't want anything left that reminds me of it. I'm grateful that people feel affection for the house, but the family has financial difficulties, and practically speaking it's hard for us to find enough money to maintain it."

Once she put it like that, it was difficult for even the most enthusiastic citizens' group members to continue their campaign. Sooner or later, the demolition work will start.

When I heard this news, however, the thought that crossed *my* mind was that she had another reason for wanting to forget about the murders. Which was – as several people I spoke to suspected – because she was the mastermind behind the crime.

Scenes I have heard described pass through my mind one after another like a parade. Hisako pumping the swing in the park, Hisako's mocking smile, Hisako looking at the crepe myrtle, Hisako being waited upon, Hisako behaving like a queen, Hisako receiving the origami cranes.

Is my image of her mistaken? Is the Hisako that everybody spoke about with such fascination really the same person I am with now?

This skinny middle-aged woman?

I glance at her in irritation. Disillusioned – if anyone has the right to be disillusioned, it's me. I'm the one who's been let down. Here I am, having finally arranged the appearance of a legendary heroine, and she turns out to be the kind of ordinary woman you might meet anywhere on the street. Where is the mysterious wicked enchantress of my imagining who lured me into all this? I cannot help but feel deceived.

Was I bewitched? Or hopelessly fascinated by an image I created myself from everything people told me about her?

All that kept me going in my research was an irrepressible desire to meet her.

Waves come rushing towards us.

Or… maybe it was simply all an illusion? One that we all created?

A powerful surge of waves breaks on the shore with a loud roar.

What if she's simply what everybody wanted her to be?

This idea strikes me almost physically. What if everybody simply desired the culprit to be a spectacularly evil, cunning, beautiful woman, rather than an impulsive, mentally ill young man?

The thought stuns me. There is no evidence, nothing at all. Only her smile, her insinuating words, and her suspect appearance. The second-hand bookshop burned down, and Makiko Saiga died. There is nothing left. Nothing that can be used to pin her down as the mastermind. Nothing apart from everybody's conjectures and hopes, that is. This woman walking alongside me is simply a shadow, a receptacle for their fantasies.

When something beyond comprehension happens people need and demand answers. Explanations such as a major conspiracy or sinister plot. The weak and powerless feel compelled to create answers or demand explanations from those in positions of superiority, because they have a need to lay the blame somewhere.

I chew on this bitter disappointment as we continue to walk.

III

"Is that how everybody sees me?" she says abruptly, with a self-deprecating smile.

The smile startles me. For a moment, her face seems to split, making her look like an old crone.

"That is all I see in people's eyes now I have my sight again. How ironic," she says, a crooked smile still on her lips.

I have no answer. Did she read my disillusion and disappointment?

"Good heavens, is this the one and only Hisako Aosawa?" she continues in a sing-song voice. "She used to be such a lovely young girl. How did that bright, beautiful child become this sorry figure of an old woman? What a disappointment. I can see it in everybody's eyes."

My cheeks flush. This thought exactly had been running through my mind.

She turns to gaze at the sea in stony silence, her humiliation whirling in the thick, humid air.

By now the sun has sunk low and sombre, ink-washed clouds roll across the sky. The evening clouds always creep up suddenly on this coast, irrespective of how fine the daytime weather has been. Where do those clouds come from?

"I used to be special. The world was mine," she mutters angrily. "Now I don't feel special or satisfied at all. When my eyes awoke, I realized the world belonged to strangers and that I never had anything from the start."

The anger in her voice turns to resignation. "Colours are the same," she says.

Casually she reaches down and plucks a withered day flower from the path's edge.

"The colours I knew in childhood from long, long ago were enough for me. I could have happily passed my whole life with the colours in my memory. The blue and red in my mind were bright and beautiful. Fresh, pure and full of energy. Much more so than real flowers."

She sounds like a small child putting on a juvenile display of bravado, bragging about how much better her home is than anyone else's.

"My husband is the same. He looks at me as if I'm a different woman," she says, the anger returning to her voice. "He's disillusioned too. I actually heard him say that once."

She swipes roughly at the tall grass with the day flower in her hand.

"When I was blind, I felt like a goddess. Full of confidence. People thought I knew everything. But once I could see again I became timid and always looking nervously around me. I aged instantly. It was like a spell had been broken."

I can't believe what I'm hearing. A spell! Is she joking? After going to America and spending all those years in clinical trials and putting up with tests to satisfy her husband?

She tosses the flower angrily aside.

I watch her in silence. *Time to bring our talk to an end,* I think, and I start to wonder about return train times.

She turns to look at me, as if she's read my mind. Her intuition certainly is good.

"So you think I did it too, don't you?"

I see her observing me, an abject light in her eyes.

"You're just like that detective, and little Maki with her book. You think I did it and that's why you're trying to get close to me, aren't you? I can tell from your eyes. Are you waiting for me to confess now the statute of limitations is suspended? Looking for a scoop, are you? Or are you here to get revenge for Jun?"

She pretends to be angry, but beneath the surface of her words I hear a pleading note. The unctuous tone of her voice revolts me. Is this what she has come to? The once divine young girl reduced to pushing her own scandal like a TV personality fallen on hard times, so she can ingratiate herself with a stranger? When I think how much time I've invested in order to hear this voice, anger and frustration surge through me in equal measure.

My contempt must be obvious, as her expression changes and she straightens her back. The change in her makes me recoil. Time seems to peel away in that moment as the haughty, proud look of the young girl returns. I, too, hastily straighten up and look at her anew.

Her calm, intelligent eyes observe me.

"All right," she says solemnly. "I'll tell you the truth, as I know it. My gift to you."

IV

The walkway overlooking the beach follows a gentle, downward curve. In the distance is a dark pine grove.

"There's a small park over there, where I was often taken as a child," Hisako says, pointing to the pine grove.

I've heard about this place. To see it for the first time fills me with a strange feeling, almost like nostalgia.

We slowly make our way towards it. Hisako's previous childish irritation and ingratiating attitude has completely disappeared. Is this quiet, composed version what she used to be like? It confuses me, puts me on my guard again. Was the grovelling an act? What if her change in attitude is a trap? Surely she wouldn't lure me here to this forsaken place and make me disappear too?

A shiver runs down my spine.

So far we have met nobody else. Has anybody seen us? Even if somebody had spotted two women walking together at a distance, I doubt if they could identify us. If I disappeared right now, there would be nobody who knew where

I had gone and why. Then Hisako could go back to America having disposed of more evidence.

"There used to be a church over there. It's gone now."

She sounds wistful as she looks in the direction of where the church presumably once stood. Has she noticed my wariness, I wonder?

"The church was also a children's home. Mother often went there with Christmas presents or cakes and biscuits for the children. I always went with her. I loved listening to the sea, so Kimi would take me to that park and I'd spend hours sitting there."

A small park comes into view. In it I see a solitary white stone bench, S-shaped, like a large love chair.

"Most of the children in the home had intellectual disabilities. Even fully grown they were just simple children at heart. They were always pleased to see me and would come running up to tell me all their news. They were so cheerful and innocent. Chattering with them made me feel all light and happy like a pretty paper balloon."

Hisako's gentle soothing voice skilfully steers the conversation. I could listen to it forever.

"Look at this bench. See the unusual shape. The backrest is so high you can't see who sits on the other side. But you can tell somebody is there through the coloured glass inset."

We sit down on the bench. The white, dry stone is warm from the sun, but not so hot as to be unbearable. Once I am seated I suddenly realize how tired and tense I am.

"I used to sit here for ages. Kimi did her knitting on the other side. Sometimes she'd say something through the glass, but mostly we sat in silence, listening to the sea. I always felt relaxed and peaceful here with the open sea breeze on my cheeks and the sound of the waves in my ears."

We both gaze at the distant horizon. She could not have seen this in the past. I try closing my eyes. The roar of the sea comes pounding at me from all directions and the world feels loosed from its foundation. Before I know it the uneasiness grows and I open my eyes again.

I glance at Hisako sitting next to me and see her stony profile fixed on a distant point, way out at sea, as if she had been gazing at this scene for years.

"When was it? I can't remember any more."

The cold face begins to speak.

"Sometimes Kimi went to help Mother and left me here alone. I didn't mind being by myself."

She puts her hand out to gently stroke the coloured glass inset.

"So this is what it looks like. Now I know why he said that," she says.

There is a red flower pattern on the glass, enclosed by a black line.

"He came from over there."

She points to the walkway we had just come along.

"He had a soft voice and sounded intelligent. He knew from my stick that I couldn't see, and called out to me first so I wouldn't be surprised. 'Hello, I'm just taking a walk along here. I'll sit down with you, if that's all right,' he said. And I could tell that he'd sat where Kimi had been earlier. I had a good feeling about him. Back then I had very good instincts about people. I could tell he wasn't a bad person. He had an air of heartache about him, as if he had suffered from grief."

Long-ago emotions colour Hisako's voice.

"After that day we got into the habit of talking here sometimes. He liked chatting with me through this glass. He often said he didn't want to be seen by anybody, that he just wanted to disappear."

Hisako slowly traces the line of the glass flower with her finger.

"That man used to call me Flower Voice."

V

They had a strange kind of arrangement.

The man hardly even attempted to look at the girl's face. Apparently he liked listening to her more than anything. Whenever he saw her in the park he would say hello, then sit down on the other side and talk through the glass. They spoke like this at irregular intervals, once every few months or so.

With the sea breeze and sound of waves washing over them in a forgotten corner of the world, they engaged in halting, guileless conversations.

Both enjoyed these brief, clandestine meetings. The man did not approach when the girl was with someone, so they never knew when they would speak again. Hardly anyone was likely to have seen them together.

They almost never talked about themselves. Didn't want to know, in fact. They talked about music they had heard. Or science. The movement of stars and the direction that morning glory vines grow in. Or myth and legend, such as the similarities between Greek myths and the chronicles of ancient Japan, the *Kojiki*. They dwelt in a world of reason and intellect, where facing up to the reality of daily life was not necessary. The formality and beauty of this world of metaphysical concerns was the main substance of their conversations.

Time passed slowly, and their voices mingled with the sound of the sea.

Once it happened that their conversation suddenly stopped and the sound of the sea vanished at the same time, as if a magical hush had been cast over them.

They discussed this moment. A moment when everything disappeared. And the sheer bliss they felt at being the only two left in the world.

The girl let slip the hope that had long been buried in her heart. The moment it left her lips, it bubbled up between them like a mad, blistering torrent. The young man listened intently to that unexpectedly fervent sound.

Abruptly, a giant roar of waves broke the silence. So suddenly and so loud that it gave them both a scare. The noise engulfed them, and they trembled.

And this was probably the moment. The moment when the young girl unintentionally uttered the comment that started it all.

VI

"It was an accident. An unlucky accident," she mutters blandly. "If you don't like the word *accident*, then call it *bad luck*," she adds, somewhat more forcefully. Perhaps she notices the lack of conviction in my face. She looks at me fiercely.

"I didn't know anything. I didn't do anything."

Oh, the brazenness in her voice.

"He asked if I had any paper," she says, folding her fingers affectedly on her lap. "He said he wanted to make a note of anything he thought of. I don't remember what that was. I happened to have some paper that we used to wrap the cakes we took to the church, but how could I know Kimi also used it as memo paper for writing down telephone messages, and that the address of Father's friend was on it? I couldn't have seen what was written on that paper, could I?"

Her tone is coquettish and wheedling. It grates on me, stirring up uneasiness and rubbing my nerves the wrong way.

"You know those paper bags used for dispensing medicine in clinics? At home we always used bags from the clinic as memo paper. With the address and telephone number printed on it. It's possible I might have given him one."

She spreads her hands out in a gesture that invites me to challenge her.

"*I* couldn't have got hold of the poison, let alone planted it. It's true, I did know the man was mentally ill. He used to talk to himself a lot, so much so that after a while I couldn't understand him any more. To be honest, I was a bit scared. I mean, if anything happened I wouldn't be able to protect myself, would I?"

I sneak another sidelong look at her. The expression in her eyes startles me.

"The last time I saw him was about six months before it happened. How could I know he'd take what I said that way? I never *dreamed* he would interpret it like that!"

But on her face is an expression of satisfaction, even pride, and her eyes glitter with the reflection from the glowing horizon.

"I couldn't see anything. I couldn't see what was happening. I couldn't have done it. I was a young, helpless girl. I would *never* have been able to do something like that."

The more she denies it, the more clearly I hear another voice: *I did it, I knew everything, I made it happen!* Her voice rings triumphantly in my head.

"The children at the church were very attached to me. And him. Children loved him. He avoided Kimi and the nuns, but he played with them. Strange, isn't it, how his own innocence attracted those poor innocent children to him?"

She smiles. No doubt staring at past glory on the horizon.

"It was no wonder those children did as he said. If he told them to make a phone call they would have done it, and if I'd told them to go to the home of a lonely old man and play with fireworks, they would have done. But of course I didn't do anything, and I have no way of knowing what he might have asked them to do."

Abruptly she turns to look at me. "Isn't that right?"

She fixes me with a smile and despite myself I cannot help staring into those eyes. Her smile is so fierce I don't know if she is angry or on the verge of tears. Is she a killer? Is this the victory declaration of a cold-blooded homicidal maniac? Or is it an unconventional confession? Does she want me to accuse her, or is she trying to win me over, or —

I realize suddenly that a human smile can sometimes look like a tree split in two. Of course, I cannot prove a thing. Even if she has just told me something that only the perpetrator could know, I have no means of proving any of it.

"It was the same for that young man, I'm sure. In the end, everybody went along with you, didn't they?" My voice is hoarse. "If you said *die*, he probably would have done as you said."

VII

One morning the young girl woke early, as usual. And as usual, the house was filled with the sound of voices, music, radio and television. She awoke with a clear head. Then a switch went on, and all the sound immediately flowed into her, helping her to gain a sense of the height of the ceiling.

Inside her room it was extremely close and hot. She was bathed in sweat and felt fatigued, as if she had already been on the move for hours. The low atmospheric pressure and clinging, sticky air signalled the approach of a storm.

Ah, she thought with a familiar weariness, *the world still goes on.* Weariness and despair were her constant companions, waiting to engulf her every time she awoke.

In addition to the usual noise, however, today the girl was aware of a cheerful note of tension in the air. In a flash, she remembered it was a special day.

A storm would come.

That's right, she recalled. This day was going to be a very special one for her family. But she was the only one in the house to know that it would be special in a different sense to what everybody else in the family or neighbourhood was expecting.

VIII

"So tell me, what does Eugenia mean?" I ask. My mouth feels parched. "The name everybody wanted to know about. Whose name was it? Who wrote that poem?"

She remains silent for a brief time. Her air of exaltation cools; it feels as if the temperature has suddenly plummeted.

"The detective asked me that too. Many times. But I don't know. It's a pretty name, though, isn't it?"

Her tone is completely different. Now she sounds flat and expressionless. She shoots me a look of piercing contempt that makes me recoil.

"Why do you ask? How could I know? I couldn't have read anything written on that paper, let alone a poem. No matter how brilliant a poem might be, it meant nothing to me unless somebody read it aloud. Do you know how cruel that is? To be in a library surrounded by books which are all meaningless unless somebody is with me."

I sense the beginning of an eruption behind that indignant profile.

"Stop pretending you're innocent!" My voice goes up sharply. "Don't you feel guilty in the least?"

My voice trembles and I know I sound foolish, but I cannot hold back any more. In my mind I see his face, looking at me with his troubled smile. The dam bursts and words come pouring out.

"Why did you do it? Why try to kill your family? All those people! Even children! Why in heaven's name? Didn't they all love you?"

Finally the accusation comes tumbling out, but it doesn't seem to make the least dent in her. Her expression remains the same. Imperturbable.

"Tell me! I'm not going to inform on you. I just want to know. I won't tell anybody. You know as well as anyone I don't have any evidence, there's nothing to prove what you did."

In her stead, the sea answers with a long boom of waves.

IX

Is it a sin to know something? To know that something *might* happen?

The girl had trouble making herself get out of bed that day. *It's bound to be a sin*, said a voice somewhere inside her.

She calmly analysed this. *In that case, am I a bad girl?* she thought. *Am I bad for keeping quiet and saying nothing?*

No voice answered this question.

I might have misunderstood, she thought. *Or maybe I imagined it. Nothing might happen at all. It might simply be a fun, cheerful day to remember. The world might go on like it always has.*

The girl lay on her bed thinking. *What if something* does *happen?*

The house rang with the sound of lively voices and patter of slippered feet rushing about. She winced and covered her face with both hands, overwhelmed by unbearable impulses of despair and despondency.

Why is it always like this? Why is there never any peace and quiet in this house?

The world she yearned for and had dreamed of for so long was a far cry from the one she knew, a world filled with vulgar music, scolding and grumbling, flattery and deference, nasty gossip, scheming in the shadows, plotting and manoeuvring behind the scenes, and her mother's praying voice filled with hypocrisy and damnation.

Apart from her sight, the girl's senses were acute in the extreme. She heard and felt all sensory input intensely. Everybody knew that, though no one grasped the degree of her sensitivity.

x

In the distance I hear the sound of a truck mounted with megaphones, blaring out advertisements for a pachinko parlour. The sound comes closer, then disappears again.

She flinches. "I hate this," she says. "Why is the world filled with such horrible noise? Loud, ear-piercing, screeching noise – as if they don't want anybody to be able to think. People try and paint over the world with noise because they can't stand the sound of their own voice or anybody else's."

She shivers and hugs herself with both arms, a gesture that provokes a strong well of revulsion in me.

"Please, don't dodge the question," I plead. "This is my only chance. Tell me, I beg of you, for his sake too. The victims didn't end that day, you know. The number keeps growing."

I grab her by the shoulder. Her bony, too skinny shoulder. But as I fear, she cannot accept what I ask.

"Hear that!" she answers in a hollow voice. "Who needs the radio and trumpets when the world is filled with all this music?"

She brusquely brushes my hand from her shoulder, stands up and walks off shakily.

XI

It had been her wish. This had been her wish for so long that she couldn't remember when it first began. What she wanted was to be alone. To spend time in the house alone. To enjoy her time in peace and quiet. And be able to listen in peace, properly, to real music from around the world.

Storm-driven rain began to fall. The din from the large drops beating against the glass door muffled all other noise. Before long it was even loud enough to drown out the voices of children playing at the back door.

The wind picked up rapidly. *A storm is coming. A storm to take away everything. A storm that will bring me everything.*

She knew she must be strong to obtain it, for what she would be required to give up in exchange was [illegible]. But she had to obtain it, at any price, in order to go on living.

She quietly inhaled and settled her breathing, searing in her mind the words she had uttered over and over: *I must be stronger and smarter than anybody else. I must be more cunning and wicked than anybody else. To obtain the world I must have the strength to accept everything.*

That was the one thing she could do for the young man who was likely to fulfil her wish, and it was her intention to be ready.

Eugenia, my Eugenia. His quiet voice echoed in her head. *I journeyed alone all this time.*

The young man and the girl had sat on the seat by the sea and composed this poem together through the glass. They had crooned it over and over, dreaming of that day.

She had introduced him as *yuu-jin*, my friend, to the children from the church. The children who wanted to know his name. They thought it was his name. *Yuu-jin, Yuu-jin*, they happily called him.

Even now the girl did not know his real name. She didn't want to know.

She had been in search of another country. A dream country that nobody else knew of. A country just for the two of them, a country of endless quiet, where the world was banished.

The two of them had called that country Eugenia.

XII

All of a sudden the sound of the waves ceases. An uneasy silence falls.

"An angel passed by," she croons in a low voice.

"Angel? What nonsense is that?"

She gives no answer to my angry question. Her hands move lightly, as if dancing.

"The world disappeared. But it's strange that it's still here. So where am I, I wonder?"

She is completely in her own world. I can't make sense of what she says.

"Did he arrive in our dream country? What about me? Am I there now? If so, my journey is over. Has my journey really ended?"

I follow behind her, this skinny middle-aged woman mumbling to herself as she walks, while I plead, "Please tell me, I beg you," over and over like a spell.

"Those people were so noisy, you know, all the time. Ever since I was little. They couldn't keep quiet. Always talking, never happy unless they were making some noise or other. They had no confidence in the value of their own existence."

She looks at the sea and spreads her arms wide.

"Don't you agree? Why, when the world is filled with such beautiful music as this."

Tired summer air hangs over the ocean bathed in the evening sun. The waves turn red. Like a sick cat, a middle-aged woman wanders along the walkway, the scene bathed in red light.

"Oh look, a beautiful flower!" she suddenly stops and happily cries. "It's the same as the flowers we had at home. Gosh, that does take me back. What was the name of that flower, I wonder?"

She points into the distance. Though I am aware she has turned to look at me I cannot see her clearly, nor the flower she is pointing to, for the tears of vexation that cloud my eyes and the evening sun at her back glaring in my face.

"I can't see. I can't see anything," I sputter, shaking my head. "Nothing at all. Not his face. Not her face."

Her outline melts into a red sea.

"*I* can see," I hear her say from a long way off, in a voice ringing with confidence. "Oh, look at that flower. Why does it make me feel so unbearably sentimental, I wonder?"

14

RED FLOWERS, WHITE FLOWERS

The author

I

The screech of cicadas in shrill chorus reverberates through her head, numbing her brain. Their voices always make her feel dazed, as if she is being bodily wrenched back into a season already past.

The heat here is as oppressive as ever, but the sun has gradually lost some of its bite.

Cities and people both generate sound in the process of change, she thinks. *The same world never exists twice, and in every moment, with every passing second, people live in a different world.*

This and other random thoughts flit through her mind as she walks alone without plan or purpose through the city she once lived in as a child. Her body retains an approximate memory of the geography that allows her to meander through the hustle and bustle like a migratory fish returning home. The self who once walked these streets subtly imposes itself on the self who walks here now, with the echo of two sets of footsteps vibrating in her bones.

Her intention is to spend just a few hours here. She is on her way back to Tokyo after visiting her husband in his latest regional posting, and has stopped off in the city on a whim.

Heat haze rises off the asphalt and the air is hot and thick, as if the city is inside a steamer. It always seems to be the last vestige of summer whenever she comes here.

She doesn't understand herself why she is here. After writing down her memories of this city in her book, it has become part of the past as far as she is concerned.

What shall I do? Perplexed, she looks around, as if the answer might be found somewhere on the streets. Signboards in the city centre robustly asserting their presence have seen better days. All have faded to a similar shade after being exposed to the same sun and rain every day, giving them the appearance of a layer of skin inseparable from the rest of the city.

Just like families, she thinks. *Though each person is an individual, people become similar while living under the same roof. Even couples like us come to resemble each other.*

She thinks about the husband she has just said goodbye to. *How many other couples are like us,* she wonders, *so alike in their indifference towards other people, including each other, naturally? But since each is equally indifferent to the other, unsurprisingly they have come thus far without discord.*

She half-expects their daughter leaving to spell the end of their relationship, but recently she has begun to think that perhaps they can continue as they are. Being able to get along without having to spend a great deal of effort on the other person means that they are in fact perfectly matched as a couple. It would not be easy to find another partner who requires as little maintenance. *In the end, we two are probably soulmates,* she thinks with a wry smile.

Unexpectedly, the image of a good-natured young man comes to mind. A young man playing a tape recorder in a hot room, drinking canned fruit juice and silently writing out transcriptions in a notebook. A kind-hearted youth, younger than her, in whose company she had once spent many days, long ago.

Why does she think of him now? Sentiment, most likely, she concludes. She had asked him to assist her way back then because deep down she liked him. The thought bemuses her as she ambles along.

The clamour of the streets on a weekday afternoon makes her feel comfortably relaxed and lethargic. And also inconspicuous, as if she could be a housewife anywhere, walking the street in the early afternoon. Nobody turns to look at her, nothing about her stands out. This knowledge sets her mind at peace.

II

She ruminates on the peculiar nature of connections to strangers, how one can never know what draws people together or pulls them apart.

Unconsciously her feet have taken her towards the famous Japanese garden in the centre of the city. She looks sidelong at the tour groups flowing through the main gate and saunters in alongside them, before peeling off alone from the standard route in the direction of *that* building.

To a quiet, still, enclosed space.

The temperature is distinctly lower inside the large wooden building and the odour of mould noticeable. A low ripple of whispers from the sprinkling of visitors inside is sucked up and absorbed by the interior. Few tourists venture away from the garden into this house.

Inside the dark old house is an open-sided covered walkway with a view of the house's garden, the view framed in such a way as to inexorably draw the visitor's gaze. She has always felt fearful in this graceful, tranquil space, a fear rooted in the powerful menacing tension that pervades Japanese gardens, one akin to a life-or-death battle, springing from the sharp separation between the observer and the observed.

The observer and the observed. *In the end, I was the observer, I suppose,* she thinks, standing fixed to the spot, gazing at the framed square of garden. She *was always one of the observed, and she knew it.*

Such are the thoughts that pass through her mind as she studies the garden and the varying degrees of colour in its greenery. If there is no observer, the observed also does not exist. A garden such as this, where every single angle of vision is calculated with thorough awareness of the viewer, would not exist without that appreciative eye. Observers and the observed can be accomplices, but the line between them does not cross.

I wanted to be an appreciative observer, she thinks, looking away from the garden. *To a proper, appreciative observer, the question of guilt – whether it exists or not – is not the issue.*

She walks along the dark corridor and goes upstairs. A creaking of steps follows her up from behind.

The fact of her existence was a kind of miracle. I knew that. But almost nobody else did. There were people who worshipped her for being a beautiful young lady and treated her with respect, but that was all.

Outside, she sees deep green pine trees.

I knew, though. I was the only one who understood. Miracles do exist, but the question is what should those with this knowledge do about it? Should they tell what they know? Should they leave a record?

A faint breeze blows, gently brushing her cheeks.

It's such a pity I wasn't able to make a decent record. If only I'd had more talent I might have been able to leave something more complete. That was the best I could do.

She bitterly regrets her failure. But how can a miracle be adequately expressed? It is altogether too difficult. This is a question that artists have always struggled with. Not that she thinks of herself as an artist.

A small room comes into view. A room that is dark, cool and serene. A room without sound, painstakingly created by craftsmen, where the walls are coated with precious blue paint. Just looking at it gives her goosebumps.

She thinks of a young girl standing here long ago. An adult holding her hand as they peer into the room. Then she turns and sees a young girl standing in the cool corridor, a girl wearing a white blouse and navy-blue skirt with shoulder straps. The girl looks at her. The two stand side by side in the corridor, peering in at the forbidding, cold room. The girl's large intelligent eyes focus with deep concentration, and she seems a little nervous.

She stares keenly at this figure of Hisako before she lost her sight.

III

"Oh, my goodness! You wouldn't by any chance be… the one who wrote a book? Oh, I thought so!"

The woman certainly had a good memory. The last time they had met was before she married, when her hairstyle and dress sense were completely different. But although their eyes had only met for a few seconds, the woman had succeeded in figuring out her identity before she could even think who this stranger might be.

The woman was plump and middle-aged, with a kindly accommodating manner that tended to distract from the fact that she was an extremely capable police officer.

The last time they had met she had been extremely

impressed by the policewoman, who was quick-witted, always chose exactly the right words, had a memory that was accurate down to the smallest detail, and never said anything vague or unsupported. She was of course also an attentive listener who was impossible to deceive with contradictions or evasions. On top of all that the policewoman radiated an emotional stability and empathy that put people at ease, making them feel as if they could trust her. Which is why, even at this unexpected meeting, she immediately relaxed and bowed her head in greeting.

They had stood conversing in a corner of the train station, on the edge of the crowd streaming through. The policewoman had mentioned her impressions of the book and they spoke about all that had happened since then. It was a short but full conversation, one that gave her a renewed appreciation of the policewoman's efficiency. She was not one to waste her own or other people's time.

Of course, the topic of *her* had come up. When she had last spoken with the policewoman she was still a student, and perhaps the policewoman had not thought the information relevant to the book she was writing, but on this occasion it fitted easily into their conversation. The information of interest concerned the police's first interviews with *her*, the survivor, immediately after it happened.

When she heard the content of this interview it came as a shock, but she tried to keep a nonchalant expression on her face while she listened.

"Of course, that child understood the appalling position she was in," the policewoman had said. "She knew vaguely that most of her family had died around her. Because of course it was hell all around. When she was taken to hospital she was in a state of panic at first. Extremely agitated and kept gabbling something very fast but didn't seem to be aware she was speaking. I couldn't catch what she said, and neither could the nurses."

She saw in her imagination an image of the young girl lying in bed. *Her*. The survivor, Hisako.

"They gave her an injection to make her rest," the policewoman continued, "and when she woke up I listened to her again. I was extremely careful to pay close attention to anything she said. Many times I tried to get her to speak, and at a slower pace, because I thought it was important for her to get whatever it was off her chest. And of course there was a chance I'd find some clues too, clues that would lead to the truth about the crime."

The policewoman had patiently listened to Hisako and kept asking her questions, straining every nerve so as not to miss anything. But still she was unable to make head or tail of what Hisako was saying. Hisako responded to questions, but not to the actual content of the questions. The police were at a loss, but they persisted, and finally they caught on.

"We couldn't believe it," the policewoman said. "It was about colour. All that time she'd been talking about when she was a young child. Gabbling the same thing over and over about when she was small and still had her sight. We didn't have the slightest idea why she'd talk about that. The doctors said she might have unconsciously been escaping in her mind to a time when she still had vivid impressions, that perhaps the fear of comprehending a tragedy that had taken place in a world where she couldn't see had driven her to a place where she could comprehend the world through her eyes.

"It left quite an impression on me," the policewoman continued. "I listened to her repeat herself over and over like a tape recorder, and my blood ran cold at times. She kept saying the same thing, like a broken record. 'Someone's with me in the blue room. The white crepe myrtle flower is scary.' That was it. But she repeated it endlessly.

"I racked my brains about what it could mean, but never figured it out in the end. She herself had no memory of saying it, despite having repeated it constantly. What on earth had that child seen in her mind as she heard her family die? Had she mentally run away to happier days when she was little?"

At this, the plump policewoman's eyes took on a faraway look, perhaps recalling that period and the young girl who had kept talking about colours. It was the only time her ageless face appeared old.

It felt as if the conversation had continued for hours, but in fact only twenty minutes had passed.

"That's right, while she was talking she kept moving her hands about. What was it… a sort of circular motion. I wonder what it meant?" The policewoman furrowed her brow and looked at her, as if to ask her opinion of this mystery she had puzzled over for many years.

But she was far from being able to give an answer, for in that moment she was struggling to control the shock that this conversation had dealt her.

IV

She leaves the old building and goes out into the lush, green garden.

She cannot remember saying goodbye to the policewoman on that occasion. No doubt she bowed and said something, but her mind was too preoccupied with what she had just heard to recall their farewell. What did she do afterwards to relieve the shock? She cannot recall that either.

The blue room and white flowers. White crepe myrtle flowers. They had been in profuse bloom that summer too.

Cries from a chorus of cicadas slice through her, fusing with the replay in her mind of the words from the memo that was left in the kitchen.

> I journeyed alone all this time
> That I might meet you again.

What did Hisako hope to achieve by leaving that memo there? Who was it meant for? Who, *really*, was it that Hisako wanted to offer everything up to?

Anger and disappointment suddenly seethe up inside her.

And I'm supposed to be the appreciative observer…

Long-suppressed emotions rise to the surface. It is all very well to be an appreciative observer, but she wishes that this ability could be recognized, by the public to begin with, and then by the subject of her observation.

Hisako should have received my message. The book was meant as a message for her alone: I see you, I can appreciate you. It didn't matter if nobody else read the book, as long as she did.

Again, she sees a vision of a young man hard at work making notes, and feels a mixture of affection mixed with contempt.

He misunderstood. He thought I asked him to be my assistant because I was making an approach. In hindsight I can't say he was entirely wrong. But he was the only one I could have asked to do that work. I was dazzled by his good breeding and happy that he seemed to like me. I envied his good nature. He knew nothing about the murders, and in front of him I could be proud of being someone connected with the tragedy.

She narrows her eyes at the green cloud over her head.

From here on we will be together, forever.

She sees Hisako in her polka-dot blouse, serenely reading the poem in a low voice.

I'm the only one in the world who knows the real Hisako. But I have no intention of accusing her of anything. I would never do anything so tedious and inelegant.

Gravel crunches under her feet and she hears a hubbub of tourists' voices. She thinks about everything for the first time in a long while.

Yes, I know why Hisako would do such a thing.

Gravel crunching. Laughing tourists. Distant cries of cicadas. A corner of her brain feels slightly numb.

I've known her all along. Even before reading that poem. I knew her long before the murders happened, I knew her before I was born.

She looks up at the sunlight filtering through the trees.

Hisako had to do something. She had to accomplish something big, something major. It couldn't be helped. If that hadn't happened, it would have been something else, maybe even bigger.

Rays of sunshine streaming through the leaves dazzle her.

It's like someone's shooting bullets of light at me. Am I being blamed? Criticized? Why me?

She staggers into the shade of a tree and sinks onto a bench. Taking a handkerchief from her bag, she mops her forehead. Sweat trickles unpleasantly down her back.

That policewoman never sweated. Her skin was always smooth, and her make-up never smudged. Just like a doll. She was a mystery, all right. Almost like a robot.

A face with a faraway expression flits through her mind.

I always tried to be somebody. Somebody other than myself. I wanted to know what it felt like to be someone who wasn't me.

Hisako.

But ultimately I was made to understand that I am merely an observer.

She clutches the handkerchief and chases images.

I'm glad Hisako lives on the other side of the ocean. Thank goodness the statute of limitations is suspended. The connection between us can continue.

She realizes that she is more exhausted than she thought. That's what comes of wandering about the streets on a hot, humid afternoon.

Why is it so dark? Maybe I've got a touch of sunstroke. She looks about for a teahouse where she can buy a drink.

I wish I hadn't met that policewoman, she thinks bitterly, fighting down nausea. *If only that woman didn't have such a good memory. If only she hadn't spotted me.*

Bitter regret, long buried in a deliberate attempt to forget, smoulders in her heart.

If only. My miracle could have continued forever.

V

She stands up ready to set off walking again, but is overcome by dizziness and sits back down on the bench. Her body feels heavy, so she decides to rest a little more first before going to buy a drink. She sighs.

White crepe myrtle flowers. The policewoman doesn't know. Probably never will.

She puts her fingers to her temples and slowly rubs them.

Hisako couldn't have seen those flowers.

The sunlight irritates her.

Couldn't have seen them.

She sees Hisako's face pointed towards the flowers in full bloom.

So picturesque. If I were an artist I'd paint that scene for posterity.

Hisako was always instantly aware of changes in the environment. She was particularly sensitive to sound and scent, and noticed any flowers immediately. She seemed to know as well as if she held them in her own hand what stage of bloom they were at, whether in bud or about to fall.

Ah, the sun hurts.

A dull pain thrums at the back of her eyes and she rubs them.

And yet, Hisako…

The polka-dot blouse. Hair lifting in the breeze…

Hisako didn't know what a white crepe myrtle looked like. She had turned her face towards the flowers in bloom on the tree outside our front door, but did not know it was a crepe myrtle. I knew that all along. Hisako misunderstood. She believed it was a different kind of tree.

I can't believe it. Nobody spotted it, not her family nor anybody else. I just happened to find out by chance.

When Hisako could still see, she saw the flowers on the tree outside the Aosawa clinic. But it was only after losing her sight that somebody must have taught her the name of it. Only it's a difficult name to read, and maybe the person who taught her didn't know it properly themselves, because it's pronounced quite differently to the way it's written.

Crepe myrtle blooms for a long period, with either red or white flowers. But she had another word for it fixed in her brain, which she was convinced was the name of the flowers that bloomed outside their house.

But Hisako knew about crepe myrtle, and in her mind she used that name for another, different flower, one she'd seen in the past.

I knew that. I'm probably the only person who did.

She stares at the pebbly gravel at her feet. Heated, round stones glowing white. Under her gaze they grow in size and form a white dotted pattern.

A polka-dot blouse. She sees Hisako facing into the wind with eyes narrowed.

The distant past seems startlingly vivid and clear. *Why now?* she wonders. *Is it being back in this city again? But I've never felt attached to anywhere. And I lost interest in this city a long time ago, after I finished the book.*

But here you are again. You came back today, didn't you? says a cool voice in her head. *If you lost interest, what are you doing here?*

She shakes her head weakly, not feeling like answering.

I don't know. But the image of the Hisako I knew as a child is strong. I recall the touch of her hair and even the air she breathed. I hear her voice as she told me things.

VI

I was in the blue room. I was only very young. This is a strange story, you see.

The room was icy blue. I was cold. Not even the air moved.

I could still see then. There was an adult next to me. I don't know who, exactly.

I was kind of scared. I don't remember why. But I stood there, afraid.

I felt signs of bats.

I was afraid. So afraid.

I felt alone, even though someone was with me.

It was the blue room. The cold blue room. The air went cold just looking at it. My skin was like ice, my bones were like ice.

I stood there for a long time without saying anything. It was awful having to stand for a long, long time without moving in the blue room.

I stared at the walls of that room. Cold blue walls. I wanted so much to get out of there, but I couldn't.

I wanted to ask the person with me to help, but I couldn't do that either. I couldn't speak. I couldn't move. The air felt weird and I was scared.

The person with me didn't move either. They just stood there behind me. Making sure I didn't run away.

That's all.

I don't remember what happened after that.

All I remember is being with somebody in the blue room, and feeling very afraid.

VII

She feels a cold wind. Every time she remembers that story, and Hisako's voice as she told it, she feels chilled to the marrow. Even now. Even on this unbearably hot, humid summer afternoon, she feels cold.

A sign of bats. That mysterious saying of Hisako's.

Hisako frequently spoke about things that were not visible as though they were and vice versa, because having lost her sight very young her knowledge of things she had actually seen was jumbled with things she hadn't. Her quirky use of language had the effect of making her seem even more mystical and miraculous, while making the other person, who did not understand, feel stupid and in the wrong. That's why if anyone had noticed that she didn't know what crepe myrtle was and was using that name for something else, nobody would have thought to point it out. They might have even wondered in the back of their mind if Hisako wasn't actually correct.

"It's a wonder. I feel anger and sadness swelling up," she used to say.

Hisako often tried to explain very carefully what she perceived. She couldn't see but she had a sense of size, and to her emotions were like balloons expanding in the dark. She knew their scale and texture. An excited cheerful mood would sparkle, because she could tell something was twinkling high up in the air. Love and adoration were like air currents, or heat. But sometimes, out of frustration perhaps, she would suddenly break off.

"We have crepe myrtle at home." She often said that too. We all thought she meant the tree outside the Aosawa house. That big crepe myrtle tree in front of the house with the round windows. That's what anyone might have thought.

We were always listeners. That was our role. Very few people could actually have a discussion with her. She told us about lots of different things. And we asked her questions. Then she would explain, and we would nod. Our conversations always went like that. She would laugh, and we would be in raptures hearing her laughing voice.

"We have a crepe myrtle tree at home."

No one knew what she meant. No one apart from me. And until I met that smooth-faced policewoman, I didn't know either.

VIII

She sits slumped on the bench. Her face is pale and contorted, her eyes are closed. Sweat pours down her forehead.

The blue room.

Behind closed eyelids she sees the small room in the old house she has just left, and a young girl in a white blouse standing in the passageway. Their eyes meet. The girl becomes Hisako in a polka-dot blouse, standing in the chilly, dark corridor. She stands in the middle of the corridor, staring at Hisako. There is a distance between them.

"I thought it was this room," she says.

"Oh, did you?" Hisako answers.

"Yes. This famous room. The one literary giants wrote about. With walls painted blue by a rare pigment. A jewel case of a room, but somehow unwelcoming. No cracks, exquisitely crafted. Where local children come on school excursions. In a building in the corner of a famous garden. A tourist destination. I thought this was the place. But when I spoke to that policewoman, I realized my mistake."

She stares at Hisako.

"There's no white crepe myrtle here. This isn't the blue room you talked about."

She looks around the cool corridor.

"That's right," Hisako answers.

"There's another blue room, isn't there." She looks at Hisako again.

"So there is," says Hisako.

She remembers the days of her childhood, and the house she used to pass by with her friends on their way home from school.

"Your house. With the porthole windows. The three round windows in a row. From a distance they looked like a ship.

"Nobody ever called the people who lived there by their name. It was always Round Windows so-and-so. At first I thought Round Windows was a surname. I went there quite a few times. To the grand house that was the centre of the neighbourhood. Your younger brother was always nice to me. Whenever he saw me he'd ask me in and give me sweets. *Ramune* lollies that dissolved on the tongue. I still remember the kick from that bittersweet taste.

"It was classy inside your house, Round Windows. Classical music always in the background and no unnecessary clutter. The floor was polished to a sparkle and the ceilings were high, like a grand house in a film.

"'Over here! Let's go to my room. I'll get us some soft drinks.'

"I can hear your little brother trotting along the passage as I followed behind him, looking round the house as I went. I was searching for those windows because I wanted to know what it was like to look through them.

"When I asked him where they were he pointed to the end of the passage. The wall with the windows was partitioned into three small rooms. One for the telephone. One had a washroom with a sink. And the third one…

"The mistress's room.

"The room where his mother said her prayers was a tiny, tiny room.

"The door was shut when I saw it the first time. I'd never heard of a special room to pray in before and was disappointed when I saw the door was closed. It was usually closed, but once I found it slightly open for some reason, and I peeked inside. What I saw when I put my head around the door gave me such a shock I immediately pulled it out again.

"Inside was blue. A pure blue space.

"I was scared, but I peeped in once more, and then I understood. There was blue glass in the window, and the light coming through the window made the room look blue.

"But it wasn't only the glass. The plasterer who had done the work had excelled himself in lining the walls with blue tiles.

"A blue room. A still, blue space.

"Then I noticed the shelf. On it was a single white lily in a small vase.

"The white lily. A pure flower blessed by God. The mistress's favourite flower.

"Time seemed to pass at a different speed in that room. For some reason, I felt robbed of words. I felt as if I'd seen something I shouldn't have.

"So, you see, I knew about that room. But I'd forgotten about it all these years. The other blue room that you repeatedly spoke of that day.

"The flower in that room was crepe myrtle to you, wasn't it? Not a lily. But you should have known what a lily was. The design at the centre of the blue glass window was a fleur-de-lis. But you called it crepe myrtle. I don't know where that misunderstanding came from. But I have no doubt that to you this flower was 'the crepe myrtle at our house'.

"Am I right?" she asks Hisako, facing her in the cool corridor.

Hisako simply stares at her with an enigmatic smile.

A long silence falls.

"Which means," she mutters, "the adult you were with..."

IX

The mistress was a fine woman. Everybody said so. She was a devout Christian, a pillar of support to her husband in his grief over their daughter's misfortune. She exerted herself in the service of the community and visited churches in all the surrounding districts, engaging in selfless activities for the less fortunate.

Hisako's mother often took her on these visits. I remember her telling me how she enjoyed hearing the different sounds of the towns they went to. How she could immediately tell from the sounds which town they were in.

The mistress loved her daughter, and no one wished for Hisako's happiness more than her. She was unassuming and retiring, not talkative, someone who stood by her family in the shadows. Which of course included Hisako.

Her emotions were never visible on the surface, but she obviously had some kind of belief that sustained her. Nobody can know now what that was.

Was it the mistress who hoped for a miracle? Did she believe that her daughter was a kind of sacrifice? Or that some kind of atonement was required? Did she think that a big sacrifice was necessary? Or was it possible that she hated those who were not less fortunate?

She crosses her arms on her knees and rests her head on them. The pain behind her eyes is becoming unbearable.

Wasn't Hisako's existence itself a miracle? But perhaps what was miraculous to me was not for the mistress.

I don't know.

She lifts her head painfully. The sun is low, and tourists are leaving.

In a room lit by blue rays, a woman in a kimono stands over a girl in a white blouse. She stands behind them, watching.

"Say your prayers," the woman says to the girl.

The girl's back twitches and trembles.

"Tell God everything," the woman orders her harshly.

The girl's shoulders tremble even more.

"What is it? What's happened between you?" she says to the woman's back and the girl's shoulders. Neither answers.

"I have to know. I'm the observer, after all," she entreats, trying to get their attention. Their backs remain turned.

White backs, blue light, fleur-de-lis in the window.

What did Hisako confess to as a little girl in that room? What did she repent of and pray for? Why did the mistress take her there in the first place?

The policewoman said that Hisako had rolled her hands round and around.

Might not that have been Hisako making the sign of the cross in childhood? What sin could such a small girl possibly need to beg forgiveness for? What was the mistress trying to make her small daughter confess to?

She doesn't know.

She rises sluggishly to her feet and sets off for the teahouse. Her throat is parched. Her body feels like lead. Her field of vision has narrowed so much she can barely see around her. Blood pools in her lower body, unable to reach her head.

I have to keep moving, she thinks. *I must get a drink and get away from here.*

She walks through the garden as twilight descends, tormented by the pain from bullets of light raining down on her from the sky.

The bullets turn into blue light. She is not thinking any more. She is a small girl alone in the blue room, wandering in search of forgiveness and water.

Through the long summer that has continued since that day. Her eternal, never-ending summer.